No Vacancy

A Black Horse Campground Mystery

Amy M. Bennett

Aakenbaaken & Kent

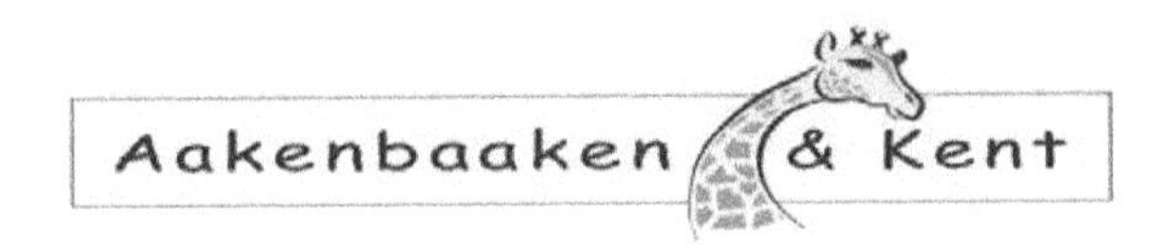

No Vacancy

aakenbaakeneditor@inbox.com

ISBN: 978-1-938436-22-2

Dedication

For Paul, for always, forever and
In loving memory of

Dawn Bennett
sister-in-law, friend, and fan
April 8, 1969 – October 18, 2016

You were the audience I was writing for.
I love you and miss you

Prologue

Life isn't fair, he thought, watching the crush of people moving around inside the crowded store.

The monsoon rains weren't supposed to visit south central New Mexico until the beginning of July, still three weeks away. But for the third day in a row, a brisk shower descended upon the Sacramento Mountains where they trailed into the village of Bonney in Bonney County. Memorial Day weekend had inaugurated the start of the horse racing season in nearby Ruidoso Downs and, with the early rains holding off the threat of wildfires, a promising summer of camping. The Lincoln National Forest and New Mexico state park campgrounds had been filled to capacity and he'd been fortunate to find an available cabin at the Black Horse Campground.

The campground served RV and tent campers as well and every site was full, including all eight of the campground's cabins. Yet despite the repeated apologies and explanations from the front desk personnel that there were no more vacancies for the night, a few persistent hopefuls still fought the crush at the front desk in the unlikely event that a space had opened up.

He watched the three women who manned the front desk. The petite older woman with the frosted blonde hair was obviously more goodwill ambassador than actual help; she kept up a steady stream of chatter with the guests who waited in line to pay for camp store purchases or registrations and probably defused many a short temper. Another woman, who was probably about the same age despite the thick, silver-gray ponytail that hung to the middle of her back, attended to the actual needs of the customers. She was brisk and capable, assisting guests with hardly a moment's hesitation. She was obviously the right hand of the younger, dark-haired woman who handled the reservations and registrations with an unflagging smile and a warmth that made even the most harried guest feel that they were, indeed, on vacation.

"Excuse ME," twanged an irritated, nasal voice that nearly drowned out the hub-bub of the customers in the store. With a start, he realized he'd been standing and staring too long, and the woman who was trying to reach a t-shirt with the campground's logo emblazoned on the front had gotten tired of repeating herself.

He gave a quick apologetic smile, though he cursed himself inwardly for having drawn attention to himself. He sidled in behind a display of coffee cups and travel mugs, keeping an eye on the front desk. To his relief, none of the women at the front counter seemed to have noticed the disturbance. Feeling a prickle at the back of his neck, he glanced sideways at the woman he had annoyed. She glared at him as she stacked her arms with t-shirts in a variety of colors and sizes — obviously stocking up on souvenirs for the family and friends back home. And he was sure she would add how hard she'd fought for them.

"Did... um, did you need some help, sir?" The voice at his elbow shocked him and he jerked around, nearly toppling the display of cups. The blond woman who had spoken to him jumped back, her tawny brown eyes grew round with dismay, and red blotches of embarrassment stained her pale face as she collided with the woman who was buying the t-shirts. She bit her lip and made a valiant effort to smile at both him and the irate customer, but neither of them was in the mood to be placated.

"Is there any way that I can possibly make a rather sizable purchase without being trampled?" the woman demanded, capturing the blond woman's attention and giving him an opportunity to slip away.

He'd been standing around too long; he knew it and he had to get out before someone else noticed him. He threw one more glance toward the front counter and snaked through the crowd toward the laundry room. The door swung open just as he put his hand on it.

"Oh, sorry, man." This time he nearly let a curse word explode from between his gritted teeth. The man stood back, holding the laundry room door open, and gave him an easy smile. "Here, let me help you escape. Unless you need help with something? I'm one of the employees here. J.D. Wilder." Of course he knew who the dark man in the black campground t-shirt was — a former lieutenant with the narcotics division of the Houston Police Department. He'd done his homework well. Once a cop, always a cop, he told himself as he managed a smile that he hoped didn't look as sick or phony as he felt and he forced himself to walk, not bolt, through the door.

It took every ounce of his strength not to glance back, although he was dying to find out if J.D. Wilder was really watching him or if it was just his nerves that were giving him the prickly sensation that tickled the back of his neck. No matter. A few more days and things would be different.

As he stepped off the covered, brick-paved patio where the Black Horse Campground hosted its social events, the rain stopped. He took it as a good sign. His smile became real.

A few more days....

~

Corrie Black scurried around the room, filling glasses for her friends and co-workers with their choice of iced tea or well-chilled Jo Mamma's White table wine. Nearly everyone, with the exception of RaeLynn Shaffer, took the wine. Even Jerry Page, who normally only consumed half a glass of red wine in the evenings, accepted a glass of the sweet white wine. “It's a celebration,” he insisted to his wife, Jackie, who pursed her lips and shook her head, sending her silver-gray ponytail swinging in disapproval.

It was well after eight p. m. and the Black Horse Campground office had finally managed to close its doors after checking in the last guest of the day. Around the campground was the low buzz of conversations, spiked with laughter and shouts from the basketball court and horse shoe pit and splashes from the pool. The scent of charcoal fires, with the combined aromas of steaks, hamburgers, hot dogs, and burnt marshmallows mingled with the refreshing pine-scented air and made the mood even more festive.

J.D. Wilder accepted his glass and hefted the wooden board under his arm as Corrie finished serving everyone and stood at J.D.'s side, holding one end of the board. “Okay, Shelli,” she announced, as everyone around the room raised their glasses. “Hit it!”

“Whomp, whomp!” Shelli Davenport cried as Corrie and J.D. hoisted the sign up for all to see and the room erupted in cheers. “No Vacancy” it stated in big, bold, black letters across a plain white background. The cheering continued as they exited the campground office and made an informal procession across the graveled parking lot and up the ramp to the big, well–lit sign that identified the entrance to the campground by the side of U.S. Highway 70. There, Buster, the campground's maintenance man, took Corrie's end of the sign and helped J.D. fasten it over the word “Welcome” and the two men stepped back. Everyone burst into applause, then laughter, as Buster ceremoniously took a bow, then joined in the laughter as he gestured for Corrie to take center stage.

"Okay, everyone!" she said as the cheers died away. "I just want to thank you all for the hard work you put in today—our first 'No Vacancy' day of the season...." she paused to let a few whoops and whistles punctuate her words. "Thanks to Shelli for providing the celebration libations," she went on.

"Hey, it was the least I could do, since it was my day off today!" Shelli said, holding up a wine bottle. Corrie grinned, then turned and nodded to Myra Kaydahzinne and Buster.

"To the maintenance crew for making us look good."

Myra dropped a curtsy and Buster again made a ceremonious bow, then waved again as if to invite further applause, which only encouraged more laughter. Corrie's grin widened and she went on.

"The office crew, Jackie and Dana, and the right-hand men, Jerry and Red," she nodded toward her long-time employees that were more family to her, "for keeping the customers happy and me sane."

"Hey!" Dee Dee Simpson, Corrie's part-time store help who was more decorative than functional most of the time, pushed her ruby-red lips into a lush pout. Dee Dee had, for once, managed to put in an appearance according to her work schedule and she couldn't have picked a better day to do it. "What about me? I think I did a pretty good job of keeping the customers happy!"

"The men, yes, their wives... not so much," Jackie murmured and Corrie bit back a laugh.

"To Dee Dee, for NOT calling in today and for exerting herself above and beyond her usual level to keep the customers happy." Dee Dee crinkled her nose and joined in the good-natured chuckles; no one could ever accuse her of striving to be employee of the month and she made no excuses for it. To her, the part-time jobs she held in Bonney County kept her body and soul together until her big break in L.A. finally came through.

Corrie turned to J.D. and to RaeLynn, who had melted into the background, sipping her iced tea and trying to make herself invisible. "And to our newest members of the 'zoo crew'," Corrie said, lifting her glass in their direction, "J.D. and RaeLynn, who made a superior showing at helping the guests in the store and in the campground. Welcome aboard and thanks for not handing in your two-weeks' notice after this crazy day!"

"Amen!" Red boomed, nudging Shelli to refill his wine glass. Dana shot him a glare. He relented and took Dana's glass for Shelli to refill first. J.D. inclined his head and lifted his glass to Corrie in a salute.

"Believe me, it's a nice break from having to chase down criminals or file paperwork. And the coffee is way better!" he added and Corrie rolled her eyes. She wondered how many cups of piñon coffee J.D. had consumed during the course of the day.

"So does this mean you're giving up a career in law enforcement for the opportunity to spend your days cleaning the pool, parking RVs, and sweeping walkways... in other words, retirement?" Jerry asked, his eyes glimmering with humor over his walrus mustache which made him look gruffer than he really was.

J.D. laughed. "I don't think the word 'retirement' will ever be in my vocabulary, not if it means not working!" The Myers and Pages nodded sagely.

"Well, I can't promise that you'll never have a dull moment around here," Corrie said, then grimaced, remembering the events of the past few months—events that J.D. had had the unfortunate luck of having been a participant. His eyes met hers and a slight smile told her that he had the same thought.

"Let's hope for a lot of dull moments," he said softly, raising his glass once more, and this time Red's "Amen" had a lot of fervent echoes.

"RaeLynn," Corrie said and the young woman jumped at the sound of her name, a flood of crimson rushing to her face. Everyone turned in her direction and she blushed harder, and busied herself studying the ice cubes in her tea glass. Corrie smiled and waved RaeLynn in closer to the group.

"Come on," Corrie coaxed, giving RaeLynn a warm, encouraging smile. "You were a great help today and I don't know what I would have done without your help. It was nice not to have to worry about customers not being helped on the floor while we were manning the counter. And believe me, we hardly had a moment to breathe at the counter!"

RaeLynn had crept closer and, to Corrie's annoyance, J.D. shifted away from her slightly. The movement was hardly perceptible and Corrie doubted anyone else had noticed... anyone but her and RaeLynn. RaeLynn kept her eyes on the ground except for a quick glance she cast at Corrie.

"You're too nice to me, Corrie," RaeLynn said softly. "I made a lot of mistakes today. You just didn't want to notice."

"It was practically your first day on the job," Corrie said firmly and Jackie nodded.

"And we were a lot busier than the other times you've helped out," Jackie said. There were murmurs of assent around the group and Corrie felt a flash of irritation that the level of enthusiasm had dropped considerably. Only Jackie and Shelli made an attempt to exhibit any enthusiasm over RaeLynn's assistance that day.

A vehicle turned off the main highway and came down the ramp leading to the Black Horse's parking area. It was nearly nine o'clock, too late for a campground guest, if there had been any more reservations they had been expecting, and Corrie's concern melted into a heat wave of surprised pleasure when she recognized the dark blue Chevy Tahoe with the words "Bonney County Sheriff" emblazoned on the side in dark gold lettering. Right behind it was a sheriff's department cruiser and Myra let out a stifled squeal of delight when she recognized Deputy Dudley Evans at the wheel of the Chevy Impala.

Sheriff Rick Sutton pulled up alongside the small group and leaned out the window of the Tahoe. "Evening, folks," he said, his dark blue eyes resting on Corrie a fraction of a second longer than on anyone else. Deputy Evans parked his cruiser behind the Tahoe and Corrie noticed Myra scooting eagerly over to speak to him. Rick went on, "Is everything all right?"

"It's wonderful," Corrie said. "First night we're filled to capacity!" She pointed to the sign and Rick inclined his head with a slight smile—the equivalent of anyone else turning cartwheels and screaming with glee.

"Not bad for the middle of June... one of the earliest 'No Vacancy' days you've had in a while, isn't it?" he asked. Of course, Corrie should have realized that Rick would know that bit of information. He'd been an unofficial part of the Black Horse for as long as anyone could remember and he knew how badly the drought had affected the campground and the tourist traffic in the last few years. The fire restrictions, while necessary, always put a damper on the summer season. No one wanted to camp when they couldn't use grills or have campfires. It was usually sometime in mid-July, when the monsoonal rains had provided enough moisture for the Forestry Service to lift the restrictions, that they had been full enough to hang out the "No Vacancy" sign. Corrie hoped—and she knew Rick shared this hope with her—that the early start to the season would help make up for the last few years when business hadn't been so great. "Looks like the celebration is in full swing," he added.

"Care to join us?" Corrie said. Before Rick could comment on everyone's wine glasses, she gestured to RaeLynn's glass and added, “We have iced tea for on-duty officers of the law.”

Rick shook his head. “I'd like to, but I've got a few reports I have to put to bed before I call it quits for the night.”

“You're working late, Sheriff,” J.D. commented, taking a slow sip from his wine glass and studying Rick over the rim. Corrie could feel the coolness of the evening drop by a few degrees. Would Rick and J.D. ever get past their first meeting and become friends? “Things have been pretty quiet around here lately.”

“Yes,” Rick said simply. “But I've got a deputy on vacation and another one on leave of absence for an appendix removal, so a few of us are pulling double shifts. Plus, I have to review a proposal I'm submitting to the county commission regarding protective gear, like bullet-resistant vests, but they're arguing that we don't need any gear that's much more protective than an extra-heavy sweatshirt.” He shook his head in disgust. “Besides, paperwork has gone by the wayside too often in the last few days. Best catch it up before tomorrow brings us anymore reasons to write up new reports.”

Before Corrie could ask how Deputy Gabe Apachito was recovering from his appendectomy, Myra bustled up to her, her pretty bronzed face glowing in the dim light from the fading evening. “Corrie, do you mind if I leave the celebration right now? Dudley—I mean, Deputy Evans, is going off duty and he offered me a ride home.”

Corrie bit back a smile. Myra's and Dudley's romance was no secret to anyone at the Black Horse or the sheriff's department. Rick cocked an eyebrow at her and one corner of his mouth lifted in a grin. “Go ahead, Myra,” Corrie said. “Thanks for all your help today and don't forget, I've got you on a split shift tomorrow so you don't have to be here before two in the afternoon.”

“However, Deputy Evans is scheduled at eight in the morning,” Rick said, mock gruffness in his voice. “Keep that in mind, or he'll be turning into a pumpkin at midnight, young lady.” He winked at Myra's blush and giddy grin.

“Yes, sir, Sheriff!” she said. She giggled and then hurried over to the cruiser and climbed in the passenger side. It was one of the perks allowed by the sheriff's department—or rather Rick himself—that the members were allowed to use the department's vehicles for personal use, as long as they conducted themselves appropriately. She and Dudley managed to wait until he had pulled the cruiser up to the stop sign at the top of the ramp before they leaned in for a kiss, then Dudley floored it, scattering gravel, as they headed off into the night.

Rick sighed and shook his head. "Wonder if she'll still be calling him 'Deputy Evans' when they get married?"

"'When'?" chorused the group and Rick's grin widened.

"He's had a little velvet box from Kendall's Jewelers burning a hole in his pocket since five o ' clock this afternoon. But you didn't hear that from me," he warned as exclamations of delight rose from the group. "If we weren't so short-handed, I'd have let him have tomorrow off."

"How sweet!" Shelli cried. "I wonder when the big day will be?"

"We'll all know soon enough," Rick said. "Don't forget that softball practice is tomorrow evening after the enchilada dinner. I don't know if Gabe will be recovered from surgery before our first game on July fourth. Might have to find someone else to play catcher." He seemed to be studiously avoiding a glance in J.D.'s direction and Corrie wondered if J.D. would take the hint. Rick went on, "I'll let you folks get back to your celebration. Have a good evening." He lowered his voice. "See you in the morning," he said to Corrie as he pulled away.

A pang shot through her; it would never go away. She could feel J.D.'s eyes on her so she fought to keep her regret off her face as she turned back to her employees. "Well, it's been a long day for us as well, and it's time we all called it a night, too."

No one argued too strenuously. Dee Dee and Buster thrust their wine glasses into Shelli's hands and made beelines for their respective vehicles. It appeared that they had plans for after work on this Thursday evening. The Pages and the Myers said their good-nights to everyone else before heading to their RV homes for the night. That left Shelli, J.D., and RaeLynn to walk back to the office with Corrie. "Do you have a ride home tonight, RaeLynn?" Corrie asked.

RaeLynn blushed furiously. "I was supposed to," she mumbled. "But that was at seven and they haven't shown up yet." Corrie suspected that some member of RaeLynn's family had, once again, forgotten to pick her up from work. This had happened at least twice a week since RaeLynn had begun working full time at the campground in late May. Twice Corrie had given her a ride home, but RaeLynn usually was adamant about walking home, a journey of at least three miles. During daylight hours, Corrie had let her win the argument, but she hated the thought of RaeLynn walking home alone during the late evening. Shelli spoke up.

"I'll be going right past your mom's house, RaeLynn," she said. Corrie knew that Shelli didn't live anywhere near the Shaffer's dilapidated double-wide, but she kept quiet, knowing RaeLynn hated to make anyone go out of their way for her. "I can drop you off if you're ready to head out."

"Sure," RaeLynn said quickly. Whether her reluctance to go to her parents' home was tempered by her gratitude or vice versa, Corrie couldn't tell. She collected the wine glasses from Shelli's hands, managing to balance them in one hand, said good night to her two friends and watched them head toward Shelli's burnt-orange Saturn Vue.

That left J.D.

He reached out and relieved her of three of the wine glasses before she had to start juggling. Corrie smiled at him. He seemed in no hurry to say good night and head to his one-man tent that had been home to him since he had first arrived at the Black Horse nearly two months earlier. He returned the smile. "You don't look like you just spent sixteen hours on your feet," he commented.

"I am too thrilled by the great start our summer season is off to," she said. "It's been rough for a while, but I think it's going to get better. Last year, the drought closed the forest from April to mid-September and it was the first time I didn't have a single 'No Vacancy' day. I checked the reservation book earlier and, except for one or two nights, I'm booked solid through the July fourth weekend. As Shelli would say, 'Whomp, whomp'!"

J.D. laughed. "That says it all!" He paused, then said, "Look, I know it's been a long day for you, so I should let you go get some rest, but I'm still wide-awake and I was thinking of making some coffee. If you'd like to join me, I'd love to have some company."

Corrie was grateful that the evening darkness hid the rush of heat to her face. She tipped up her wine glass and drained the last few drops. "I don't suppose it would be piñon coffee?" she asked to hide her eagerness to accept the invitation.

"What else is there? With the exception of beer, water, and an occasional glass of Noisy Water wine, it's about all I drink."

"It would probably keep me from sleeping through the alarm in the morning. Let me take the glasses back into the kitchen and I'll meet you in a few minutes."

"I'll help you. The coffee's all set up and I just have to push a button when we get to my tent."

"Oh?" Corrie raised a brow at him. "You have a coffee maker now?" Previously, he'd used a camp coffee pot on his Coleman stove to make coffee. His definition of "roughing it" had been modified. "How'd you manage that? Your site doesn't have electricity on it."

He grinned as he scooped up the glasses left behind by the Myers and Pages and nodded toward the camp office. "I had to switch sites with a guest who wanted to be closer to the RVs because his family was in that section. So now I'm closer to the campground store and I've entered the twentieth-century... at least as far as coffee making goes. Takes less time and it's easier to clean. Plus it's less likely to boil over."

Corrie smiled and they walked toward the camp office in companionable silence. The cool breeze sighed in the pine trees and the babble of the nearby river made a soothing finale to a busy day. She reflected that, despite the hectic day, things had gone quite well. There had been a few incidents where ruffled feathers had to be smoothed and her staff had risen to the challenge admirably. But she also knew that, no matter how well things ran, there would always be a guest or two that would have some complaint about something. It came with the territory. She sighed and shook her head as she and J.D. entered the camp store.

"What is it?" J.D. asked, shouldering the door open. From upstairs, where Corrie had had to relegate them, Renfro, her late father's ancient black Lab, let out a dutiful "woof" at the sound of the bell tinkling over the door and her black and gray tabby, Oliver, let out a mournful wail. The dog and cat were fixtures in the camp store, often spending the day in blissful slumber behind the counter. However, the crush of the guests in the store and the extra helpers crowding the area behind the counter convinced Corrie that everyone would be more comfortable if the two mascots remained in her upstairs apartment. But now that it was quiet, both pets wanted the run of the building as they were accustomed.

"Hold on," Corrie said, scooting past J.D. and hurrying up the stairs to open the apartment door. Oliver practically leaped down to the ground floor, purring ecstatically at his freedom. Renfro yawned, thumped his tail gratefully, and carefully navigated the steps as quickly as his arthritic old limbs would carry him. Corrie didn't have the heart to tell him that he'd probably be making the arduous trek back up the stairs within the hour. With a chuckle, she followed him back down to where J.D. was waiting.

"Just leave the glasses on the counter, J.D., and I'll... what?" she asked, stopping short at the bottom of the stairs. J.D. had already set the glasses down and stood, holding an envelope and a sheet of paper in his hands. The expression on his face was grim and he jerked his head toward the phone.

"Call the sheriff," he said quietly. "I think he'd better see this."

"What is it?" Corrie said, coming up to him, her heart pounding. J.D. held out the paper, to her, carefully holding it by the edges so as to preserve any fingerprints. In huge dark letters were the words, "CLOSE THE CAMPGROUND SATURDAY. THIS IS YOUR ONLY WARNING. YOUR LIFE IS IN DANGER."

Chapter 1

Corrie swatted off the alarm Friday morning, hoping that the previous night's events had merely been a bad dream. She opened her eyes and, despite the serene familiarity of her bedroom, everything rushed into her mind with sickening clarity.

Rick's plans to wrap up paperwork at the sheriff's office were shelved as he returned to the Black Horse to see the anonymous note J.D. had found. It had been shoved under the door, so close to the hinges that neither J.D. nor Corrie had seen it until J.D. had pushed the door closed while Corrie went to release Renfro and Oliver. Not taking the time—nor having the heart—to call in Deputy Evans to dust the note and the door for fingerprints, Rick did it himself. It did nothing to alleviate Corrie's apprehension when none turned up except for J.D.'s. She and J.D. racked their memories but neither of them recalled seeing anyone approach the front door of the camp store while they were engaged in the celebration by the campground sign.

The phone had rung; Jackie and Jerry had seen the sheriff's Tahoe come roaring back into camp at the unusual hour and, naturally, were concerned. Since Jerry had a reputation for being a night owl with the ears of a cat, Rick asked them to come over for coffee and questioning—the coffee had been Corrie's suggestion—and, since they had to pass by the Myers' restored Airstream, Red and Dana had ended up joining them.

No, they hadn't noticed anyone lurking around the camp store while they were at the sign. No, no one had been hanging around the camp store after closing hours, not that they noticed. No, there hadn't been any suspicious people hanging around throughout the day.

"I'm glad you didn't ask if there were any 'strangers' hanging around," Jackie said wryly. "With the exception of the staff, that's all we had around here today."

"You didn't notice any suspicious or strange behavior, anyone who seemed to be casing the place, anyone asking a lot of questions?" Rick's patience was rapidly evaporating as the heads of all the Black Horse employees kept shaking. He sighed irritably. "Someone had to have seen something!"

"Well, the only ones missing from this meeting are Dee Dee

and RaeLynn. They were both helping out in the store today," Corrie said, a little irritated herself at Rick's impatience. "And Myra. She came in early to clean the laundry room, TV room, and kitchen, then she did the bathrooms from eleven to one, then she had to run some errands and take her grandmother to a doctor's appointment. She was back at five-thirty and stayed till closing, cleaning my apartment. And Buster was out working on the grounds with J.D., Red, and Jerry...."

"And we had those three kids working today—Darrell, Jon, and Will. But I think they all left by five o'clock," Jackie added.

"Do you want me to call them all in?" Corrie asked Rick, almost—but not quite—embarrassed at her testiness. Rick shot her a look.

"I doubt Buster and those three boys had much interaction with any of the guests, but you never know. I definitely want to talk to Myra, Dee Dee, and RaeLynn. If anyone had an opportunity to see anything suspicious, they would be the most likely. " He shook his head. "But I can wait until tomorrow to talk to them, if they're scheduled to be here."

"All of them, except Myra, should be here by eight in the morning although, to be honest, I can't guarantee that Dee Dee will show up," Corrie sighed. She noticed J.D.'s lips twisting in half-grin, half-grimace and she realized that Dee Dee had become far more conscientious about showing up for work, on time and as scheduled, since J.D. had begun working here. "But none of them mentioned any odd or suspicious behavior."

"Just because they didn't mention it doesn't mean they didn't see it," Rick said. He slipped his ever-present notepad back into his shirt pocket. "Do you have anything special scheduled for this particular Saturday?" he asked Corrie.

"Just the usual... pancakes for breakfast and pizza party at dinner time."

"Nothing scheduled personally?" The question almost came out too casually and his eyes flicked in J.D.'s direction for a split second. Corrie didn't know whether to be amused, flattered, or annoyed.

"Nothing."

"All right," Rick said. He had sealed the letter and envelope in a clear plastic evidence bag and he held it up, eyeing it with distaste. "It could just be a prank, but let's not take any chances. I'm checking all your windows and doors to make sure they're secure...."

"Surely I can manage to lock my own windows and doors, Rick," Corrie said, her testiness rushing back in full force. To her surprise, J.D. spoke up.

"It won't hurt to be extra cautious," he said. He looked at Rick. "I know you're short-handed right now, Sheriff, but I can keep an eye on the camp store and office tonight."

"Wouldn't want to interfere with any plans you might have, Wilder," Rick said, his courteous tone tempered with coolness.

"Nah," J.D. said with exaggerated casualness as he leaned on the counter. "Corrie and I were going to have a cup of coffee anyway, so...."

"I think we've all had enough coffee, and...." Rick stopped, his face flushing. He avoided Corrie's eyes and busied himself putting away the fingerprint kit. "Whatever. Lock up behind us and I'll check the doors and windows from the outside before I leave. Call if you see anything remotely suspicious." His eyes locked with J.D.'s for a moment, then he glanced at Corrie. "I'll be back in the morning."

A chorus of "good nights" came from the Pages and Myers as they left to go back to their respective RVs and Rick followed them out. Then he and J.D. made a circuit around the building, J.D. locking all possible points of entry and Rick testing them for security from the outside. Before he left, Rick pointed to the side door and J.D. nodded. "What was that?" Corrie asked, her brow furrowing as Rick headed to his Tahoe and left.

"He was telling me to use only one door to go in and out and to use that one," J.D. said, nodding at the side door. "We don't want to compromise any more windows or doors than we have to, now that we know they're all secure."

"Lovely. I suppose this means that I won't be able to open my bedroom window tonight?" she said. J.D. grinned.

"Not unless you want me to sleep outside it all night. Got any heavy-duty Velcro to keep me from rolling off the roof?"

Corrie laughed. "That won't be necessary. Thanks for checking the building, but you don't need to put yourself out. If everything is secure, then I'm sure I'll be fine. You and Rick were very thorough."

He seemed ready to say something, then changed his mind. "All right," he said. "I'm trusting you to lock your window. And if you hear or see anything suspicious," he held up his cell phone, "call me first, then the sheriff. I don't care if he breaks the sound barrier, I'll still be here faster than he can be."

"Good night, J.D.," she said as he headed out the side door and waited for her to secure the locks.

Now she sat up, eyeing the clock on her nightstand dismally. The time read five-thirty and she was positive that the last time she looked at it was shortly after four, and before that, at ten to fifteen minute intervals since she'd gone to bed at nearly eleven. She'd tried to keep her concern and anxiety hidden from both J.D. and Rick but she was sure they knew exactly how she felt.

She slipped out of bed and headed to the bathroom, shooting a glance at the window to make sure it was still locked and testing the door of the apartment that led down to the camp store to make sure it was secure. She shook her head, annoyed at herself for letting her nerves get the better of her, and took the quickest shower of her life before heading downstairs. Renfro and Oliver followed, glad to not be relegated to the apartment. It occurred to Corrie, with a pang of regret, that if she had let her dog and cat out of the apartment before they went to go hang the "No Vacancy" sign out, then Renfro would have definitely sounded an alarm when her mysterious "messenger" had arrived.

She flipped on the light switch at the bottom of the stairs, but no aroma of piñon coffee greeted her. To her chagrin, she remembered that she hadn't set up her coffee maker to go off this morning as usual. With a groan, she went to make a pot of coffee, only grudgingly admitting to herself that she had allowed herself to be spoiled by her auto-start coffee maker. As she filled the pot with water from the kitchen spigot, she let her mind sift through the disconnected pictures in her mind of the dozens of people who had filed through her office and store—her home, really—over the course of the last twenty-four hours. Most were merely blurs, like unfocused photographs, and none really stood out clearly. Perhaps Jackie or Dana could recall someone who might seem to be the type to shove that note under the door.

But what did that type look like?

She started the coffee and moved to her seat behind the counter. She stared at her paperwork and her computer, not seeing either of them. What did the note mean anyway? Why would her life be in danger? And why should she have to close on Saturday? Was the writer of the note an enemy or a friend who was trying to warn her? And did he—or she—mean just Corrie, herself, was in danger, or were her friends and employees at risk as well? She shook her head to clear it and glanced at the wall clock. It was barely after six, too early to expect Jackie or Dana to show up. She wondered if J.D. had gotten any sleep at all.

As if he'd heard her thoughts, he suddenly materialized at the side door of the office. His alert look relaxed as she flashed him a smile and he held up his thermal mug that held three times the amount of coffee as the Styrofoam cups on the courtesy table. She laughed as she let him in.

"Did the smell of piñon coffee wake you up or did you bother to go to bed at all?" she asked as she let him in and locked the door behind him.

He gave her a sleepy smile. "I must have heard every snore, every cricket chirp, every leaf rustle all night long. And you had eighteen campers make trips to the restrooms," he added. He shook his head as he filled his coffee cup and filled one for her as well. "Thinking on it now, it seems silly to think whoever left you that note would try anything last night. I mean, if that were the case, why bother to warn you? Why not just take action?"

"IF," Corrie said, "they were the ones planning whatever 'action' that note was warning me about. Or they might have panicked after seeing all the attention their note got last night and maybe decided to do some damage control."

"Like what? A note saying, 'April fool!'" J.D. shook his head and took a sip of coffee. He took a moment to close his eyes and sigh with pleasure before he went on. "Have you given any thought about what that note might mean?" he asked, his steel-gray eyes suddenly snapping open with alertness.

She shook her head. "I don't have a clue, J.D. To my knowledge, I haven't done anything to tick anyone off. Not so much that my life would be in danger from it."

He set his mug down on the counter and leaned back, folding his arms across his chest. "Do we know for a fact that the message was aimed at you, personally? Or someone else who works here?"

"Or all of us collectively," Corrie added. She shrugged. "Honestly, I don't have any idea who that warning—I'm taking it as a warning, that's how it was worded—was aimed at." She looked at him for a long moment, wondering where his thoughts were going with his question. "J.D., no one who works here has the authority to close the campground. I'm the only one who can do that. That message had to be for me... and it did seem more like a warning than a threat."

"I'd like to see you convince the sheriff that the person who shoved that note under your door was a friend," J.D. said dryly. "Why didn't they sign the note? Or how about this—warn you in person?"

"Maybe," Corrie said slowly, a chill snaking down her back as the thought in her mind unfolded, "maybe they're in as much danger as I am."

They looked at each other for a long moment, then a knock on the door made Corrie jump and nearly drop her coffee cup. J.D. spun around, his hand dropping to his side as he reached for a firearm he no longer carried, a habit he couldn't seem to kick whenever there was a stressful situation.

"It's Rick," Corrie said, hurrying to the door, her heart still hammering in her throat. J.D. didn't answer, just took a long pull on his coffee cup. "You're here early," she said as she opened the door.

Rick stepped in, looking very much like he had just a few hours earlier and Corrie wondered if he had bothered to go to bed. He removed his Stetson and gave J.D. a nod as Corrie went to get him some coffee. J.D. raised his cup to him. "Nothing to report, Sheriff," he said.

"That's good news," Rick said as Corrie placed the cup in his hand. He took a sip, grimaced, and threw her a look of disgust.

"The bad news is, you're almost an hour early and I haven't brewed any regular coffee yet. You'll have to make do with piñon coffee for the next ten minutes."

"I'll wait," Rick said, handing the cup back to Corrie. Most people fell in love with the New Mexico piñon coffee she sold and served in the camp store. But Rick Sutton wasn't like most people. He turned his attention back to the matter at hand. "Have you given any thought as to who that note might have been referring to?"

"We were just discussing that," Corrie admitted. She told him what she and J.D. had talked about before his arrival. "What's puzzling me is, why Saturday? And why give me two days' warning?"

Rick shook his head. "Can you think of any reason why shutting down the campground would be of any benefit to anyone? Are you expecting anyone to arrive on Saturday that might be considered a threat to anyone?"

Corrie let out a laugh. "Unless known terrorists or criminals are in the habit of making reservations in their own names, no." She went around the counter to her seat and brought up her reservations list on her computer. "The majority of people who checked in today—make that yesterday—are booked straight through to Sunday, Monday, or Tuesday. A total of three are due to check out today, but they've been here since last weekend. Six are supposed to check out Saturday...." She paused, eyeing the list for a long moment.

"What?" The question burst from both J.D. and Rick simultaneously and with the same degree of impatience. She looked up at them.

"Well, for Saturday, I only have two vacancies left. Of the six that check out that day, there are four more reservations to replace them. And those were made a week ago or longer," she added. "But there's still room for two more reservations or drop-ins...."

"RV or tent sites?" Rick asked. She shook her head.

"Both are cabins."

J.D. broke the silence. "Do you suppose whoever wrote that note is trying to keep someone from checking in that day?"

"But who? A guest who already has a reservation... or do they know that someone will be coming in that day who needs one?"

Rick shook his head. "It's too risky to assume that there will be a space available without making a reservation. They have to know that someone is going to be here who already has a spot secured for them. So it's either someone who's already here or someone who will be getting here on Saturday."

"And... what?" Corrie asked. "What is it that they expect this 'someone' to do? They said my life is in danger if I don't close the campground. What will they do if I don't? Blow up the place? Shoot me? Poison the pancake batter?"

"Well, you can just rock us to sleep tonight," J.D. muttered. Corrie threw him an exasperated look.

"Don't you see, J.D.? All of those threats involve other people getting hurt, not just me. It doesn't make sense!"

"No, it doesn't," Rick said shortly, his eyes darkening to the color of midnight. "And that, frankly, is what scares me, Corrie." He glanced at the clock. "I have to get to the office, but I'm coming back at eight. I want all your employees who were here yesterday to be here when I get back...."

"Even Shelli? She isn't on the schedule to work today and, yesterday, she didn't get here until almost closing time. All she did was bring the wine for the celebration." Rick shook his head.

"Call her and tell her she needs to rack her memory for anything that might have seemed out of place or if anyone else mentioned something to her in passing. They might have mentioned it then forgotten about it. We can't ignore the least suspicious thing."

They all became quiet. Corrie took a deep breath, trying to calm her hammering heart. It all seemed like a nightmare, but she refused to let herself be paralyzed with fear. Whatever this threat might be, it threatened her employees—her friends, her family—as well, and she wasn't about to let that happen. She looked up, saw that both J.D. and Rick were watching her. "I'm fine," she said, her tone a little sharper than she intended. "We'll carry on as usual, unless you think I should close the campground. The safety of my staff and my guests matters most to me. I just don't see what difference it makes that I close on Saturday."

"It has to be someone who's arriving that day," J.D. said. He looked at Rick, then nodded at Corrie. "Who are the people arriving on Saturday? And don't," he added, giving her a stern look, "start with any invasion of privacy stuff."

Corrie threw Rick a rueful smile. "Got a warrant, Sheriff?"

"I could get one," he said, not smiling.

"I'll save Judge Sedillos the trouble," she muttered, reaching for a notepad and scribbling the names and addresses of the guests who were scheduled to arrive Saturday. She tore off the page and handed it to Rick. "Two things I noticed," she said as Rick scanned the list. "One, all of those guests are from Texas, but from different cities."

"Dallas, Lubbock, Abilene, and Ft. Hancock," Rick said for J.D.'s benefit.

"Two," Corrie went on. "They're all couples. No family groups, no singles. Just double-occupancy on the reservations."

"Married couples?" J.D. asked.

"They all have the same last names," Rick answered. He shrugged. "These are all points that might matter, or might not matter. I'm not going to overlook anything, no matter how minor a point it might be. And that's what I want to impress on your employees, Corrie," he said, his voice turning stony. "No matter how trivial, stupid, insignificant, funny, coincidental... you get the idea. I want to know about anything or anyone that drew their attention, even if only for a split second."

Corrie looked back at the guest list and sighed. "With over eighty people checking in during an eight-hour period, you're sure not asking for much, Sheriff."

Chapter 2

Despite his misgivings, J.D. had to admit that Sheriff Sutton certainly knew how to conduct an inquiry without making a public event out of it.

The sheriff had returned to the campground at ten minutes to eight and drew a double-take from every one of the employees of the Black Horse, including J.D., himself. Instead of his usual pristine Bonney County sheriff's department uniform and Tahoe, he arrived in a pair of Wrangler jeans, a light blue button-down Western shirt, and a well-worn pair of Tony Lama's. He'd left his Tahoe at home and arrived in his late-model dark blue Silverado.

And he had the good sense to conduct his questioning in Corrie's living quarters where he would be less likely to be noticed by the female guests populating the campground.

He'd called in Deputies Dudley Evans and Mike Ramirez to assist in patrolling the campground. Like the sheriff, they had arrived in their own personal vehicles and, upon arrival, had been presented with Black Horse Campground t-shirts to enable them to circulate around the campground and among the guests without announcing their status as law enforcement officers. J.D. wondered aloud how long it would take them to blow their cover if they were asked any questions regarding the day-to-day operations of the campground.

Mike Ramirez, who sported a magnificent handlebar mustache, grinned, tipped back his straw Stetson, and affected a Mexican accent, "I just say, 'No hablo inglés, amigo'," and he proceeded to belt out a few lines from a Mexican ballad. "Then I better hope they don't decide to call Immigration and Naturalization Services on me!" he added reverting back to his usual drawl.

"That's all I'll need," Corrie groused. She glanced over at a rather subdued Dudley Evans. "What's your cover story?"

"First day on the job," he said shortly. Though Dudley Evans was usually quiet and kept his face expressionless during the course of his work days, he seemed tired and out-of-sorts... not unexpected, considering that he and Myra had probably been up half the night discussing wedding plans. Since Rick had warned them not to bring it up until Dudley or Myra did, J.D. noted that

Corrie kept her questions to herself despite the fact that she had to be bursting with the urge to offer congratulations. However, Dudley didn't look like a man who was recently engaged, but perhaps he was too concerned over how this threat might affect his intended to be in a very celebratory mood.

The deputies headed out, led by J.D.—Buster, not surprisingly, was late for work—to be given the yard tools that would serve as props for their undercover work. J.D. just hoped that Buster wouldn't see them before the sheriff had a chance to talk to him, or he would be right over, blowing their cover and demanding to know what was going on.

After stationing the two deputies where they could "work" and perhaps overhear any interesting conversations, J.D. went back to the camp store. He walked in just as the three teenagers, Will Davis, Jon Comanche, and Darrell LaRue, were being allowed to leave the questioning. Will and Jon looked as if they were doing everything they could to keep their excitement and pride over being considered witnesses in a sheriff's department investigation under wraps. They walked with their heads up and chests out, practically strutting over their imagined importance. J.D. doubted that they'd given the sheriff any useful information; he had seen them over the course of their work day with their ear buds effectively blocking out the world and their eyes and hands constantly checking whatever important information might be found on their cell phones. Darrell LaRue slouched out of the camp store behind them, his expression sullen and his hands deep in his pockets. Being questioned by the police in an investigation was nothing new to him, and perhaps memories of his last experience, where he discovered that the girl he cared for had only been using him to get to one of his friends, still rankled.

Corrie came down the stairs and motioned for Red Myers to follow her up to the "interrogation room" as they had dubbed her personal sitting area. Jackie and Jerry Page had already been questioned and neither of them seemed to recall any incidents or conversations with or among the guests that merited a second thought. Corrie came back down the stairs, shaking her head.

"No one remembers anything being said or anyone acting strange, though I think the boys would have liked to be able to say they did."

"I figured as much," J.D. said. Despite the look of calm control on Corrie's face, J.D. could tell that she was worried. The threat had been so vaguely worded as to sound like a joke, but still had enough directness and no-nonsense feel to it for them to take it seriously. He shifted restlessly. "I should be out on the grounds with the deputies; maybe I might hear something...."

Corrie shrugged. "I have over fifty campsites for RVs and tents, plus eight cabins, that are currently occupied. The entire sheriff's department and village police department combined doesn't have enough man power to monitor all the people on site, even if Rick didn't have two deputies out." She bit back a sigh. "I wish someone would remember something, anything, that would give us a clue so we can get this issue taken care of."

J.D. eyed her. "Sutton wants you to close the campground?" he asked.

"He thinks it might not be a bad idea, from a safety standpoint," Corrie said. "Financially, J.D., it's a hit I'd rather not take. But I have to think of the safety of my guests and employees...."

"And your own," J.D. added and Corrie gave a slight shudder, as if she would have rather he hadn't mentioned it. She looked at him and the depth of helplessness and anger he saw in her eyes was like a punch in the gut.

"What is this all about, J.D.? Is it aimed at me, the Black Horse, or someone else, someone I don't even know? And if it is, why choose this place, my home and business, to threaten them?" Her words came out in a desperate whisper and he reached for her hand and squeezed it. She clutched back as if she were drowning and he were a life preserver.

"We'll find out, Corrie," he said, keeping his voice low, but capturing her gaze with his and hoping she could see his determination to keep her safe. "Whoever it is, whatever they're up to, we'll find them and you and your family will be safe."

She managed a shaky smile then pulled herself together. To his dismay, she also pulled her hand out of his. "I know," she said, her voice stronger. "I know you and Rick won't let this person hurt me or anyone else."

Rick. J.D. felt the sheriff's name like another punch in the gut. No matter what, it seemed like she couldn't get the sheriff out of her mind or heart. Never mind that he was, and would always be, out of reach for her... it took all of J.D.'s strength to manage a smile without choking on it.

"Yeah," he said, then cleared his throat. "Guess I'd better...." He stopped, feeling a gaze like a laser beam drilling into his back. He turned and saw that Sheriff Rick Sutton had followed Red

Myers down the stairs and now his eyes were aimed directly at Corrie and J.D.

Corrie straightened up and went to him immediately. J.D. followed her, not at all sure that he should, but unable to stop himself.

Sutton glanced around the room. "Who else are we missing?" he asked, keeping his voice low. He didn't pointedly ignore J.D., but it was clear that his question was aimed at Corrie.

"Myra, but she's not scheduled until two o'clock," Corrie answered. "Dee Dee is running late, which isn't unusual, but at least she hasn't called out yet. And normally RaeLynn would have gotten here a short while ago, but I forgot I told her to come in a little later and she usually walks to work. And you haven't talked to Dana yet," Corrie reminded him and Rick let a grimace slip out before he could stop himself.

"I don't have all day," he muttered and both Corrie and J.D. bit back a grin. Dana's habit of embellishing and drawing out a narrative made a simple "yes" or "no" question into an essay question. Corrie gave him a raised eyebrow.

"You know, Dana was being very chatty with the guests all day yesterday. She defused a few storm clouds because of the crowds we had. Short tempers all around. She might have heard someone let something slip out."

"I'll keep that in mind," the sheriff said and sighed. "All right, bring her up."

Corrie flashed a smile at J.D. then went to get Dana, who could barely contain her excitement at being questioned so closely. J.D. noticed Jackie roll her eyes as Corrie led Dana up the stairs and he managed to hold in a grin. He figured Corrie would be tied up for the next hour at least, so he told himself he might better make use of himself trying to pick up some information around the campground on his own and he slipped out the side door.

Dana settled into a chair at Corrie's dinette table, practically bouncing from the excitement at being considered a possible witness in what might be a potential terror attack. It WAS a terrorist threat, wasn't it? People's lives were being threatened... well, at least Corrie's was, but since the whole campground had been ordered to be closed, didn't that mean all the campers and employees were at risk as well? Who would do such a thing? And what did they want? The silence in the room, in addition to Rick's stony gaze, caused Dana's chattery exclamations to grind to a halt.

She gave Rick a weak, apologetic smile. "I'm sorry. What did you want to ask me?"

Rick cleared his throat and nodded to Corrie to have a seat. She knew that protocol demanded that another woman be present when the sheriff questioned a female witness and since Deputy Angie Mirabal was the deputy who was on vacation, it was just easier for Rick to ask Corrie to sit in rather than try to pull in his dispatcher, who was needed at her post.

"Okay," Rick said, his manner brisk and capable. "Tell me what you did yesterday, Dana."

"You mean, from the time I got here till the time I left?" Dana asked.

Both Rick and Corrie suppressed a sigh. "Yes," Rick answered.

"Well," Dana said, drawing the word out as she furrowed her brow in thought. "Well, I came over from our Airstream about ten minutes till eight. It only took me a couple of minutes to walk over, so I probably left our trailer at about seven forty-seven... of course, Red came over, too, but he was still finishing up brushing his teeth and I didn't feel like waiting...." Rick shifted in his chair and Dana quickly went on, "Anyway, I got here and we already had quite a few guests milling around the store. Not new guests, actually, because they can't check in until two o'clock, but the ones who were already here wanted change for the laundry room and were buying some last minute supplies. A few of them just wanted some information on local attractions. The phone was ringing off the wall, too. Probably a lot of people checking to make sure their reservations were secure or maybe even wanting to make a reservation although that would have been impossible yesterday, right, Corrie?"

"Right," Corrie said, wishing Dana would get to the point before Rick's patience ran out.

Dana nodded. "Well, Jackie was taking care of customers at the register and Corrie was taking care of the ones on the phone, so I decided it would be best if I checked with the ones who were still shopping around and help them find what they were looking for. I mean, I didn't want them to get up to the counter and then hold up the line because they couldn't find toothpicks!"

"Did you notice if anyone seemed particularly agitated or nervous? Anyone who seemed to be just hanging around?" Rick said, hoping to focus Dana's attention on the matter at hand.

"Well, some of the men were just waiting for their wives to

finish shopping, but they didn't look like they were in any kind of a hurry or out to kill anyone, not even their wives for spending too much money! And we had plenty of coffee and pastries on the courtesy table, so they probably didn't mind the wait very much." She laughed, then frowned. "Oh, there was one couple who seemed to be in some kind of argument, though. They were huddled together by the laundry room door and practically hissing at each other. I didn't really want to approach them...."

Sure, you didn't, Corrie thought ungraciously.

"... but I thought, 'What if they're arguing over something I can easily help them with', you know, like a place to go out to eat or where to go for a hike. So I asked them if they needed help and they did kind of spring apart and look uncomfortable. I didn't actually hear what the argument was about, but they left right away, through the laundry room door."

Rick jotted down a few notes. "They didn't stay to buy anything?"

"No, they didn't," Dana said and coughed self-consciously. "But I DID hear a snippet of what they were arguing about."

Corrie doubted it was merely a snippet. She managed to rein in her impulse to ask what it was and let Rick ask.

"It was about the weather," Dana said, looking as if she had just given the sheriff the name of the person who had written the note. Rick's brows rose and he threw a glance at Corrie. She was sure she looked just as mystified as he felt.

"The weather?" he repeated as if he hadn't heard right.

"The fact that it was raining off and on most of the day," Dana explained. "It did, you know. Of course, WE think it's wonderful, but if you've traveled all the way from Texas to camp and hike...."

"They were from Texas?" Rick interrupted, and Corrie's attention was riveted on Dana's next response.

"Well, really, Sheriff, I honestly couldn't say for sure," she said unblushingly. "I just assumed since the majority of our guests are from Texas...."

"Okay," Rick broke in, his impatience tempered by the fact that Dana was a friend and he didn't want to upset her and cause problems for Corrie and the rest of the staff. "Do you suppose you would recognize them if you saw them again?"

"Oh, of course!" Dana exclaimed. "And, in fact, I can tell you which site they're on!"

Corrie knew that sheer will-power kept Rick's head from

thumping onto the table top in front of him. He didn't ask Dana how she knew, he merely said, "Yes?"

Dana told him the site number, adding that it was a tent site not too far from the horseshoe pits and basketball court, but practically the furthest from the store and bathrooms. Corrie knew she would be questioned after Dana left, to see if she recalled the guests on that site. Sure enough, no sooner had Dana left the room than Rick shot a look at Corrie.

"Young couple, probably in their mid-to-late-twenties," Corrie said. She sighed and shook her head. "They looked like they were in a bad temper from the moment they checked in. They argued over the location of the site—neither of them wanted the site I originally assigned to them—but they couldn't agree whether they wanted to be closer to the pool, the sports area, the front of the campground, the back. I finally told them that there was only one other site available or else the first one I assigned them. I think they took the current assignment only because they didn't want ME to make the decision where they would be. But if their complaint was about the rain, then they should have taken the site I originally assigned; they wouldn't have had to walk so far in the rain to get to the restrooms or camp store!"

Rick grunted. "I doubt that would be enough to make them threaten you with bodily harm if you didn't shut down the campground on Saturday, but I'll have Dudley ask them some questions." He looked at his notepad. "So the only ones left to talk to are RaeLynn, Dee Dee, Myra, and...."

"Here I am, Sheriff!" Buster practically shouted as he pounded up the stairs. Rick grimaced and Corrie shook her head. The burly maintenance man burst through the door of Corrie's apartment and then skidded to a halt, his mouth hanging open, partly from his exertion, but mostly from awe that he was in his boss's "inner sanctum". Corrie cleared her throat.

"Hello, Buster, come on in, have a seat," she deadpanned. He jumped, then glanced at his massive work boots furtively as if checking, far too late, to see if he had any mud on them. "I'll leave you boys alone to talk," she said as she got up and headed for the door.

"Uh, what? You're not staying? Oh..." Buster threw a worried look at Rick. Rick's expression was bland and Corrie knew he was fighting the urge to laugh at Buster's sudden discomfiture.

"No, Buster, gentlemen don't need a female chaperone when talking to a male officer of the law," she said dryly. "But I'll be down in the store if you need me," she added as she headed down the stairs.

~

She went to the counter where Jackie and Dana were deep in conversation and slid onto her stool. "Got it all figured out yet?" she asked.

Jackie shook her head. "I don't know how Rick expects any of us to recall some random comment or conversation among so many strangers."

Dana pursed up her lips. "What if the person who left the note wasn't a guest after all? What if they just came in from off the highway when we weren't looking and then sneaked out again? Isn't that possible?"

"Anything's possible," Corrie said glumly. "Even the possibility that this is all just some kind of sick joke."

"Well, we're not about to take any chances," Jackie said stoutly. "Even if it means closing down the campground for one day...."

Corrie groaned and let her head drop onto her arms folded on the counter top. "Let's not even go there, Jackie, okay?" she pleaded.

The bell over the front door rang and RaeLynn Shaffer walked in. She carried a brown paper bag with the words "Dulcie's Bakery" printed on the side and the delightful aromas of cinnamon, sugar, and other sweet things emanating from it. She smiled shyly and held up the bag. "Sorry I'm late," she said, "but I was passing by Dulcie's and she must have just opened the oven 'cause the smell dragged me in and I had a hard time making up my mind!"

"Oh, RaeLynn, how sweet!" Corrie said. She threw a glance at the clock and shook her head. "I think I can let you being late by three whole minutes slide under these circumstances!"

"Oh, my, I'm going to gain twenty pounds just from the smells coming from that bag!" Dana exclaimed. RaeLynn blushed furiously then hurried to the kitchen to get a platter. Corrie had pulled out Jackie's banana bread and applesauce bread from the freezer for the courtesy table and, though a few customers had already visited the camp store and helped themselves to free coffee and sweets, she knew that pastries from Dulcie's were sure to draw some interest even if they managed to keep most of the goodies for the employees.

RaeLynn pulled out an assortment of two dozen pastries—empanadas with apricot, peach, apple, and cherry fillings; flaky, crown-shaped corona pastries filled with cream cheese and pineapple or strawberry filling and drizzled with white frosting; cinnamon rolls, still warm and bursting with raisins and dripping with sweet white frosting; and Corrie's favorites, conchas, high-domed round yeast rolls, flavored with anise and topped with colorful sugar paste that made them look like shells—hence the name—in chocolate, vanilla, and strawberry. RaeLynn gave Corrie a bashful glance.

"I know you like the vanilla conchas best, so I had Dulcie pack me an extra two for you," she said, handing the bag to Corrie with the two extras still in it.

"You didn't have to do that, RaeLynn. Thank you," Corrie said, wondering how anyone could doubt RaeLynn's sincerity in her efforts to turn her life around. She still had a lot to overcome; she'd been clean for over a month and making strides in putting her life in order. Corrie knew that some of her friends had misgivings about Corrie hiring RaeLynn to work full-time at the campground; they weren't sure that RaeLynn wouldn't succumb to the temptation of having money to support her drug habits, even though she seemed to be succeeding at staying sober and drug-free, and they feared, perhaps justifiably, that RaeLynn couldn't be trusted around the cash drawer should the pull of addiction be too great for her. And of course, there was always the real concern that RaeLynn's family would pressure her to do something to support their habits, even if it meant that she jeopardize her job and her friendships. So far, she seemed to be doing well and all Corrie could do was pray and continue to offer her as much help and encouragement as she could.

J.D. stepped back into the camp store through the side door and the minute he did, Corrie could see that he picked up on the mouth-watering scents from the pastries. He looked at her with a cocked brow. "You been holding out on me?"

"No," Corrie said. "You had your requisite one helping of each item on the courtesy table this morning along with your three cups of piñon coffee," she said. "This is a bonus, courtesy of RaeLynn," she said, nodding in RaeLynn's direction. RaeLynn, not surprisingly, dropped her chin and made the briefest eye contact with J.D. before scurrying toward the employees' coat closet under the stairs to stash her battered denim purse before starting work. She mumbled a brief "good morning" to him before taking a feather duster to the souvenir shelves along the wall furthest from the side door.

"Oh?" J.D. said, moving toward the counter. It irritated Corrie that J.D. always acted so suspicious of RaeLynn, as if he enjoyed making her feel uncomfortable, making sure she knew he was keeping an eye on her and didn't trust her. It didn't help matters that RaeLynn always reacted in such a manner as to raise suspicion, either. J.D. eyed the pastries and raised a brow. "She make these?"

Corrie held up the Dulcie's bag. "She treated. No one makes pastries like Dulcie."

"You got that right. Holding out on me?" Rick said, coming down the stairs preceded by Buster. Buster, relieved at being found faultless by the long arm of the law, made a beeline for the pastries and grabbed a cherry empanada and a cinnamon roll. Rick gave J.D. a cool nod then looked over the tray. "Did you save me a peach empanada?"

Corrie pointed. "Grab it before Jerry comes in," she warned him and Jackie laughed.

"There were two in the bag and I already set one aside for Jerry. You have to hand it to RaeLynn. She knows what everyone likes!"

Corrie felt her cheeks flush with heat. Apparently RaeLynn accepted Rick's daily visit to the campground as a given event and had planned for his arrival this morning. Before she could say anything, Buster stopped at the door before heading out to take care of his duties. "Oh, hey, Corrie?" he said, his mouth full of cinnamon roll and a smear of white frosting adorning his mustache. "Listen, do we got any tent stakes, you know, the metal kind? Some guy, a guest, says one of his is missing and he don't want the plastic ones we got in the store."

Corrie shook her head, relieved at having an ordinary problem to distract her. "He'd probably have to check in town or in Ruidoso at a hardware or camping store or at Walmart. Why can't he use the plastic ones?"

"He's ticked off that one stake got lost. Says he borrowed the tent from somebody and doesn't want to return it with any parts missing."

"Well, maybe there's an extra one in the storage shed. You or Jerry or Red can check and see if there's one you can just give him."

"Okay, I'll go look right now!" Buster said, shoving the last bite of empanada into his mouth and licking the cherry filling off his fingers, happy to be given a task that might take a long time but would excuse him from doing any actual hard work. He gave a cheery wave as he scooted out the door.

"Got a minute, RaeLynn? I'd like to ask you a few questions." From across the room, RaeLynn gave a startled glance when she saw Rick in civilian clothes.

Corrie cringed at the sight of RaeLynn's face growing pale; she looked like she had a guilty conscience and it didn't make Corrie feel any better when J.D. raised a brow and aimed a piercing gaze at the young woman. She threw Corrie a confused look and Corrie came out from behind the counter. "It's okay, RaeLynn. Rick—I mean, the sheriff—is asking everyone some questions about something that happened yesterday."

RaeLynn turned even paler for a split second, then her face flushed a deep crimson. "Oh... okay. Something that happened here, at the campground?"

It was painful to hear and see her attempt to sound casual. Corrie sensed waves of suspicion emanating from J.D. but she didn't look at him. She put her hand on RaeLynn's shoulder and they headed toward the door to the apartment where Rick was waiting. "The sheriff—Rick—just wants to know if you remember anything...." She stopped when Rick cleared his throat and she said nothing else as they headed up the stairs.

Once in the apartment, she waved RaeLynn to the chair at the dinette table where everyone else had sat during their questioning. RaeLynn perched on the very edge of the wooden chair, gripping the seat with both hands, her knuckles turning white. Rick had to notice that as he took his seat opposite of her. Corrie forced herself to go to her chair in the corner behind RaeLynn and keep quiet. Rick flipped his notebook open and gave RaeLynn a curt nod and a brief smile.

"It's all right, RaeLynn. It's just that something happened last night and I need to know if anyone saw or heard anything suspicious anywhere on the camp grounds or in the store yesterday." RaeLynn nodded and her grip eased slightly—at least, the color returned to her knuckles—but she remained on the edge of the seat. Rick waited a few moments, ostensibly to allow the young woman time to gather her composure, but Corrie wondered if it merely made RaeLynn even more nervous. "RaeLynn, did you work all day in the camp store yesterday?"

RaeLynn looked up at Rick, then looked down again and nodded. "Yes," she whispered.

"Were you in the store all day or did you go outside at all?"

Her head jerked up and she threw a wide-eyed look in Corrie's direction, which Corrie couldn't comprehend. RaeLynn licked her lips. "I... I went outside twice. Just to take a break. It was... it was kind of stuffy and crowded in the store."

Rick's eyes met Corrie's and she nodded. Everyone, at one time or another, throughout the course of the day, had stepped out to catch a breath of fresh air. Rick turned back to RaeLynn.

"What did you do all day in the store?"

RaeLynn stared at him. "What did I do? You mean, everything I did all day?"

Rick leaned forward, his manner a little less formal, when RaeLynn appeared to be on the verge of panic. "I'm not asking for a minute-by-minute account of everything you did, RaeLynn," he said gently. "For instance, did you help customers find things?"

She relaxed. "Oh, yeah. Yeah, I did that a lot."

"So you talked to a lot of the customers?"

"Um, sort of. I mean, I just asked, you know, 'Can I help you find anything?' and sometimes they said 'yes' but mostly they said, 'no, just looking, thanks'." She seemed to relax a little more and her brow furrowed. "You mean, stuff like that?"

"Yes," Rick said, nodding encouragement. "How were the customers with you? Pleasant, friendly, nice? Any problems with them?"

"Well," RaeLynn began, and squirmed in her seat. "For the most part, they were nice. Most of them were. Even when they said 'no' they didn't act like I was bothering them. Corrie told me to be helpful but not persistent," she added, glancing at Corrie. Corrie gave her a smile then Rick a shrug as if to say that was business. RaeLynn bit her lip then blurted out. "Did someone complain about me?"

The question took Corrie by surprise, but Rick merely raised a brow at RaeLynn. "Not that I've heard," he said, then looked at Corrie. She shook her head. "Did you have a problem with a customer?"

"Well, no, not really... maybe, sort of." The words tumbled out of her mouth. "I... I didn't think anything of it at the time. No, actually, Corrie," RaeLynn said, turning in her seat and fastening beseeching eyes on her employer, "the truth is, I was embarrassed and I didn't want you to find out what happened."

"What? What happened?" Corrie said, half rising from her seat. She sat back down as Rick waved at her to wait for RaeLynn to finish.

RaeLynn gulped and tears shone in her eyes. Her lip trembled. "I was trying so hard to do just what you asked, Corrie. You know, help the customers. And I thought I was doing so good.... But then I asked this man if I could help him and he jumped, like I scared the daylights out of him and it scared me and I jumped back and I bumped into this woman. She had her arms full of t-shirts and I didn't see that she was right behind me and I don't know if I scared her, too...."

"Hold it, RaeLynn," Rick said, his sharp tone bringing her scrambled narrative to a complete stop. "You said this man acted scared when you spoke to him?"

She twisted her hands in her lap. "Well, like I startled him. Like, he didn't hear me come up to him from behind and maybe he was thinking about something and when I said, 'Can I help you?', it startled him." She grimaced and shook her head. "But it was the lady who was really upset, the one who I bumped into that had all the t-shirts in her arms. She got... kind of upset...." RaeLynn's voice trailed away and the acne scars on her face bloomed like red roses against the snow-white paleness of her skin. She swallowed hard. "The lady was buying a lot of stuff. It was a good sale and I tried to be really nice and apologize. See, it really wasn't ME she was mad at, not really. It was that man, the man I startled."

Corrie exchanged a look with Rick and she knew he was thinking the same thing. It took all her strength to let him ask the next question. "Why was she angry at the man you startled?"

RaeLynn stared at the floor. "She said he was in her way earlier, when she was trying to pick out t-shirts. She said he was just standing there 'in a fog', staring off into space, and not paying any attention to any of the people around him. He was just staring up at the front counter, she said, like...." She gulped and looked at Rick with frightened eyes then at Corrie. "Like he was mesmerized—that's the word she used—by the pretty lady behind the counter."

"Get Jackie and Dana up here now!" Rick snapped at Corrie and she was out of her seat and dashing down the steps before he could finish the sentence.

She stopped herself before she burst into the camp store and tried to look collected and nonchalant. Jackie looked up from the counter, where she had been talking to Dee Dee who had finally managed to make an appearance, and her calm dark eyes widened with alarm. Corrie gave her what she hoped looked like a real smile. "Jackie, could you get Dana and come upstairs with me for a minute?" Jackie nodded once and hurried toward the laundry room. Corrie turned to ask Dee Dee to watch the store for a while when a touch on her shoulder nearly sent her through the wall with shock.

"Easy," J.D. said, his brows rising as he stepped back, his hands in the air.

Corrie's lungs unfroze. "Good God, J.D.," she croaked as she sagged against the wall. Before either of them could say anything, Dana and Jackie appeared. Corrie barely managed to nod up the stairs and the two women scurried past her and J.D. who looked completely perplexed.

"What...?"

"Dee Dee," Corrie managed to say clearly, "Don't go anywhere. Watch the store for a while."

"That's what I'm paid to do, Boss!" Dee Dee chirped, apparently unaware of any drama that was unfolding in her presence. Today, Dee Dee was affecting a "country-girl-next-door" look with a casual light brown ponytail, sparkling green eyes, and a red-and-white checked shirt tied at the waist, but still showing her belly-button ring. Corrie made a mental note to remember to ask Dee Dee to tuck her shirt in and button at least one more button. "Well, hello, Mr. Wilder! Are you working today, too?" Dee Dee sang out.

Corrie felt J.D. grow tense and before she could take into consideration what Rick would say, she blurted, "Oh, J.D., I'm so glad you have a minute to come by and get my kitchen window unstuck!" then she grabbed J.D.'s arm and yanked him into the stairwell.

"Your kitchen window?" he whispered as she tugged him up the stairs.

She shook her head. "RaeLynn... she saw something... a man who was acting strangely yesterday... she said he was watching me...."

J.D. took the rest of the steps two at a time with Corrie right behind him.

~

He entered the sitting area of Corrie's apartment where

Sheriff Sutton was interviewing the employees. RaeLynn sat at the table, her face pale with shock, shaking her head back and forth.

"Come on, RaeLynn, you have to remember something more about the man," the sheriff was saying, his soothing tone holding a current of impatience.

J.D. turned to Corrie but she had already brushed past him and pulled up a chair next to RaeLynn's. "Do you remember what he looked like?" she asked, ignoring the sheriff who, for once, didn't seem to mind.

RaeLynn's eyes swam with tears. "Oh, Corrie, I'm trying. I didn't really look at him, I was so embarrassed when I startled him. I know he wasn't very tall, not as tall as Rick—the sheriff, I mean—or Lt. Wilder," she added. "And he wasn't really skinny or fat, just average. He had on a baseball cap, a blue one. Dark blue." She pressed her lips together and her brow wrinkled with the strain of trying to remember. "He had on a windbreaker. It was maroon-colored. I think he was wearing jeans." She stopped and shook her head miserably.

"Honestly, Rick, that sounds like every other man who was in the camp store yesterday!" Jackie said hopelessly. "I doubt any of us would remember any particular person dressed like that!"

Sutton shook his head. "RaeLynn said he was just standing in the store, 'in a fog', the other customer described it. None of you noticed someone just staring off into space?" he added, shooting disbelieving looks at Corrie, Jackie, and Dana.

"We were too busy," Corrie snapped. "When that rain storm hit, everyone in the area just crammed into the store to get out of it. Some were in here just to get out of the rain, so not everyone came up to the counter. We had a crowd at the counter trying to buy things and get registered. RaeLynn was working the floor to take some of the pressure off of us."

Dana had been frowning. Before the sheriff could respond to Corrie, she suddenly asked, "RaeLynn, the woman who was upset... did she have very bright yellow hair and wear a lot of eye makeup? Kind of heavy-set, a little shorter than me, maybe?"

"Yes!" RaeLynn said, her head bobbing eagerly. Rick turned to Dana.

"You remember her?"

"I remember her bringing up about eleven t-shirts that she wanted folded neatly," Dana said, nodding. "Jackie rang her up, remember?" she asked, nudging Jackie.

"I remember the sale," Jackie acknowledged. "And she paid

with a credit card."

"I'll get the slips from yesterday," Corrie said, jumping up and heading back down the stairs before the sheriff could ask. So far, no one had questioned J.D.'s presence, then RaeLynn looked directly at him, her eyes growing wide, and her mouth formed a perfect "O".

"What is it?" Sutton asked sharply. RaeLynn pointed at J.D.

"Lt. Wilder... YOU saw him! He headed to the laundry room right after I startled him! You opened the door just as he was about to go in...."

Everyone turned to look at J.D. He hadn't officially been a law enforcement officer for almost three months, and he wasn't exactly sure what it was about that brief encounter with the guest that mattered to this case, but it hadn't taken him long to figure out what the question was going to be and he nodded at the sheriff. "About five-foot, ten; one-hundred sixty pounds; eyes either blue or gray—he made a point to avoid eye contact, so I only caught a glimpse—and probably around fifty-five years of age. I didn't see any hair under that ball cap, so either he didn't have much or he was bald. Dressed just like she said," he added, gesturing toward RaeLynn, who was nodding in triumph at having her observations validated. "And before you ask, no, I didn't see where he went after he went into the laundry room. I figured he was trying to escape the crowds in the store, so I just let him go. Besides, I was supposed to be helping out so I didn't spend a lot of time dwelling on him since Corrie had a full house in the store."

Sutton was jotting down notes and he looked up at J.D. "Think you'd recognize him if you saw him again?" J.D. shrugged.

"Maybe. There was nothing particularly outstanding about him, no physical characteristic that I noticed that would make him stand out. He was pretty ordinary looking. Out there," he said, jerking his head to indicate the world outside the Black Horse, "I might not recognize him if I ever saw him again, but the field's narrower here and if he's a guest, I'm pretty sure I'd know him if I saw him."

"Good enough," the sheriff said as Corrie came back up the stairs.

"Here it is," she said, holding two slips of paper in her hand. "The sale was made around two-thirty in the afternoon and the credit card was issued to a Thomas W. McMillan. I've got a Tom and Marjorie McMillan registered through Sunday and they've been assigned site twenty-one.

“That's right next to the Westlakes,” Jackie interjected.

“And they're driving a red Toyota Camry. They towed it in.”

“I know the lady you're talking about,” Dana put in. “She stopped in this morning for coffee... said she and her husband were going to Alamogordo for the day to visit her niece and her family.”

The sheriff stood up and nodded to RaeLynn. “Thanks for your help,” he told her. “I might have to ask you some more questions later on.”

“Okay,” RaeLynn said. The tension seemed to have left her body and her breathing was easier. She looked at Corrie. “I'll go down and start the preparations for the enchiladas for tonight.”

“That's fine, RaeLynn,” Corrie said. She looked at the sheriff. “I don't suppose you want any of us to say much about what we've been talking about up here?”

“Let's keep it between us for now,” he said. “Thank you, everyone.”

It was a dismissal. Jackie, Dana, and RaeLynn filed out silently, but J.D. stayed behind with Corrie and the sheriff. After the door closed behind the three women, J.D. spoke up. “Do you want me to grab a rake or a leaf blower and start doing some unnecessary work around the campground and see if this guy shows his face?”

“You might have to,” the sheriff said. “This description is so vague, I might end up having half the men in the campground pulled in if I ask my deputies to go with it.”

“Sorry about that, Sheriff,” J.D. said, but Sutton waved away his apology.

“Let's get started. It'll be late before this woman, Mrs. McMillan, returns from her trip to Alamogordo. We might have some luck in finding this man before she gets back.”

“And what do you intend to do if you do find him?” Corrie asked quietly. “I mean, can you suspect him of writing that note just because he was a little jumpy yesterday?”

The sheriff didn't answer right away. J.D. wasn't sure if it was because J.D. was standing right there listening or if it was because he didn't have an answer. Finally he said, “I don't know, Corrie. Someone left that note. That's all I know. I don't know if they were serious about the threat, I don't know a lot of things.” It occurred to J.D. that Sheriff Rick Sutton wasn't used to admitting that he didn't know something. “For now, we're taking it seriously and if this man knows something, either about the note or the threat it implies, then we're going to find out."

We? J.D. covered his surprise. He'd fully expected to be asked to bow out, but thinking about it now, J.D. realized that when it came to Corrie's safety, the sheriff was willing to accept any and all help he could get.

Even from J.D.

Chapter 3

Corrie sighed as she sank onto her stool behind the counter. Even though they weren't nearly as rushed as they had been the day before, they'd had a steady stream of customers in the camp store all day long. Dee Dee had been taken aside and informally questioned by Rick—a heroic act if there ever was one—and once he'd managed to get Dee Dee's attention off his civilian attire and back on to the questions he was asking, it became clear that the only men Dee Dee had noticed the day before were the ones who came up and specifically talked to her and she had their names and cell phone numbers as well. And a date with a few of them.

Which was why, at a quarter to two, she begged off the rest of the day's work, promising to make it up on Sunday—which was her next scheduled day to work. Corrie let her go, knowing that it really didn't make a difference whether Dee Dee was around or not in the amount of work Corrie actually got from her. Besides, RaeLynn had gotten most of the work in preparing the enchiladas for the Friday night dinner done, even getting all the lettuce and tomatoes chopped, and she was busily helping Jackie re-stock the t-shirt shelves. Dana, as usual, was making herself useful helping the customers in the game room and laundry room and flitting out to the patio from time to time to check on any guests who might be needing help out there.

Promptly at two o'clock Myra Kaydahzinne walked in and Corrie had to admit that her impatience was getting the better of her. She had fully expected Myra to show up earlier, flaunting her new engagement ring and bubbling with excitement over her wedding plans. But when Myra entered the camp store, it was as if she had dragged a dark rain cloud in with her.

"Myra?" Corrie said, slipping off her stool and coming around the counter. Myra raised her eyes to look at Corrie and Corrie was shocked to see tears streaming down the young woman's face and, judging from the swollen redness of it, it was apparent that she had been crying for a long time. "Myra, what's wrong?"

"Nothing," Myra whispered, an answer so obviously false that Corrie was speechless for a few seconds.

"Don't tell me this is just an allergy attack!" she said when she found her voice. "Come on, now, what's wrong? You don't look like someone who just got engaged... oh, my gosh, Myra, is your family all right?" It suddenly occurred to Corrie that some serious health threat or death in her family would be the only reason Myra wasn't brimming with joy and excitement.

Myra's face crumpled and she pulled a wadded-up tissue out of her pocket and tried to wipe her tears and blow her nose at the same time. Corrie reached over the counter and grabbed several tissues from the box on her desk and thrust them at Myra, who nodded her thanks.

"My family's okay... and I'm not engaged." The words came out so flat that Corrie wasn't sure she heard correctly.

"What? I mean...." Corrie realized that she had spilled the beans that Rick had specifically asked her not to spill and she winced. Best to just come clean, now that she'd put her foot in it. "I mean, Rick mentioned something about Dudley... that he thought Dudley might be proposing... Dudley picked up a box from the jewelers...." She stopped, tired of babbling.

"I know," Myra said dully. "It's a beautiful ring. And he did propose," Myra added. A wistful smile brushed her lips and she sighed. "It was so romantic. We walked down by the river and the moonlight on the water was so beautiful. Then he got down on one knee and took my hand, just like in the movies. And he pulled out the ring and asked me to honor him by becoming his wife." She took a deep shaky breath and stared at the floor."And I turned him down."

Corrie was truly speechless this time although a million questions spun through her mind. Finally only one managed to come out and it was the one that summed up the rest. "Why?"

Myra shrugged. "Oh, Corrie, it would never work out." The indifference in her voice was belied by the fresh tears that leaked from her swollen eyes.

Corrie blinked. Never work out? Corrie had watched this romance blossom and if there was one thing she was sure of, it was that Dudley and Myra had found "the one" in each other—kindred spirits or soul mates, if one preferred the term. "That's ridiculous, Myra! Why wouldn't it work out? You love Dudley, don't you?"

"Yes," Myra said, simply and without the need to add any modifiers like "with all my heart".

"And he loves you. You know that, right?"

"Yes." Again, a plain statement of an undeniable truth.

Corrie shook her head. "Then I don't understand. What makes you think it wouldn't work?"

Myra sighed and shifted her leather purse from one shoulder to the other. Corrie remembered Rick mentioning that Deputy Evans had pulled a few double shifts to buy that purse for Myra's birthday a few weeks earlier. Myra had seen it in the window of a leather shop in mid-town Ruidoso when she and Dudley had taken a walk after he'd taken her to lunch to celebrate. She had merely commented on what a nice purse it was and they had kept on walking. She'd been so excited to show everyone her gift, amazed that Dudley had remembered her passing admiration of it. Of course, Myra was equally considerate in remembering Dudley's likes and dislikes regarding food—she'd made it her mission to keep him from wasting away from hunger when she discovered that his bachelor cooking skills extended only as far as picking up the phone and ordering carry-out. Everyone who saw them together always commented on how well they seemed to fit. For Myra to state that their relationship wouldn't work stretched credulity. "Corrie, it's hard to explain. I don't think anyone would understand. Even Dudley doesn't understand." She sighed again, and it seemed to come from the deepest pits of her heart and soul. "It's my grandmother."

"Your grandmother?" Corrie knew Myra was especially close to her grandmother, driving the nearly-ninety-year-old woman everywhere she wanted and needed to go—church on Sundays, to visit relatives in Mescalero or Tularosa or Roswell whenever the whim hit her, and tending to the old woman's garden of herbs and numerous cages of songbirds and parakeets, all the while holding down a full-time job at the Black Horse and helping her mother with her three youngest siblings who were all still in school. And it wasn't just out of a strong sense of family duty. Myra truly loved her grandmother and Corrie knew that the crusty old lady loved her granddaughter with a fierce protective love. But surely she would approve of a man like Dudley...?

"Yes," Myra said sadly. "It's not that she wouldn't like him for who he is...."

"That sounds like she's never even met him," Corrie said raising her brows. Myra's coppery face took on a rosy tint.

"She hasn't," she said, her voice a mere squeak. "She doesn't even know I'm dating anyone."

"Why not?"

Myra shifted again and pursed her lips, frowning. Corrie

wasn't sure if it was because she disapproved of Corrie's prying questions or if it was because she didn't know how to answer. "It's complicated," she said at last.

Corrie wasn't going to leave it at that. "How?"

Myra looked her square in the face. "Oh, come on, Corrie. You, of all people, should be able to figure it out. You know what your dad went through for marrying your mom."

Corrie sucked her breath in so hard it hurt her chest. Of course. Myra was right, she SHOULD have guessed. Myra's grandmother, despite the fact that she lived so far off the Mescalero Apache reservation, was still very much a traditional Mescalero Apache. She may have left the reservation for reasons of convenience to be with family who could look after her, but the reservation had never left her. "She wants you to marry a member of the tribe."

Myra nodded gloomily. "It's not even that he's black... that wouldn't bother her if Dudley could claim even half, or even a fourth, of some kind of Indian heritage... but no luck. He's from Cleveland by way of New York City and Washington, D. C. Not a single drop of Native American blood anywhere in his veins. Grandma won't stand for that."

Corrie nodded as well. It was useless to protest, to say that Myra's grandmother was being unreasonable. Corrie's own paternal grandmother was still, nearly forty years later, getting ulcers over the fact that her youngest son, Billy Chee Black Horse, had defied tradition and her own well-laid plans and married a woman who not only wasn't a member of the tribe or a Native American, she wasn't even a U.S. citizen when they got married. That Corrie's parents went on to have a happy marriage that lasted until the day Corrie's mother succumbed to a heart aneurysm when Corrie was twelve didn't make a difference to Billy's family. Before that, he and Corrie's mother had had fifteen years of wedded bliss, despite the opposition of both their families. That didn't mean it didn't hurt when family members refused to accept or be anywhere around the person you loved most in the world.

"I'm sorry, Myra," she said and felt the inadequacy of her words. The look of quiet sadness on the young woman's face tore at her heart. "Dudley is having a hard time accepting that?"

Myra wiped a tear away. "He thinks it shouldn't matter what my grandmother thinks, that the only thing that matters is what WE think. But his family doesn't live here, so he doesn't know—or maybe he doesn't care—if they approve of me. He says it's silly, old-fashioned prejudice... and I know he's right. That doesn't mean that I can just pretend it doesn't matter. I still love my grandma, even if she is prejudiced, and I don't want to hurt her any more than I want to hurt Dudley." She sighed. "And if my grandmother disapproves, it could cause a lot of tension in the family. She's the glue that holds the family together. If I go against her, then a lot of my family members will hold me responsible for the rift in the family."

"You mean, no one in your family has married anyone who wasn't a member of the tribe?" Corrie asked skeptically. She knew Myra had nieces and nephews and cousins who were half-Native and half-something else—black, white, or Hispanic, even Asian. Myra gave her a ghost of a smile.

"That's the operative word. 'Married'. A lot of my nieces and nephews have parents with different last names. My sisters have just settled into living with their boyfriends without bothering to make it legal. Of course, my mother and father aren't happy about that, but my grandmother, I think, tolerates it because there's still a chance their relationships are just temporary and they'll end up marrying someone from the tribe...."

"This is so ridiculous!" Corrie couldn't help blurt out. Was it possible that in this day and age, people still clung to such narrow-minded ideas and held such sway over their families that no one challenged them? "I can't believe you and Dudley are being kept apart by something so trivial as this!"

Myra went to stash her purse in the coat closet and returned with her work smock over her arm and pushing the upright vacuum cleaner. "I guess it's no use dwelling on it," she said. "I told Dudley that it wasn't fair for me to keep on seeing him if our relationship wasn't going to go anywhere. And I told him if it wasn't going to be marriage, then it couldn't be anything more than just friends. Of course, he agreed... he'd never suggest anything like that," she added, a note of virtuous pride in her voice. "But he doesn't want to give up. He still thinks something will work out. I just don't want to raise his hopes only to see him be knocked down." She hesitated for a moment, fingering one of her dangling silver earrings. It made Corrie wonder if they, too, were a gift from Dudley. "We decided it might be best if we didn't see each other for a while," Myra said in a tiny, trembling voice.

"Oh," Corrie said, unable to hide a grimace. "Well, then, you should probably know, Myra, that you might be running into him today."

"Where? Here? At the campground?" Myra's eyes widened and her mouth dropped open. "Why? What happened? Is there something wrong?"

"You could say that," Corrie said and proceeded to tell Myra about the anonymous note that had been slipped under the door while they were all celebrating the campground's first "No Vacancy" night. Myra shook her head, her brow puckered with worry.

"No one has a clue who did this? Or what it means? How is your life in danger?"

"Not just mine, Myra," Corrie said, folding her arms. "If I'm being threatened here, at the campground, then I have to assume all of your lives are in danger, as well as those of my guests. Otherwise, why demand I close down the entire campground?"

Myra took a deep breath. "And you say Dudley—that is, Deputy Evans—is here today?"

It bothered Corrie that Myra chose to refer to Dudley by his professional name, but decided not to make an issue of it. "The sheriff has him and Deputy Ramirez on the grounds, undercover as employees of the campground, to see if they pick up anything that might give them an idea who slipped that note under the door. So if you run into him, make sure you don't call him "deputy". Better yet, you might try to avoid making it sound like you know him at all. His cover story, should anyone ask him anything about the Black Horse that he doesn't know, is that it's his first day on the job."

Myra nodded. "Well, Buster should have taken care of the bathrooms by now, so it's unlikely I'll even run into Deputy Evans unless he comes into the laundry room, or the kitchen, or the TV room. And since all the cabins are occupied I won't be out there to clean any of them, so it's unlikely I'll see him on the grounds."

"Something will work out, Myra. Don't give up."

Myra gave her a wan smile. "Sure, Corrie. I'd better get to work so I can be ready to help you with the enchilada dinner later on." She pursed up her lips in concern. "So ARE you planning to close the campground for tomorrow?"

It was a question Corrie had been asking herself over and over and one she didn't know how to answer. "Rick hasn't asked me to... not yet, anyway. I just don't know, Myra. He's following up on some leads. You don't remember seeing anyone suspicious around the campground yesterday?" She went on to give Myra a description of the man that RaeLynn and J.D. had described, but

Myra only looked dazed.

"Corrie, that sounds like half the men here. Even the windbreaker isn't that unusual considering all the rain showers we've been having!"

"Jackie said the same thing," Corrie sighed. "Well, I just thought I'd mention it, see if you remembered something. Let me know if you do," she added as Myra nodded and headed toward the TV room with the vacuum cleaner in tow. A few customers browsed among the shelves and racks in the camp store, nothing that Jackie and Dana couldn't handle with RaeLynn's help. Automatically, Corrie found herself studying the men closely, even as RaeLynn kept shooting furtive glances at them, but none seemed to fit RaeLynn's vague description.

Corrie decided it might not hurt to take a walk around the campground herself.

Chapter 4

J.D. bit back a grin when he saw Corrie leave the campground store with a small notepad in her hand and an air of brisk inspection about her. Of course, she wasn't going to sit around the camp store waiting for Sheriff Sutton and his deputies to find out who had threatened her and her friends and guests. He aimed his golf cart, loaded with trash cans and cleaning supplies, in her direction and pulled up alongside her.

"Need a lift?" he asked. She raised a brow at him.

"Buster let you use the cart? That's unusual," she commented and J.D. chuckled.

"He's keeping an eye on things in the pool area. Where else would you find someone wearing jeans and a windbreaker?" J.D. said dryly. He nodded toward the dog yard and then toward the playground area where the basketball court and horseshoe pit were located. "The three teens are taking care of those areas. I checked on them and they seem to be doing well. For once, they've got their ear buds out and their phones put away. I think they're enjoying the idea of possibly helping out with a sheriff's department investigation. And they're getting an impressive amount of work done as well."

"It's a game to them," Corrie sighed. A strand of her long dark hair escaped her braid and, caught by the summer breeze, blew across her lips. It was all J.D. could do to keep his hands on the golf cart's steering wheel and not reach up to brush it away. She caught it and tucked it behind her ear and looked at J.D. squarely. "Has Rick said anything else about closing the campground?"

"Not to me," J.D. answered. He shrugged. "It's still early. His two deputies are still trying to see if they can find the guy that was in the store yesterday."

"You haven't seen him?"

He shook his head. "Or else I just haven't recognized him. Kind of sad that this guy isn't exactly the kind that sticks in your mind after a brief encounter."

Corrie nodded and looked around the campground. A great many guests were lounging around their campsites in lawn chairs, some grilling a late lunch, others reading or playing card games.

Shouts of laughter and splashing came from the pool and J.D. could hear the far-off "chink" of horseshoes making contact with the steel pegs and basketballs bouncing off the pavement. He could guess what Corrie was thinking—with all these guests here, and many others who had gone off on excursions for the day, how on earth were the sheriff and his deputies going to find the person who slipped that note under her door or the man who was startled in the camp store? Was there a connection? Were they the same person? J.D. cleared his throat.

"I took the liberty of making a list of all the campsites where the occupants were gone," he said. "I mean gone as in taken their car and left the campground. Thought maybe you and Jackie could go over the list, see if any of them stand out in your mind."

She seemed to perk up. "That's a good idea, J.D." She took the sheet of paper from him and frowned as she scanned it. "What's this question mark by one of the cabin sites?"

"That one," J.D. said, nodding toward the cabins that lined the road near the patio area. "I can't really tell if the guest who's renting it is in or not. His car's there, but the curtains are drawn and there's no sign that he's used the grill or fire pit or even his trash can."

"'He'?"

"Well, 'he', 'she', 'they', whatever," J.D. said with a shrug, "might have decided to go for a hike just by leaving the campground on foot. Or 'they' might have decided to take a stroll into town." He caught her gaze; it had narrowed and confirmed his own gut feeling. "Earlier, you said that all the cabins had been rented by couples... Mr. and Mrs. Fill-in-the-Blank. But if you'll forgive me for sounding a tad chauvinistic, I've never known a woman who hadn't tried to make temporary living quarters more home-like." He nodded toward the other cabins, with tablecloths on the picnic tables, lanterns and camp stoves neatly set up on the porch, water coolers set up for convenience. "Maybe we should have Sheriff Sutton present when we look up this guest's information."

"You mean the occupant of cabin A-6?" came Sutton's voice from behind them. He had opted to wear a Dallas Cowboys baseball cap instead of his usual Stetson with his civilian outfit. It didn't make him look any less professional, in J.D.'s opinion, but many, if not all, of the guests wouldn't know he was the sheriff anyway. His gaze, hidden behind his mirrored shades, also turned in the direction of the cabin J.D. had indicated. "I've noticed all that, too, Wilder. Could be the occupant is taking advantage of the peace and quiet to catch up on his or her rest...."

"What peace and quiet? It's the closest cabin to the pool area," Corrie said. Sutton nodded and went on.

"... or left on foot. But let's find out who that person is before I go up and knock on the door to ask them a few questions."

"What are you planning to ask him... or her?" Corrie asked as J.D. stepped off the golf cart and fell in step beside her and the sheriff on their way to the camp store.

"Depends on what he or she looks like when they answer the door," Sutton said.

~

Corrie settled in behind the computer at her desk. The camp store was quiet except for a small group of kids who had come in to buy soft drinks and ice cream bars before scooting back out to the patio area, with Dana trailing behind them to remind them that the empty wrappers, cans, and bottles needed to go into the trash bins and not on the patio floor or in the pool. Corrie tried not to smile at the fact that Rick and J.D. were both failing miserably to look inconspicuous as they hovered over her at the counter. Within a minute she had pulled up the name of the person in cabin A-6. "Timothy H. Jenkins of Dallas, Texas. Says two guests are checked in. Driving a Honda," she added, looking up.

"A gray one," both J.D. and Rick said simultaneously.

"He checked in sometime yesterday, during the busiest part of the day. No one else's name is registered with him," Corrie said.

"I don't suppose you remember what he looked like," Rick said, and Corrie shook her head.

"Nope. But then if you picked any of my guests' names at random and asked me to remember what they looked like, I probably couldn't do it. I don't have the photographic memory of most law enforcement officers," she said with a nod toward J.D.

"All right, then," Rick said, straightening up. "I guess I'd better go see if Mr. Timothy Jenkins of Dallas, Texas or his plus one is awake and willing to talk to me." He slipped his badge out of his jeans pocket and clipped it to his belt, then went out to his Silverado and retrieved his side arm. He surprised Corrie by coming back into the office rather than just walking around the outside of the building to the cabin. "I'll need your key to the cabin, Corrie. Just in case. Wilder," he said, turning to J.D. "Care to join me?"

"Do I look like I need an engraved invitation?" J.D. asked.

"Wait a minute," Corrie said. "I don't need any kind of invitation to accompany you, either, Sheriff. In fact, unless I'm mistaken, aren't I supposed to escort you to my guest's accommodations if you're visiting them on official business?"

Rick sighed and rolled his eyes. "Corrie...."

"She has a point, Sheriff," J.D. put in, a sly grin on his face.

"Of course I do." Corrie rummaged through her desk and pulled out the master key to the cabins. She kept it out of Rick's reach as she scooted around the counter and toward the door. "Let's go!"

Rick blocked her way out of the building. "Corrie, do I have to remind you that this person just might be the one that slipped a note threatening your life under your door?"

"He's got a point, too, Corrie," J.D. added. She threw him a look that made him shrug.

"MIGHT be the person who slipped the note under the door. And if he isn't, and I don't follow proper procedures in allowing the police to question a guest, then he MIGHT be the guy who sues me and causes me to lose my business," she said, folding her arms across her chest. Although both men topped her height by well over ten inches, she wasn't about to give in. "Unless you're planning to break his door down, Sheriff, I'm going with you."

Rick threw his hands up in exasperation. "Fine!" he snapped. "On the condition that if we have to use your key, I'll unlock the door and you step out of the way. For all we know, he's got a bomb wired to the door. And you'll do exactly as I say. Is that understood?" His glare included J.D. as well.

"You're the boss," J.D. said, bowing and showing Rick to the door.

"Don't expect me to agree with him," Corrie warned. "But it's a deal."

Rick gave a curt nod, then strapped his gun on and slipped his cell phone out of its holster and briefed Deputies Ramirez and Evans. "Let's go," he said to Corrie and J.D.

~

They crossed the gravel road toward the cabins with J.D. and the sheriff flanking Corrie. J.D. knew that Sutton was doing the same thing he was doing—scanning the area for any signs of potential danger. So far, the area around the cabins was deserted; it seemed as if all the cabin occupants were either engaged in activities away from their temporary homes or were inside their cabins out of the summer heat. As he pointed out earlier, all but one of the eight cabins had some sign of habitation around them: coolers on the porches, damp beach towels hanging on the railings, ashes of campfires in the fire pits or remnants of charcoal fires in the grills. Only two of the cabins were missing their respective occupants' vehicles. They approached cabin A-6 in silence and stopped at the foot of the three steps leading up to the porch.

The sheriff gestured for Corrie to go ahead and jerked his head at J.D. to precede her. J.D. took up a station to the side of the door where it would open and Sutton stood directly behind Corrie, with enough space between them in case he had to make a swift defensive move. Corrie took a deep breath and knocked loudly on the cabin door. "Hello? Mr. Jenkins?"

Not a sound came from the cabin, not the creak of the bunk as Mr. Jenkins got up, not a chair scraping across the floor, not a footstep. Corrie glanced at the sheriff and raised a brow. He reached around her, gently nudging her aside, and pounded on the door. "Mr. Jenkins? Sheriff's department. Open up."

J.D. looked in the window beside the front door. The heavy light–blocking curtains were drawn completely over the window, not permitting the thinnest slice of light to enter the cabin. He slipped under the railing off the porch and went around to the back where another window might allow him to see inside the cabin. He went up to the back window and peered in. The curtains here, too, were closed, but not as tightly as the ones at the front window. They were open the merest slit. Just enough for him to see what was inside.

He dashed around to the front of the cabin, vaulting over the railing just as the sheriff had inserted Corrie's master key into the lock. Sutton looked up, immediately alert.

J.D. nodded once. "He's in there but I think we're too late. Corrie, get back."

"Oh, dear God," Corrie gasped as the sheriff turned the key and pushed the door open. As J.D. stepped in behind the sheriff, he heard Corrie whisper, "Not again!"

Chapter 5

Corrie sat numbly in her father's overstuffed recliner in her apartment, waiting for Rick to finish wrapping up his business in cabin A-6. Normally, she would have insisted she was fine and have continued to carry on her regular campground business, but shock and relief had overwhelmed her. She'd managed to keep herself together long enough to take a look at the body of Timothy Jenkins of Dallas, Texas and assure Rick that she didn't know him or, she acknowledged with a twinge of guilt, even remember him checking in.

The relief came from the realization that the threat against her and her campground seemed to have been averted. And that brought on another wave of guilt.

A soft tap on the door made her sit up. "Who is it?" she asked.

"J.D. The sheriff wanted me to check on you."

"Come in," Corrie said, leaning back and closing her eyes as a wave of weariness swept over her. The rich, nutty aroma of piñon coffee suddenly jerked her to full alertness and her eyes snapped open as J.D. entered the room, steaming cup in hand.

"Bless you," she murmured and took a bracing gulp. She welcomed the warmth of the coffee almost as much as she did the warmth in J.D.'s silver-gray eyes. She took a deep breath and set the cup down as she straightened up. "So it's official? He's really... dead?"

J.D. perched on the arm of the wing chair that sat opposite the recliner and nodded solemnly. "I'm afraid so, Corrie."

She closed her eyes and tried to shake off a shudder. "So this isn't just a bad dream, either?" She stood up before J.D. could say another word and went to the window that looked out over the campground. Cabin A-6 was just beyond her view, but she could see a couple of sheriff's department cruisers and the medical examiner's van, along with several guests milling around just beyond the yellow police tape. "I can't believe this is happening again!"

"Corrie...."

She turned to him, not wanting to hear any soothing platitudes, not in the mood to be comforted. "What's going on,

J.D.? I thought things were back to normal. I never thought they would be after Krista Otero's death, but everything was going well, and now when word of this gets out, people will be afraid to come here, they'll think the place is jinxed or dangerous, they'll...."

"Whoa, whoa, whoa," J.D. said as he stood up and came toward her, gesturing with his palms down to stop the hysterical flow of words. She swallowed hard and hiccuped, feeling the salty sting in her eyes, and then J.D.'s muscular arms went around her and she welcomed his strength and allowed herself a few tears as she clung to him. "It's all right," he said softly. "You've had a shock and no one will blame you for being upset. And no one's going to blame you for what happened to this man. You didn't even know him."

"What happened to him, J.D.?" she asked, pulling herself out of his arms. She tried not to think about the flash of disappointment she saw in his eyes, tried not to think about how good it had felt to be held by him. She swiped her fingers across her eyes and took a deep breath. "It wasn't a natural death, was it? It wasn't a heart attack or stroke. I saw his face. He looked shocked. I mean, not like what I would have expected if he...?"

"It wasn't suicide, if that's what you're asking," J.D. said grimly. "He didn't write that threatening note to you then have a fit of remorse and kill himself. He was stabbed."

Corrie winced. "Stabbed? But I didn't see any blood."

"It was done with a long, thin instrument. The M. E. found a puncture mark right near his heart. He can't tell till he runs some tests and gets a toxicology report back from the lab, but it's possible he was injected with something that killed him but the stab wound alone might have been enough."

Corrie found herself staring at the center of J.D.'s chest and not because he favored tight-fitting t-shirts that accentuated every rippling abdominal muscle. "Whoever did it... they had to be standing pretty close to him," she said, her voice a mere whisper.

"He knew his murderer. Yeah, that's probably safe to assume," J.D. said. Corrie looked up into his eyes and he nodded toward the stairs. "The sheriff wanted to give you some time to collect yourself, but he's probably biting at the bit to ask you some more questions. Are you up to it?"

"Do I have a choice?" she asked. She moved toward the stairs and squared her shoulders. Then she glanced at J.D. "Mind grabbing my coffee cup for me?"

~

She emerged at the bottom of the stairs and Rick glanced up. He nodded toward the TV room. "Let's talk."

She led the way into the TV room which was strangely deserted for this hour of the afternoon. She tried to ignore the unusual quiet of a regular Friday afternoon in the campground—the camp store was empty and even the laundry room was silent. She couldn't hear anymore shouts or splashes from the pool or voices of any of the campers. For a moment, she wanted to stop and ask how many guests had checked out in the last thirty minutes, but decided that she could wait a little longer before getting any more bad news.

She waited for Rick to enter the room and wasn't too surprised when J.D. came in as well. He handed Corrie her coffee cup then sat in one of the wooden chairs at one of the game tables and tipped it back against the wall... a habit of his. Corrie turned to Rick. "Well?"

"I'm sure Wilder's filled you in on some of the details," Rick said, concentrating on his notepad which seemed filled with jottings. "What I want to know is, are you sure you don't remember having had any interaction with the deceased at all?"

Corrie sighed. "Rick, I've been racking my brain. I don't even remember checking the poor guy in." She raised a brow at him. "Was he the man RaeLynn was talking about?"

Rick nodded, then shook his head. "I hated to ask her to look at him. It was all she could do to hold it together. I tried to send her home, but she said she couldn't go and leave you at a time like this."

"Poor RaeLynn," Corrie said. "Did either Jackie or Dana remember him?" Rick snorted.

"Dana thinks she might have checked him in but since you and Jackie do the majority of the guest registrations, I'm betting she's engaging in wishful thinking. Jackie says if any of the guests do an on-line registration, it's simply a matter of them handing you their printed-out reservation form and paying for it. Timothy Jenkins is listed as having paid cash for his cabin rental. Is that unusual?"

"Paying cash? Not really. For a cabin rental, I'm surprised it didn't stick in my mind. Most people who pay cash are in the least expensive tent sites," she said, nodding toward J.D. "The cabin sites are the most expensive, but I suppose there are still a few people who pay cash for everything when they can." Rick gave a grunt of assent and made a few more notes.

"What if he had paid for it on-line?" J.D. asked. Corrie frowned, wondering what his question had to do with the situation at hand.

"He'd have had to have done it with a credit card and we would have probably asked him for the card and his I. D. to verify that he was the account holder. For security reasons," she added. "For cash customers, all we ask is payment in advance when they arrive and their vehicle's license plate number."

"Not even a photo I.D.?"

"No," Corrie said, feeling a flash of resentment at the questions. She'd never had problems before so why was J.D. asking questions that implied that she ran her business incorrectly? She raised a brow at him as if to ask if he wanted to know anything else, but he shook his head.

Rick cleared his throat. "I've got Dudley running a check on his plates. The victim—assuming he is Timothy Jenkins—had a wallet full of cash, but no I. D. of any kind. No driver's license, no military I.D., not even a library card. And no credit cards. If he was driving that Honda, he should have at least had a driver's license. But too many things aren't adding up." Before he could continue, Deputy Evans appeared in the doorway.

"Sheriff, sir," he said in his quiet voice and held out a sheet of paper to Rick. Rick took it with a nod and Dudley took it as a dismissal. Corrie wondered, fleetingly, if the young deputy had run into Myra or sought her out after this tragic turn of events.

"Huh!" Rick said and Corrie immediately turned her attention back to him. J.D. had been leaning back in his chair, his hands locked behind his head as he frowned toward the ceiling, but he glanced over at Rick as well.

"What?" Corrie said, her impatience getting the better of her when Rick said nothing else.

He looked up. "That Honda isn't registered to a Timothy Jenkins. It belongs to a Robert Moreno from Lubbock and it was reported stolen three days ago."

There was a "thud" as J.D. brought the front legs of his chair down and got up and walked over to them. "What are the odds that the fellow we found in the cabin isn't named Timothy Jenkins after all?"

Rick shrugged and looked at Corrie. "Can you find out when this Timothy Jenkins made his reservation?"

"I should have that in the computer," Corrie said, feeling a twinge of relief that she would at least have that information to give Rick. She went to her desk, noting the time and grimacing at the thought that she was supposed to be hosting her campground's weekly Friday night dinner. It was enchiladas tonight, a meal that didn't require as much attention as the fish fries that took place on alternating weeks, and she knew that Jackie and Dana, with RaeLynn's help, already had the meal ready to go. Despite their shock, they had welcomed the opportunity to stay busy, though Jackie dreaded having to face the questions the guests were sure to have... and to keep Dana from giving out more information than was prudent. RaeLynn had made herself useful in the kitchen and was doing everything she could to avoid having to face any questions herself. With Red and Jerry's help, it was unnecessary for Corrie to have to make an appearance at the dinner and she felt a grudging relief that she didn't have to go out and see just how many people had opted to skip the enchilada dinner and how many had attended out of morbid curiosity.

As before, Rick and J.D. hovered over her as she brought up the information. "Looks like he made his reservation on Tuesday, two days before he checked in. And he did give a credit card number to hold the reservation, but since he showed up and paid cash, I never bothered to run the card or check to see if it was valid or not."

"So it could be just a random string of numbers he made up or a stolen card... probably Robert Moreno's," J.D. murmured.

"Or it could be his and he just used it to make reservations with," Rick said. Before he could ask, Corrie jotted down the number and expiration date and handed it to him.

"I presume you want to check this out," she said. He nodded as the bell over the front door rang.

"We'll be getting in touch with this Robert Moreno...."

"I beg your pardon? Did I just hear my name?"

The three of them swiveled toward the front door. A distinguished looking man in his late fifties stood in the doorway, his bronzed face wearing an expression of concern. He was dressed rather formally for a weekend camper, with a dark blue sports jacket over a white polo shirt, khaki slacks, and black loafers. He had an overnight bag in his hand and beside him stood a rolling suitcase. He raised his brows and glanced from one to the other, his gaze finally resting on Corrie as she stood up.

"Mr. Robert Moreno? Of Lubbock?" she said.

The man nodded, relief on his face. “Yes. Are you Corrie Black, the campground owner? I take it that means you were able to hold my reservation till today. I got held up—quite literally, as it turns out—at home and wasn't able to leave till late this morning. My travel agent said he'd make sure you'd hold my reservation and not give it up to someone else. I understand you're full.”

“Mr. Moreno,” Rick interrupted, stepping forward and holding up his badge. “Sheriff Sutton. I wonder if I could ask you a few questions.”

“Is this about the theft of my car? The police in Lubbock didn't seem to think it was anything but a couple of kids just out joy-riding, though I would have thought they'd have found it by now if that was the case.”

“You drive a gray Honda Accord?”

“You found it? Where? Here?” Mr. Moreno looked dumbfounded. Rick held up a hand.

“Mr. Moreno, you mentioned a travel agent. Did your travel agent book your reservation here at the Black Horse Campground?”

“Well, yes. That is, that was my understanding. Why? Is there a problem with my reservation?”

Corrie broke in before Rick asked another question. “Mr. Moreno, is your agent's name Timothy Jenkins?”

Mr. Moreno glanced at her and frowned. “Timothy Jenkins?” He shook his head. “No, it isn't. My agent's name is...,” he fumbled for his wallet and pulled out a white business card, “David Duncan.”

“May I?” Rick asked, reaching for the card in the man's hand. Corrie only caught the briefest glimpse at the card, but it seemed smudged and dog-eared and remarkably amateurishly printed. Robert Moreno surrendered it without a word then shook his head.

“I don't understand. Is there a problem with my reservation? I was told that the owner of the campground would understand that there were circumstances that would prevent me from checking in yesterday as scheduled and would make adjustments accordingly.”

“Mr. Moreno, I am the owner of the campground. Corrie Black,” Corrie said, extending her hand, which Mr. Moreno shook dubiously. “And you are correct; if I had been notified about your situation I would have made arrangements. However, as far as my records show, you, Robert Moreno, don't have a reservation with us at all.”

The man's mouth dropped open in shock. "That's ridiculous!" he sputtered, his face darkening. "I paid this agent well in advance for my reservation and I have the receipt to prove it!"

"You paid in advance?" Rick echoed, fingering the agent's card. "How far in advance, Mr. Moreno? And how did you pay?"

"Why, with my credit card, of course!" he snapped turning to look at Rick as if challenging him to prove him wrong. "And I paid in full three weeks ago when I booked my trip!"

"Three weeks ago?" Corrie looked at Rick, but he didn't seem to notice her outburst. In fact, his face registered no emotion or reaction whatsoever. J.D. slipped his cell phone out of his holster and began fiddling with it, before handing it to Rick. He glanced at it, then nodded at J.D.

"Would this man be your travel agent?" J.D. asked quietly, handing the phone to the irate Robert Moreno, who calmed down long enough to slip his glasses out of his shirt pocket and put them on. He studied the photo that J.D. had apparently taken with his phone and raised his brows, then grimaced.

"I think so. Yes, it looks like him although this man looks... er...." He handed the phone back to J.D. "Is this man, er...?" he hesitated, looking at J. D then Rick.

"Yes, he is," Rick said bluntly. "I assume you had asked him to book you a cabin here?"

The man's face paled alarmingly. "Are you saying he was found dead in the accommodations he rented for me?" He didn't wait for an answer. "Now wait one minute, Sheriff!" he thundered, suddenly regaining his composure. "Are you insinuating that I had something to do with this man's death? Because if you are, then I want to talk to an attorney before I say one more word to any of you!"

Rick straightened up. "Mr. Moreno, I do have some questions and if you wish to have an attorney present when I ask them, then that is certainly your right. However, there is something else you should know; there is a strong possibility that this man may have had something to do with an anonymous threat that was delivered to the campground office...."

"A threat? What kind of threat? Against whom?"

"Against the campground itself. Whether that included the guests and staff as well, or just the owner, really isn't an issue. The threat stipulated that the campground be shut down Saturday—that's tomorrow."

"You think that this man threatened the campground? Well,

then, if he did and he's now dead, then that should take care of the threat, shouldn't it?"

Rick put on his most patient expression. "It should, IF we can prove that this man was the one who issued the threat. But even if he was, Mr. Moreno," Rick went on, although the man's foot had begun tapping over his apparent irritation at what he perceived to be typical police run-around, "we have no guarantee that the threat, whatever it was, has been averted. Then there is the matter that the man was murdered. Whether he was killed by someone who was trying to prevent him from harming anyone in the campground, or he was killed by someone who had other reasons for wanting him dead remains to be seen."

Mr. Robert Moreno finally set down his overnight bag and sighed. "Well, is it possible, then, that I could get some kind of accommodations for the night? After all, I did have a reservation."

Technically, he hadn't; the reservation was in the name of Timothy Jenkins who, apparently, was not the man Mr. Moreno had originally contacted about his reservation. Regardless of that fact, however, was the fact that Corrie didn't have any accommodations to offer Mr. Moreno. It was obvious that his overnight bag and suitcase were all the luggage he brought—no tent, no sleeping bag. And the only cabin that was vacant at the moment was a crime scene. Furthermore, he had just been told that the campground had been threatened, but that didn't seem to faze him in the least. Most people, it occurred to Corrie, would have demanded a cancellation and refund of their reservation. She glanced at Rick and, despite the expression on his face which was carefully devoid of interest, knew that the same thought had occurred to him. He cleared his throat.

"Mr. Moreno, I'm afraid you'll have to find accommodations elsewhere. The campground is full tonight and the cabin you were assigned is now a crime scene. And there is a possibility that the campground might need to be closed down, in light of everything that has happened." He didn't look at Corrie or make any visible signal, but something in the tone of his voice kept her from protesting.

But not Robert Moreno.

"Other accommodations elsewhere? You've got to be joking, Sheriff! You expect me to go and find a place to stay when I already had a reservation here?"

It was evident that Mr. Moreno was going to cause problems. Corrie was about to make a scathing reply to his objection when

J.D. spoke up. "May I ask why you're so set on staying here at the Black Horse, Mr. Moreno... especially in light of the fact that we've had a murder here and there is still a possible threat to your safety and that of the other guests?"

The man pulled himself up to his full height, which meant he was still about eight inches shorter than either J.D. or Rick. His face took on a reddish glow and he cleared his throat. "I have very important work to do and I was assured that I would have more privacy here than at a hotel...."

"You have to be kidding!" Corrie said in disbelief. "Hotels have private bathrooms. Here, you have to walk to a public bathroom and shower house. Not to mention there isn't any room service or even a restaurant, unless you count our weekend social meals," she added, jerking her head in the direction of the patio. "Perhaps you've been misled as to just how luxurious your accommodations were going to be!"

Robert Moreno's shoulders sagged. He slid a glance at Rick, as if wishing he were having this conversation anywhere but in the presence of a law enforcement officer, then he sighed. "All right," he muttered. He reached for his wallet and removed another card from it and handed it to Rick. This time the card was printed on professional light-gray card stock with maroon and black ink. Rick took the card and his brows rose. He shot a look that carried more than a hint of disbelief at Robert Moreno.

"Private investigator?" he quoted off the card.

"What?" Corrie's stunned squawk burst from her as her mouth dropped open. She reached for the business card which Rick surrendered without a word. Sure enough, the card had a small photo in the corner of the man standing in her camp store with his name, an address, and phone number in Lubbock, and the words "Private Investigator" printed in bold black letters. J.D. plucked the card from her fingers and studied it as well, before handing it back to Rick.

"Let's start over, Mr. Moreno," Rick said, his voice edged with ice and his blue eyes turning glacial. Corrie sensed J.D. brace himself for the storm as well; Rick could be the epitome of patience when he wanted or needed to be, but anyone who deliberately yanked him around brought out a side of him that was instrumental in his success as a sheriff in keeping Bonney County peaceful and law-abiding. Even Mr. Moreno turned a shade pale. "What, exactly, is your purpose for coming here and, more importantly, for keeping your profession a secret?"

"I wasn't keeping it a secret, Sheriff Sutton," Mr. Moreno blustered, although his bluster was, at best, half-hearted. "No one asked me what my line of work was."

"We just got done informing you that your cabin was found to be inhabited by a man whom you claim to know as someone else and was discovered murdered in it. That there was a possibility that this man may have sent a threat to the campground and its guests and staff. That this man was registered as a guest with your vehicle that was reported stolen three days ago. And it never once occurred to you to mention that you were a private investigator? Not to mention that this," Rick added, flipping the travel agent's business card onto the counter, "has to be one of the most blatantly fake business cards I've ever seen. I doubt your 'travel agent' actually exists. You don't need a travel agent to book a reservation at an RV park!"

He hadn't raised his voice, but Mr. Moreno cringed as if Rick were giving him the dressing down of his life. He cleared his throat and flicked an imaginary piece of lint off his sports jacket. "Sheriff, perhaps you're not aware that there is such a thing as client confidentiality...."

"If your client had anything to do with the death of that man in your cabin, then your 'client confidentiality' could very well become 'accessory to a crime'. Perhaps you're not aware of that," Rick shot back and the man flinched.

"Very well, Sheriff. But is it possible for us to talk somewhere else?"

"How about my office at the sheriff's department?" Rick said and Mr. Moreno nodded, then took a deep breath.

"There's one more thing you need to know, Sheriff... and you as well, Miss Black," he said, inclining his head toward Corrie.

"What's that?" Corrie said, her heart beginning to pound with dread. Robert Moreno's face had paled again and he ran a nervous hand over his slicked-back hair.

"There's a reason I wanted to stay in the campground tonight in spite of everything,. "It's about that threat you received."

"What about it?" Both Rick and J.D. barked the question and Mr. Moreno jumped, his gaze darting nervously between them.

"I have reason to believe the threat you received is very real. I don't know what it is or who it's from or why you're being targeted. But in light of what has happened, I strongly recommend that you follow the directions in the note and close the campground down for the weekend."

Chapter 6

Corrie stared out the front window as the last of the vehicles carrying her guests pulled out of the campground and onto the highway. She felt sick to her stomach. The words had no sooner been out of Robert Moreno's mouth than both Rick and J.D. had mobilized to start evacuating the campground. To Corrie had fallen the task of finding other accommodations for the guests. She'd made the owner of Bonney's only motel very happy by filling all thirty of his rooms in a matter of twenty minutes. Two hotels and another campground in Ruidoso had also benefited from her threat. She had tried not to think of what this was going to cost her; she either had to refund her guests' fees or pay for their new accommodations. She had wanted to protest, but she knew she couldn't take a chance that Mr. Moreno was just trying to scare her.

She had sent her staff home, Buster offering to drive the three teenagers home and Deputy Dudley Evans insisting on escorting Myra safely back to her house. It had taken a great deal of persuasion to get her year-round guests to leave as well. Most of them resisted leaving their homes, especially the Westlakes, since Rosemary hated the thought of missing out on what was happening. Still, Rick had successfully managed to get them to leave with stern orders to stay put until the threat was over and it was safe to return. Afterwards, he had taken Robert Moreno to his office at the sheriff's department to question him more closely and then returned to supervise the evacuation of the campground after securing a room for Mr. Moreno at a local bed-and-breakfast, the River's Edge, and admonishing him to stay put and not tell anyone where he was.

Now the only people remaining at the Black Horse were the Pages and the Myers and J.D. And they had made it perfectly clear that, if Corrie was staying, then they were staying, too. RaeLynn had refused to leave as well. And Rick was having no luck in persuading Corrie to leave.

"Where would I go, Rick? I just sent all my guests to take up every available vacant room and campsite in Bonney County and the village of Ruidoso. Besides," she added, folding her arms and leaning against the counter, "you and your deputies checked the campground over and didn't find a bomb or anything, right? So now that my guests are safe...."

"I want YOU to be safe as well!" Rick barked. "If you're worried about a place to stay, I have a couple of vacant beds at the county lock up. Not a four-star resort, but at least we—or I—won't have to worry about what might be happening here at the campground tomorrow!"

"And where are YOU going to be, Sheriff?" she fired back. "I doubt you'll be safely far away from the campground. You'll be right here, to see what happens tomorrow!"

"That's my job!"

"And this is my home!"

A piercing whistle froze their next words in their mouths and nearly shattered the windows and the glass display cases. "And you both need to chill out!" J.D. said, raising his voice and his hands. He gave both Corrie and Rick a sharp look. "We're assuming that the threat had to do with that Timothy Jenkins or David Duncan or whatever other alias he may have had. But maybe there's someone else who is at risk. Maybe it's someone here at the Black Horse, on the staff, or maybe it's a guest who was supposed to arrive tomorrow." He glanced at Jackie. "Offhand, do you know if there are any guests who are supposed to arrive tomorrow?"

Jackie frowned. "I think we determined that there were a few guests checking out tomorrow and a few reservations are supposed to be coming to replace them, but I think we still have a few sites available in case anymore reservations or drop-ins arrive." Jerry's walrus mustache twitched.

"You thinking that maybe there's someone who might be coming tomorrow that might actually be the threat that was the subject of the letter?" he asked, his instincts as a former investigative reporter kicking in.

J.D. looked at Rick. Rick chewed his lower lip, furiously thinking.

"It's a possibility, sure," he said at last. "But there's also a threat that's already here. That's whoever took it upon themselves to murder Timothy Jenkins. Even if their intention was to protect the campground from the original threat, anyone who commits murder in cold blood can't be trusted... and therefore, no one is safe until we find them."

"'We'?" J.D. and Corrie echoed and Rick glared at them.

"The Bonney County Sheriff's Department," he clarified.

"And in order for us to do our job, we can't be worrying about the safety of all of you. If you want to help us, then please, leave the campground, just for tonight." He looked directly at Corrie and his voice dropped. "Please."

Corrie's breath caught in her throat. The look in Rick's eyes was a mixture of raw worry and pure exasperation. She knew she was being stubborn and defiant only because... well, because it was Rick. She looked around the room, at Jerry and Jackie, who had been like an uncle and aunt to her; at Red and Dana who had selflessly jumped in to help her keep her business going during the most difficult year of her life; at RaeLynn, who, despite her fear and uncertainty, stood loyally by Corrie's side; and at J.D. who had demonstrated that Rick Sutton wasn't the only man of honor left in the world. And while he might be nothing more than just a friend, he would never leave her to face troubles and danger on her own. Corrie knew what Rick was really saying: her friends—her family—would not leave her here at the campground to face whatever threat or danger there might be alone. If she stayed, they would stay, and if she was in danger, then they were in danger as well. She swallowed her pride.

"All right," she said. She looked at Rick. "So how many beds do you have at the jail? Do we need to bring our own linens?"

She saw the relief in his eyes. "I was kidding about the jail. But I do have an idea. The Enriquez ranch has some RV hook-ups for their annual family reunion. Let me give Joe a call and see if he wouldn't mind putting a few guests up for the night. And they're just a few miles down the road, outside of Tunstall, so you won't have to travel too far."

"Sounds good. I'll go start unhooking the Airstream," Red said immediately and headed out the front door. Dana went with him. There was no questioning the Myers' loyalty and love, but that didn't mean that they weren't relieved at Corrie's decision.

Jerry and Jackie nodded soberly, knowing Rick was right, but like Corrie, loathe to be chased out of their home by some senseless threat. "You'll stay with us, honey?" Jackie asked Corrie. "Of course, Oliver and Renfro are welcome, too."

"I suppose so," Corrie said, her reluctance to leave her home evident in her lack of enthusiasm. She looked at RaeLynn. "I'll drop you off at your place on our way, if you like."

RaeLynn's nod, like Corrie's, was half-hearted, but Corrie knew that it was because RaeLynn would rather be anywhere else but "her place", which was her family's home, even if it meant being in a potentially dangerous place, as long as she was surrounded by friends and people who cared about her. Then she shook her head. "I think I'll just walk, Corrie. It's a nice evening."

"Are you sure? I don't mind...." But RaeLynn was already heading for the storage closet and getting her purse.

"It's okay. When can I come back to work?" she asked, her honey-colored eyes clouded with concern. Corrie knew it was just as much from fear over the threat to the campground as it was dread of having to deal with her family for too long a period of time.

"How about Sunday morning? That should be okay, shouldn't it, Rick?" Corrie asked, turning to him. He gave a shrug.

"Should be. Wish I could guarantee it," he said, but he, too, noted the look of desperation in RaeLynn's eyes. "Why don't you plan on it and if, for some reason it isn't safe, someone will get in touch with you."

"Okay," she said. She looked at Corrie and the concern in her face made her look so young and vulnerable. "If you need me, Corrie—not that there's much I can do—let me know. Okay? For anything at all," she added and Corrie nodded. RaeLynn gave Rick and J.D. each a hesitant smile and then headed out the door. Jerry and Jackie followed her.

That left J.D. Corrie turned to him. "What about you? I don't know if Jerry and Jackie have enough room in their RV, but the Myers will...." But he shook his head before she could finish.

"If I decide to take advantage of the Enriquez's hospitality, I can just set up my tent down there."

"What do you mean, 'if'?" Corrie asked, narrowing her eyes. J.D. nodded toward Rick.

"I was going to see if the sheriff would object to any help I might be able to give him and the sheriff's department. That means staying on site," he added. Rick inclined his head slightly, just enough to give his assent.

"Now wait a minute!" Corrie sputtered, feeling the heat rise in her face. "Did you two conspire to convince me to leave so you could just move in and take over my home and business?"

"We're not the I.R.S.," Rick said dryly. "We're trying to protect your home and business... and YOU."

"What about your safety?" she asked, fear overcoming her anger at the thought of the risk that they were taking on her behalf. And there WAS a risk, or Rick wouldn't have been so adamant about making everyone leave the Black Horse.

"We're law enforcement officers, Corrie.," he said. "It's our job to protect and serve. That doesn't mean we throw our own personal safety out the window. We'll take every precaution, but we have to do our job, regardless of the risk."

Corrie felt as if there was a ton of lead sitting in the pit of her stomach. The seriousness of his expression and the fact that he gave his consent for J.D. to help out, even though he wasn't officially a member of any law enforcement agency in Bonney, or anywhere else for that matter, made her realize that he DID expect danger of some kind to rear its ugly head. She swallowed hard. "What did Mr. Moreno tell you?" she asked.

Rick didn't answer right away. He stared at her for a long moment until she squirmed and before she could repeat the question, he said, "You've met Timothy Jenkins before."

His statement took her completely by surprise. "What? The man who was murdered?" She shook her head. "You're wrong, Rick! I've never seen him before in my life until he checked in, and he obviously didn't make an impression on me because I didn't even recognize him after he was killed!"

"You were ten years old the last time you saw him. And you knew him as Bill Woods."

Corrie's mouth dropped open and she sank onto her stool behind the counter. She felt as if the room were closing in on her. She swallowed hard and finally managed to squeak out two words.

"Uncle Bill?"

Chapter 7

“You were related to him?” J.D.'s incredulous voice snapped her out of her shock.

“No. Not blood related. He was... he was one of my dad's best friends. Him and one of my dad's cousins, Toby Willis.” She cleared her throat. “Rick, are you sure?” she asked, not wanting to think because her thoughts were a tangle of confusion, hurt, and surprise.

The last time she had seen the man she had known as Uncle Bill was, as Rick had said, when she was ten years old and her father had been all but exchanging blows with the man who had once been his best friend. What had conspired to break up a decades-old friendship was never clearly explained to her, only her mother's tearful assurance that Billy was doing what was best for all of them. Uncle Bill's departure left a gap in their lives and a lot of unanswered questions in Corrie's mind. She learned quickly that Billy's good nature would turn sour if she insisted on asking questions about why Uncle Bill had left, so she stopped asking. Her parents must have assumed she had gotten over his leaving and never talked of him again.

And now, he had reappeared in her life and, just as mysteriously as before, left again. Leaving more unanswered questions.

Rick nodded, giving her time to digest the information he had given her. “He's had about three or four false names over the last twenty-some years, but there's no question about who he is.” Corrie nodded absently, noting that at least one question was answered—Uncle Bill was still alive.

Or had been alive.

J.D. spoke up. “What's the reason he's had so many identities?” Rick looked at Corrie, silently asking if she minded talking about it in front of J.D. She nodded at him, also curious but dreading what she might hear about a man she had once trusted and loved enough to consider him a part of her family.

Rick pulled out his notepad and flipped it open. “First off, he's left a string of wives from New Mexico to Texas to Oklahoma. No divorces,” he added, “and no children, either, except those of the women he'd married. He'd just take off and leave without a word, find another woman in a town where he wasn't known, and settle down again."

"Criminal record?" J.D. asked. Rick shook his head.

"Nothing official. Meaning he's never been convicted of a crime, not even bigamy, although he was suspected in some shady dealings, such as illegal gambling, money laundering, real estate fraud."

Something clicked in Corrie's mind—a long-ago snatch of an argument. Billy and Uncle Bill shouting and Toby Willis trying to intervene and prevent possible bloodshed. She sat up straighter. "He was selling property that didn't exist or that didn't belong to him?"

Rick raised an eyebrow. "You remember that?"

Corrie nodded slowly. "Something about it. Billy was upset about a call he got from someone asking him about some river front property that was being offered for sale. The tract wasn't up for sale. It was part of the National Forest and the Bureau of Land Management also owned part of it, but it joined up to our land." Rick nodded.

"According to the court records, he listed your father as a co-owner in the land he was selling, but he was the principal owner. All inquiries were supposed to go through him, but he didn't answer his phone or failed to return calls one time too many so the prospective buyer called your dad directly at the campground. Of course, Billy didn't know what the buyer was talking about, things got heated, and then your dad...."

"Yeah, I know my dad," Corrie sighed. She rubbed her eyes with her hands. "That was when the big blow-up took place and Uncle Bill left."

J.D. had been taking in the entire conversation silently. He cleared his throat. "Your dad called the cops on his friend?"

"No. No, he didn't do that," Corrie said. "He couldn't bring himself to do it. Uncle Bill had been his best friend for too long. But Billy wasn't going to let anyone who had tried to break the law or risk having his property taken away just get off without him saying a word. He told Uncle Bill that he was no longer welcome and that he didn't want him anywhere near his wife or daughter or his home and that if he ever tried to tie the Black Horse or the family name to any of his business dealings, he'd report him to the police and then Uncle Bill better hope the cops caught up with him before my dad did. Uncle Bill tried to tell him that he hadn't intended to get Billy involved, that the whole thing was a mistake, that the wrong parcel of property had been listed, but my dad wasn't stupid. He'd often wondered where Uncle Bill would get his money and why he never stayed around for very long. He never could get hold of him, either, never a phone number or address. He'd just show up without warning, stay a few weeks, then take off again. He was always generous," she went on. She smiled and tears stung her eyes. "One year when the campground was struggling to make ends meet, he gave my dad and mom the money to give me a birthday party and a new bike." She went on, almost to herself. "Of course, Billy would have never taken the money if he'd known it wasn't earned legitimately. I think that was what hurt him most of all. That Uncle Bill lied to him."

"And Toby Willis, your dad's cousin? What happened to him?" Rick asked.

"I'm not sure, Rick. He had been the one to introduce my dad to Bill Woods. I think maybe he... I don't know, felt guilty that he got my family—our family, really—involved with someone who was involved in shady, or outright criminal, activities. I remember Billy asking him 'What would your aunt think of the people you're associating with and introducing to your family?' That was the last time I remember seeing Toby Willis. Last I heard, through the family grapevine at Billy's funeral, was that he'd moved his family to Oklahoma."

"He didn't attend the funeral?"

"No."

"And you never saw Bill Woods again, either?"

"No." Silence descended on the room and she looked up at the two men. "Why did he come here? Did he not know that my dad's been gone for over a year? Did he find out and come to pay his respects? Or was he hoping to come and make amends?"

Rick sighed and leaned his forearms on the counter. "We'll probably never know now."

"Why was this Robert Moreno keeping tabs on him? Did he know who he really was? Was he Moreno's client?"

"According to Moreno, he was asked to keep an eye on him," Rick said. "He claimed he couldn't give me the name of the person who hired him—client confidentiality," he added dryly. "But he did tell me it was a woman, probably an ex-wife. His speculation, not mine."

"Wouldn't be the first time a woman hired a private investigator to find an errant husband," J.D. commented, leaning back against the counter with his thumbs hooked into his belt loops. “The question is, was she mad enough to use the information to kill him?”

“Moreno claims he never had the chance to tell the woman where her husband was,” Rick said. “His story is that the woman called him from Dallas, hired him, and then he tracked Woods, known as Timothy Jenkins to his client, to this travel agency in Lubbock, where he was supposedly posing as an agent named David Duncan. He said he told 'Duncan' he wanted to take a vacation somewhere away from it all and that Duncan recommended this campground.” Corrie felt a smile tug at her lips in spite of herself, which faded as Rick continued. “But then Moreno's car was stolen three days ago and that threw his 'vacation' off....”

“He was actually planning to come here?” J.D. interjected. Rick shrugged.

“Apparently he was trying to get as much information about Duncan-slash-Jenkins as he could before reporting to his client. Said he didn't want to arouse suspicion by not booking a vacation and this was the least expensive one that the agency offered.”

“Somehow, I doubt the agency even has us on their list of top ten vacation destinations, or even the top ten thousand,” Corrie said. She stood up. “I'll bet Uncle Bill recommended us on his own.”

“And then stole his client's car to come down and... what?” J.D. said sharply. Corrie threw him a startled glance and was surprised to see a glint of anger in his eyes. She looked at Rick and wasn't too surprised to see the expression mirrored there.

“All right, calm down,” she said, holding her hands up. “I knew him as 'Uncle Bill', not Timothy Jenkins, not David Duncan, or any other alias he might have had. That doesn't mean I think he was an innocent party in this whole thing.”

“He may have been the one who threatened you and your campground,” Rick said. Corrie shook her head.

“I don't agree, Rick. He may have had dishonest dealings and my dad may have almost gotten burned by one of them, but I don't believe that Bill Woods would have threatened my life.”

“You haven't seen the man in over twenty years, Corrie,” J.D. said. “You were just a kid and probably don't know as much about him as you think. And people do change,” he added darkly.

“If Uncle Bill had been that dangerous, I doubt my father would have just let it go without giving me a clear warning,” Corrie argued. “And he definitely would have reported him to the police, not just told him to get out and never come back."

"It doesn't matter," Rick growled, sparks flying in his dark blue eyes. "Whether he was the one who threatened you or not, he's dead now and that means that there is a killer out there somewhere, probably a lot closer than you care to think," he said.

"So that's who we need to be focusing on—whoever killed Uncle Bill," Corrie said.

"No, YOU need to be focusing on getting yourself ready to go with the Pages to stay at the Enriquez ranch!" Rick shot back. "WE," he gestured to himself and J.D., "will be focusing on this murder investigation and those threats you received. So grab your toothbrush and a change of clothes and be ready to go when the Pages are ready!"

"Now just wait one minute, Sheriff!" Corrie said, planting her fists on her hips and holding her ground. "You're overlooking one thing."

"Oh, am I? And what would that be?" Rick said, folding his arms across his chest and preparing to stand his ground as well.

"That note merely told me to close the campground for Saturday. It didn't say one word about me having to leave it!"

"So?"

"So, I'm not leaving! Everyone is gone, the campground is basically deserted, it's just me, here in my own home, and nothing was said about me having to leave!"

"Do the words 'Your life is in danger' ring a bell? Because I'm pretty sure I saw them on that note and as far as I'm concerned, they mean the same thing as 'Get the hell out of Dodge'!" Rick snapped.

"My life was in danger if I kept the campground open. That's what the note actually said!"

"We're not going to argue semantics here!" J.D. thundered, taking hold of Corrie's arm, an action that took them all by surprise. He quickly let go and stepped back just as Rick straightened up, his jaw tightening. He held up his hands. "Easy, Sheriff, I wasn't going to throw her over my shoulder and carry her off caveman-style."

"That might be what it takes to get her attention," Rick growled, transferring his glare back to Corrie.

"Okay, you know what? Spare me your fantasies!" Corrie said, throwing her hands up in exasperation. A ghost of a smile flitted across both men's faces, but it only served to annoy her even more. "But let me tell you one thing: if you want to catch whoever is making threats or killed Uncle Bill, then sending me away might not be the smartest move. All it will do is scare them off. They'll know the police are watching the campground and they won't try anything. If all you want to do is avert the threat, then fine, but if you want to catch this guy, you'll need bait." She took a deep breath and looked at them both in turn. "That would be me," she said firmly.

"They're going to know the cops are watching the place anyway," Rick said after a moment's hesitation. J.D. looked away, muttering under his breath. Corrie kept her smile hidden and raised a brow at Rick.

"Right. And if I'm not here, they might just decide to try whatever it is they're going to try some other time, without any kind of warning. They want something, Rick, something besides me closing down for one day. And they think I have it, or can get it for them. You need me here, whether you want to admit it or not," she added firmly.

Rick's face reddened and J.D. shook his head, his gray eyes looking like thunderclouds. "It doesn't have to be you, Corrie," he growled. "They just have to think it's you. The sheriff has a female deputy. She can be here, posing as you...."

"If she weren't on vacation," Corrie said, unable to keep a smug smile off her face. This time J.D. didn't bother to mutter as he slapped his hand down on the counter in exasperation.

"Corrie," Rick said, his voice barely above a whisper, a sure sign that he was trying not to lose his cool, "you don't know what you're proposing. Someone killed Bill Woods; that person may kill again. For me to allow you to expose yourself to danger would be irresponsible and possibly deadly. I'm not going to allow you to put yourself in that position. If anything happened to you...."

"Billy would come back and knock your head off. Yeah, I know," Corrie said, unable to keep the undercurrent of hurt out of her voice. Whatever reasons Rick may have had for breaking up their relationship fifteen years ago and marrying someone else ten years ago, the fact that he stayed close and kept a watchful eye on her only because he had made a death-bed promise to her father was something that she'd never been able to fully accept. It was times like these that her pride was assuaged by the fact that Rick's marriage in the Catholic Church and his subsequent divorce kept any possibility of a reconciliation between them—let alone a future relationship—out of the question. She wanted to believe that Rick still cared for her, and she knew he did, as a friend and nothing more, so he said. Not that he ever acted like a mere friend. Part of her wanted to believe that his care and concern were the product of a love that had never died. But that would only make having to live with his decision even harder. So much easier to believe he only wanted to protect her to keep Billy's spirit at peace. "Billy's probably doing flips in his grave right now. First off, I didn't recognize his best friend, the man I thought of as an uncle for most of my childhood years, and then this man ends up dead in Billy's home. I might end up getting MY head knocked off. Rick," she said, daring to lay a hand on his forearm. The muscles were as tight as steel cables and she fought the urge to let go and retreat. "You have to let me do this. You'll be here. J.D. will be here," she added, turning to J.D. She caught him shooting a glance at her hand on Rick's arm and she made herself let go. She leaned back against the counter and sighed. "I don't know if it's the right thing to do and I know you're only thinking about my safety. I understand that. But I can't see letting this person, whoever he or she is, walk away from threatening me and my home and murdering someone I used to care about as if he were family without doing something about it. Surely if anyone can understand that, you two can."

Her words touched several nerves in both men; she could sense it in the air around them before either of them said a word. She wanted to say more, but she kept quiet, knowing that if she pushed too hard, they'd both push back. Finally, Rick let out a sigh. "You are not to set foot outside this building. You are not to let a single soul IN to this building." She didn't ask how that was supposed to help catch the person who threatened her or killed Uncle Bill. She simply nodded. "And both Wilder and I will be staying here with you tonight and tomorrow. No arguments or you'll be staying at the Enriquez ranch with a round-the-clock guard, is that clear?"

"Yes, sir," she said with a mock salute. She looked at J.D. "Anything you care to add?"

"Yeah," he deadpanned. "I get the Barcalounger in the TV room. Sutton gets the rollaway bed."

Chapter 8

J.D. managed to get through the evening without letting his mind wander to places he didn't want it to go. While he went back to his tent for a change of clothes and other necessities, Corrie provided linens and towels for him and the sheriff and then heated up a pan of the over-abundant enchiladas left over from the campground dinner. Despite the half-hearted protests from both men, she also threw together a cherry cobbler—insisting it was because she had a bag of fresh cherries in the freezer she needed to use. Both J.D. and the sheriff knew she was simply trying to stay busy though they wisely kept the thought to themselves. The three of them ate in the TV room with very little conversation, with both J.D. and the sheriff getting up periodically to check out the windows and doors to see if anyone approached the camp store. Corrie had the cordless phone at her side, but so far there hadn't been any calls from anyone. Sutton had made several calls from his cell phone to check in with the deputies he had stationed out of sight around the campground and with Deputy Evans who was keeping an eye on Robert Moreno at the bed and breakfast.

J.D. didn't say much, but it was evident to him that both Corrie and the sheriff were glad that he was there and for the same reason. And it had nothing to do with the threat against the Black Horse. He had known for a long time that there had once been something between them—Rick Sutton and Corrie Black had, at one time, been very close. Why that changed was something that was never explained to him and something he doubted he'd ever understand. If he were in the sheriff's place, if he'd had a woman like Corrie who had once loved him and still did, in spite of everything that had gone wrong between them, there wasn't anything he wouldn't do to make things right again. But for some reason, Sutton had made a decision that made no sense to J.D.—and possibly even less to Corrie—and now they were both living with that decision, even if it meant having to deny whatever feelings might still exist between them.

And anyone who believed that those feelings were merely "friendship" wouldn't know what love was if it came up and slapped them in the face.

After dinner, Corrie invited them up to her sitting room for coffee. J.D. knew that Corrie had never encouraged visitors to her private quarters, but lately—at least, since he'd met her—the rules had been relaxed. It made J.D. feel a bit better to see that even the sheriff seemed a little ill at ease being there, even though he had used it as an informal interrogation room earlier in the day. It was obvious he wasn't used to being in her apartment socially. Corrie had set up two coffee makers which were brewing away; one with piñon coffee, for her and J.D. and one with regular coffee for Sutton. She had just poured them all a cup when the sound of tires on gravel filtered in through the open window. She moved to look out, but Sutton got there first, gently edging her aside. His cell phone buzzed and he flipped it open. "Sutton." He listened for a moment, then said, "We'll be right down."

"What is it?" Corrie asked as the sheriff released the strap on his holster and checked his service automatic.

"Mike says a couple just drove into the campground. They claim they're guests and have been gone all day. The McMillans."

"Rick, that's the woman who RaeLynn said got all irate when Uncle Bill was in her way when she was picking out t-shirts yesterday!" Corrie said. He nodded.

"Let's go down and explain the situation to the McMillans and see if they have anything to add to what we know so far about your Uncle Bill and this threat you received."

J.D. stood up as well and moved to the door. "These are the people that spent the day visiting family in Alamogordo?"

"That's what Dana said they told her they were going to do," Corrie said. She shot J.D. a look. "Why? Don't you believe them?"

He shrugged. "No reason not to. But it just seems a tad suspicious that they've been gone all day after that run-in with Bill Woods yesterday. Then he was found dead in his cabin, and then they show up after the campground's been evacuated. But I could be overreacting."

"You know I don't believe in coincidences, Wilder," said the sheriff, leading the way down the stairs, with his hand resting on the butt of his gun. "But let's see what these people have to say before we jump to any conclusions."

They reached the bottom of the stairs and went to the front door of the camp store. Deputy Mike Ramirez was standing just outside and he turned and nodded. "Bring them in," Sutton said and Deputy Ramirez inclined his head then went to the driver's side door of the red Toyota and spoke briefly with the occupants. No clear words could be heard but an angry nasal twang reached their ears and J.D. grimaced. They were going to be in for an interesting interview.

"Well, I just don't understand," huffed the female voice. "We paid up front, cash on the barrel, for our RV site and spent a great deal of money in the camp store, too. You can't tell me you're not going to let us use our RV for the night!"

"Now, honey, just calm down, now, I'm sure it's just all a big mistake, now," soothed a softer, male drawl. The woman had disembarked from the car via the passenger door and she looked more than just a little put out. J.D. recalled the description Dana had given of the woman that RaeLynn had described and it matched, from the bright yellow hair to the heavy eye makeup. The woman also favored lipstick color that bordered on orange, J.D. noted with a grimace.

She huffed her way into the camp store with her husband trailing along behind her, offering an apologetic grin to anyone who happened to make eye contact with him. Mr. Thomas W. McMillan lacked the forceful personality of his wife and probably wouldn't have made much of an impression on anyone who only gave him a cursory glance. If anyone were asked to give description of him, it wouldn't differ very much from the one RaeLynn had given Sheriff Sutton of the man she had startled in the camp store. It occurred to J.D. that a lot of men, like Mr. McMillan and Bill Woods, a.k.a. Timothy Jenkins, might easily pass through life without being noticed.

Mrs. McMillan caught sight of Corrie, who had retreated to her station behind the counter, and immediately made her way toward her, her huffing and puffing as a result of extra padding on her petite frame making her look and sound like a train engine. Her lips were an angry slash of orange in a face that was otherwise white with indignation. "Miss Black? Do you know who I am?" She didn't give Corrie a chance to answer before she went on, "I am Marjorie McMillian and I have given your campground a great deal of business in addition to a reservation for a deluxe RV site which was supposed to be for two weeks, but now, since it appears that we have been evicted from our site, I will probably have to cancel and will expect a full refund for our time here!"

She stopped speaking long enough to catch her breath and that gave Corrie an opportunity to speak. "Yes, Mrs. McMillan, I understand why you're upset," she said, and J.D. could tell it was a struggle for Corrie to keep her voice carefully neutral. "And I have every intention of reimbursing you for your site rental and finding you accommodations elsewhere...."

Apparently Marjorie McMillan had had enough time to recover her breath to continue her tirade. "Find accommodations elsewhere? Are you saying we have to leave the campground? You're kicking us out?" Her voice had scaled up, her nasal twang bordering on an ear-splitting screech. Corrie blinked, but managed to keep from flinching too obviously. Mr. McMillan winced and gently patted his wife's shoulder, giving Corrie a weak smile.

"Now, now, Margie, darling, just take it easy now," he murmured. His eyes darted toward J.D. and the sheriff. Deputy Ramirez had backed toward the door and shot a look at his boss as if asking for permission to depart. But Sutton either didn't see it or chose to ignore it. He cleared his throat.

"Mrs. McMillan," he said, stepping forward. "I'm Sheriff Rick Sutton, and if you have a problem with the campground closing, you might want to speak with me rather than Miss Black. She is merely following a safety recommendation made by me."

Mrs. McMillan turned toward the sheriff and a rainbow of eye shadow hues ranging from turquoise to midnight blue appeared as she raised her brows even as her violently cat-green eyes narrowed. "A safety recommendation? And what is it about this campground that would create a safety issue? And why weren't we told earlier?"

She appeared ready to go on, but her husband shook her arm gently. "Now, honey, let's just hear what the sheriff has to say, all right?" It was a plea, almost as much for her not to take his head off for suggesting it as it was for her to hear the sheriff out.

She thrust her orange lips out in a pout and glared at her husband then at the sheriff. "Well?" she demanded.

Sutton, to J.D.'s mean satisfaction, didn't answer Mrs. McMillan immediately and when he did, he didn't make any apologies for any inconveniences. "Mrs. McMillan, I understand you were in the store yesterday afternoon, making a purchase."

"Yes," she huffed. "A rather sizable purchase, Sheriff," she added, shooting a glare at Corrie. "And what about it? Don't tell me you had a problem with my credit card?" she asked suddenly, her voice scaling up again. "That card, I'll have you know, Miss Black, is in perfect standing, as is our credit score, and, even if it weren't, I can't believe you would call in the sheriff for such a trivial matter!"

"Mrs. McMillan," Sutton said, this time raising his voice, which caused Mr. McMillan to wince again and pluck at his wife's sleeve, “this has nothing to do with your purchase. But I understand that you had a brief run-in with another guest here at the campground?”

“Oh, I suppose you mean that man who was constantly in my way,” she said, rolling her eyes as she let out a sigh of exasperation. “I swear, some people think that they're the only people in the entire world and that no one matters but them!”

“Did he give you some trouble?” the sheriff asked.

“Well, I suppose you could say so, Sheriff,” Mrs. McMillan said, appearing to be mollified by the idea that the sheriff was inquiring about an incident and person that had annoyed her. She straightened her shoulders. “And I'm sure I'm not the only person he inconvenienced, although I'm certain that no one else would have the backbone to speak up about it.”

“Margie,” her husband said, his voice holding a weak note of warning. Not surprisingly, she ignored him.

Sutton gave a nod. “Would you tell me exactly what this man did, Mrs. McMillan?”

“Of course, Sheriff,” she said, straightening her shoulders and fixing a hard stare on Corrie. “I'm pleased to see that my concerns are being taken seriously.”

“Ma’am?” Sutton prodded, saving Corrie from having her eye roll seen by Mrs. McMillan. J.D. barely refrained from joining her and forced himself to look, he hoped, appropriately interested in the woman's story.

“Well,” she said, eyeing the circle of faces around her, to make sure they were listening, “I first noticed him after I'd been shopping for a while. I have a lot of grandchildren and nieces to buy souvenirs for and, of course, I can't forget the folks who are keeping an eye on things at home... you know, the lady who's feeding our cat and picking up our mail and newspaper and the boy who's coming over to cut the grass, to make the place look inhabited. Why, I even asked one of the neighbors to please park one of their cars—they have about three—in our driveway, just to make it look even more realistic.” She paused, whether to catch her breath or to collect accolades from the sheriff for her clever burglar-deterrent methods, J.D. couldn't tell. Sutton merely inclined his head.

“Go on, Mrs. McMillan.”

She pursed her tangerine-colored lips in mild disapproval. “Well,” she went on, “I like to take my time to pick out just the right gifts for people. I like to take their tastes into consideration, like colors and such, just so you know I don't grab the first thing I see." She nodded. "And that's just what I was doing when this man just suddenly stopped dead right in front of me while I was looking at some coffee mugs. You DO have a nice variety of gift items," the woman said, half-turning to Corrie. Her compliment sounded more grudging than gracious, but Corrie gave her a faint smile of thanks. "And there I was, with a couple of coffee mugs in my hand when this man just stopped walking and stood in front of the display, blocking my view of the other items on the shelf. I can't imagine he didn't see me...."

I can't, either, J.D. thought with a grim smile.

"... but there he stood, as if I wasn't right there. I mean, I almost dropped the mugs in my hands and then I would have had to pay for them, not him!" She shot Corrie another look, this time as if accusing her of taking advantage of honest customers who were at the mercy of inconsiderate bystanders.

"Did you say anything to him?" the sheriff asked, politeness masking his impatience.

"Well, of course, I said, 'Excuse me'... twice," Mrs. McMillan huffed. She shook her head. "I swear the man was deliberately ignoring me. I mean, I know I'm petite, but I'm not invisible! I shouldn't have had to repeat myself twice!"

"Then what happened?" Sutton's patience was waning rapidly and it appeared that even Mrs. McMillan noticed. She shook her head.

"Well, then, he moved off and, wouldn't you know, there he was again, standing in front of the shelves where all the t-shirts are." She waved a hand in the direction of the t-shirt display although no one bothered to glance in that direction. "Most people, especially kids and teenagers, like a souvenir t-shirt, so of course, I had to get a few. Very nice selection," she added, with a nod in Corrie's direction, "and, as I said, I did have several people to buy for, so I was quite busy in that area when that man came and stood right in front of me again! It was almost as if he were deliberately trying to annoy me!"

"What was the man doing?" asked Sutton, hoping to cut to the chase, J.D. thought. Marjorie McMillan frowned then shrugged.

"Well, really, Sheriff, how should I know?" she asked. "He was standing there, just staring...."

"Staring at what?"

"Well...." She frowned again and shook her head. "Well, I

suppose at nothing, really. He appeared to be staring off into space. Or he might have been staring at Miss Black." She looked at Corrie and arched a brow as she looked her up and down. "She is a rather attractive young lady and I'm sure this man noticed that."

"But you're not sure he was actually looking at Miss Black?" Sutton asked.

Mrs. McMillan hesitated. "No... no, I suppose I really can't say for sure that's who he was staring at. But it would make far more sense for him to be staring at something or someone than to just be staring off into space, wouldn't it?"

Sutton didn't respond. He turned to the woman's husband. "Mr. McMillan, did you notice anything unusual about this man?"

Thomas McMillan jumped and his face flushed a bright red. He stammered, "Well, now, Sheriff, you know...." He licked his lips and tried to force a smile. "You know, I just didn't see the man at all. You see, it was Margie who was shopping in the store, not me. I was sitting outside on the patio you know, just staying out of the way."

J.D. could sense the question even if the sheriff neither glanced at him or asked him directly and he gave the merest of nods. Yes, he HAD seen Mr. McMillan on the patio. Or, at least, he'd seen a man who would have matched his nondescript description. He'd just passed the man on his way into the laundry room, just seconds before he'd run into Bill Woods making his escape from the camp store and Marjorie McMillan's irate scrutiny. Sutton cleared his throat.

"Mrs. McMillan, have you had any interaction with this man either before or after this incident in the store?"

"No," Marjorie McMillan said firmly with an equally firm head shake. "Absolutely not, Sheriff. I've never seen that man before in my life and I have no idea who he was or even what his name was. Now, it's my turn to ask you a few questions," she said, leaving no room for argument. If the sheriff was surprised at the turn of events, he didn't show it. He merely nodded and gestured for her to go on. "Why are you asking questions about this man and what does this have to do with the campground closing down? What has he done? And are you thinking that whatever it is, that Thomas and I had something to do with it?"

"Mrs. McMillan, late yesterday evening, Miss Black discovered a note shoved under the door of the camp store, warning her to close down the campground for this weekend. It also went on to say that her life was in danger. What the threat was, we don't know and we'll probably never know. This man was found dead in his cabin today."

"What?" Mrs. McMillan's brows rose nearly up into her hair. "Dead? What on earth happened? Did he have a heart attack or stroke or some accident...?"

"He was murdered, Mrs. McMillan."

"And... what? You think Thomas and I had something to do with this man's death? You think that I was annoyed enough with him to actually do something to harm him?" Her voice had risen sharply and her glare was enough to melt steel. Sutton held up a hand.

"No, ma'am, that's not what I'm suggesting," he said. "I'm just trying to find out as much about him as possible, to see if I can find out who did have a reason to kill him."

"Well, it certainly wasn't us!" she said, her indignation coloring her cheeks even darker than her garish lipstick. "The idea!" She shot a look at Corrie. "You probably think that we aren't very sociable just because this man happened to cause problems for us, but I'll have you know that I've gotten quite friendly with our neighbor in the campground...."

"That would be the Westlakes?" Corrie said. The woman nodded.

"Yes, and Rosemary told us that this isn't the first time there's been a mysterious and violent death in this campground." She seemed to take a mean satisfaction from the sudden reddening of Corrie's face. Fortunately, the sheriff spoke up before the woman said anything else.

"Mrs. McMillan, how did you happen to choose this campground for your vacation?"

"What do you mean?"

"I mean, did a travel agent suggest the Black Horse Campground for you? How did you happen to hear about this campground? This is the first time you've ever stayed here, isn't it?"

"Well, yes, it is. And, really, Sheriff, why on earth would I engage a travel agent to find me an RV park? My niece told us about this place. She's stationed at Holloman Air Force Base and she and her family have camped up here in the past. Even though it's further away from her, she told us it's less expensive than staying in Ruidoso and just as convenient to all the attractions there. There really isn't much to do here in Bonney, you know.

Why do you ask?" she demanded.

The sheriff shrugged. "Just wondered if you'd had any interaction with a travel agent by the name of David Duncan."

"Not to stay in a campground," Mrs. McMillan snorted. "We haven't contacted any travel agents, period."

"Okay," Sutton said smoothly. He straightened up and seemed to signal that the interview was over. "Well, Mr. and Mrs. McMillan, I thank you for your cooperation and I'm sorry that we have to inconvenience you by having you move to another place...."

Mrs. McMillan looked as if she had bitten into the most bitter lemon in the world. "You want us to unhook our RV and move it tonight? But I thought the threat was for tomorrow," she said petulantly. Corrie shook her head, barely suppressing a sigh. J.D. decided to speak up.

"We're not asking you to move your RV, ma'am," he said forcing a respectable tone into his voice. "We're just asking that you consider staying in a hotel for tonight, at the Black Horse's expense," he added, when it seemed that Mrs. McMillan was going to protest.

"Now, Margie, honey," Mr. McMillan said earnestly, tugging at her arm, "let's not make it harder on everyone. These nice people are offering us a place to stay, free of charge, so why don't we just cooperate and we'll be able to come back tomorrow night. Isn't that right, Sheriff?" the man said, his gaze pleading.

Corrie was beginning to look sick at the repeated reminders of what this threat was costing her, but Sutton spoke up. "Miss Black has a place to recommend and she'll be more than happy to call and get a room for you for tonight. The River's Edge Bed and Breakfast," he added for Corrie's benefit. She gave him a puzzled glance, but picked up the phone and made the arrangements. Mrs. McMillan seemed only slightly mollified.

"Well, I suppose this will have to do," she sniffed. "May we get some clothes from our RV before we go to this place?"

"Certainly. Deputy Ramirez will escort you to your RV," Sutton said. Deputy Ramirez looked as if he'd rather hand-feed a piranha, but he inclined his head and said, "Yes, sir," before showing the McMillans out of the camp store.

Corrie waited until the door had shut and the sound of their engine starting reached them. "What's going on, Rick? You're going to put them in the same place that Robert Moreno is staying?"

He shrugged. "I'll call Dudley and let him know. It would be interesting to see if they recognize each other or not. Besides, where else are they going to stay? Every other place is booked up, unless we send them to Ruidoso."

"I just wonder if the Kellermans are going to appreciate me sending the McMillans to stay there. Mr. Moreno might not be expecting a four-star place, but I'm sure Mrs. McMillan will be expecting this to be an upgrade," Corrie murmured with a pained expression.

"Well, she's going to be disappointed," the sheriff said bluntly. "But she's got a place to stay that should be safe and it's not costing her a thing."

"Right," Corrie said, looking even more glum than ever herself. "Well, if you two are still up for it, I guess we'd better enjoy our coffee and dessert so we can get some rest. Then I'll set up the coffee makers down here so you guys will be able to have it through the night."

"Sounds good. We'll be right up," J.D. said, hoping Sutton would take the hint. He did, turning back toward the counter without a word, just a lift of his brows. Corrie didn't seem to notice as she headed up the stairs. J.D. waited until he heard the door at the top of the stairs open with a slight creak.

"Something you want to talk about, Wilder?" the sheriff said, keeping his voice low.

"Yeah," J.D. said, before he could back out. "Have you stopped to think about what this is going to cost Corrie?" The sheriff straightened up, his stare turning icy. J.D. caught it and held it. "Look, I know that closing down the campground is the only smart and safe thing to do, but it stinks that she's going to be losing money just to keep herself, her staff and friends, and her guests safe."

"Wilder...."

"And I know she doesn't have a choice," J.D. went on doggedly. "It's only right and fair that she pays for her guests' new accommodations, but a lot of them are going to cancel the rest of their reservations here—not that I blame them—and that's going to be a tough hit for her to take."

"Wilder...."

"What I'm trying to say," he went on, ignoring the sheriff's attempts to speak, "is that there has to be some way we can help this not be such a huge financial hit for her. She's finally getting her business back on track and...."

"Wilder!" The sheriff didn't shout, didn't really raise his voice, but the tone he used had the same effect. "I know what you're saying, I've thought about it, and it's been taken care of."

J.D. stared. "What?"

"Just trust me. It's taken care of."

"How's it been taken care of, Sheriff?" J.D. asked, his eyes narrowing. Sutton returned the gaze steadily and apparently in no hurry to explain. "You're not going to tell me?"

"No one needs to know anything about it, except that it's been taken care of."

"Corrie's going to have to know."

"You're not Corrie. And she'll know when the time is right. I don't have time for a fight on my hands right now."

"A fight? Come on, Sutton, we're supposed to be helping her together. This is no time to go all 'lone gun' on me."

Sutton went to the bottom of the stairs and glanced up to make sure that Corrie was still in the apartment. Then he returned to the counter and spoke in an even lower tone than he had been using. "If you say one word to her, Wilder, I'll never trust you again. Hear?"

"Loud and clear," J.D. answered, his voice barely above a whisper. The sheriff took a deep breath.

"I paid for her guests' emergency lodging at all those other places. Made sure they had the best that was offered, because I don't want any of them to hold anything against Corrie. I made sure that they knew it was MY doing that they were being asked to leave for the day, not hers. And I also got most of them to promise to come back after the danger had passed." He stopped and glanced back over his shoulder. "And if Corrie finds out, I'll be in for the worst butt-chewing of my life, not to mention she'll feel awful that I took on what she perceives to be her responsibility. If I'm lucky, I'll get away with her only having a minor meltdown when she finds out... and you know, as well as I do, that she WILL find out, but I'm hoping that won't happen until after this case is solved. I know, better than you do, that she can't afford a crisis like this. It's not her fault, it's not fair, and I'm trying to do everything in my power to help her get through this as painlessly as possible." He no sooner finished speaking than Corrie's voice drifted down the stairs.

"Guys, this coffee's getting cold and so is the cobbler."

The sheriff gave J.D. one last, long look and J.D. nodded. "Come on, Sheriff," he said, slapping Sutton's shoulder. "If we let that coffee and cobbler get cold, we'll both be in the dog house for sure."

Chapter 9

The squeal of brakes and the blast of a horn, followed by a frantic, high-pitched bark from Renfro, shocked Corrie out of a surprisingly sound sleep at three in the morning. She threw the covers—and Oliver—to the floor and flew out of bed, barely avoiding tripping over both frightened animals, and barreled down the stairs. She burst through the door at the bottom of the stairs to have a strong hand grab her shoulder in the darkness and shove her to the ground. "Get down!" Rick hissed before she had a chance to shriek.

The safety lights outside the building illuminated the inside of the camp store through the windows and Corrie could see the silvery outline of J.D. standing beside the front door, carefully keeping himself back out of sight. Rick had moved to the front window, all but his face in the shadows, and a mere glint of his drawn gun in his hand. Corrie's heart was hammering wildly in her chest, but she didn't dare move, not even to draw a breath. From outside, she heard car doors slamming and loud, angry voices. Rick's hushed voice sounded like thunder to Corrie. "How many do you see, Wilder?"

"Two. Male and female." It occurred to Corrie that J.D. was unarmed; though he had been a lieutenant with the Houston Police Department, to her knowledge, he no longer carried a weapon. She felt herself go icy cold at the thought of him placing himself in the line of any possible fire. He ducked back away from the door as footsteps pounded on the wooden walkway leading to the front door and the irate voices preceded insistent knocking.

"Hey! Open up! What's going on?"

Rick had slipped quietly through the store, a silent shadow, to the side of the door and then two sheriff's department vehicles, bubble lights flashing, converged on the parking lot, blocking the vehicle in. A brief chirp of the sirens and then spotlights pierced the night followed by Deputy Andy Luna's booming voice. "Sheriff's department! Turn around and put your hands up!"

By this time, Corrie had made her way to the front counter, half-crawling, half-slithering along the floor, and she crept up to the front window. Two figures were silhouetted in the bright glare of the spotlights and she heard a man's petulant voice. "Hey, what is this? What's going on? We're just trying to get back into our campsite!"

Deputy Luna had stepped up and asked for identification, which was produced with much mumbling and muttering of profanities. The man's voice snarled, "What the hell is all this? We've got reservations here and now the campground's closed?"

Rick unlocked the front door and stepped outside, J.D. right behind him. "Getting in kind of late, aren't you?" he said quietly.

"What, there's a curfew? There's nothing in the campground rules that says we gotta be in by a certain time!"

Rick didn't answer, just held out his hand for the couple's I.D.s. He looked them over and said, "So, Mr. Jamie and Mrs. Lisa Carson, you have a tent space rented through Sunday night?"

"Damn straight, we do!" barked Mr. Carson and Corrie cringed at the thought of what that response would do to Rick's patience.

"I'm just verifying facts, folks. Where have you been all day?"

"What's it to you?" the woman snarled.

"Depends on what your answer is and how you cooperate," Rick said, a thin thread of ice running through the words. "I could make this easier on myself and just arrest you for trespassing since the sign on the gate clearly says the campground is closed...."

"Yeah? Well, the gate was open...."

"... and we could continue this conversation at the county jail," he finished as if they hadn't spoken. "It would probably be in your best interests to answer my questions honestly and without any attitude."

The couple had quieted down and had been glancing around uneasily. It had taken some time, but apparently the sight of a closed and darkened campground, populated by nothing but law enforcement officers, had registered with them as a sign that something might be seriously wrong. Finally, the man spoke after his wife nudged him. "We went out for the day... did some hiking around the area. We left early this morning, right after breakfast."

"Where did you go?"

The man's face contorted, as if he were about to make a scathing reply, but he calmed down after another nudge. "I don't remember every place we went. We got a map and a brochure on hiking trails in the National Forest from the lady in the store. We drove into Ruidoso then went up Ski Run Road toward Sierra Blanca, then we did a short hike around Grindstone Lake and had a picnic there. We thought about doing a horseback ride, but changed our minds and decided to hit the casino at the Inn for a couple hours. We ended up staying for dinner and drinks at the sports bar. Then we decided to check out the nightclub, but it wasn't for us. Someone told us there's a place in Ruidoso we might like better so we went there...."

"Would that be Win, Place and Show?" Rick asked quietly.

"Yeah, we went there, then we went across the street... place called The Quarters."

"And then?"

"Well, we closed the place down," the man said. "But we hung out in the parking lot, talking to people we met, making plans to meet up with them while we were going to be in town."

"And did you make plans to meet up with anyone you met?"

"Sort of. I mean, you know, it was those kind of plans, like, 'Hey, we should get together', but nothing definite. I figured we'd probably end up meeting at the bar again some night. They looked like it was a regular hang-out for them."

"It's a popular place for locals," Rick said. "So you were out in the parking lot at The Quarters until, what? About a half hour ago?"

"More or less," the man said. "Is there a problem we need to know about, Sheriff? Can we go to our campsite now?"

"Deputies Luna and Ramirez will escort you to your campsite and you can get what you need for the night, but you can't stay here. We have evacuated the campground for the night."

"WHAT?" The woman's voice sounded like a startled cat screeching and Corrie wondered if perhaps Oliver had reacted in alarm at the sound. "Why? It's late and we're tired and we paid for the whole week and we're not going anywhere!"

"Yes, ma'am, I'm afraid you are," Rick said coolly, his voice registering none of the deference that he had shown earlier to the McMillans. "This campground is a crime scene and there has been a threat made to the residents and guests of this campground."

"Crime scene? Whoa, whoa, wait a minute, what do you mean 'crime scene' and what kind of threat? We didn't do anything! We haven't been here all day!" Mr. Carson's voice had scaled up nearly to the same octave his wife was reaching.

Rick, however, continued in a calm, even tone. "Are you folks acquainted with a man by the name of Timothy Jenkins?"

"No!" Two simultaneous denials without hesitation.

"How about David Duncan?"

This time there was a slight hesitation and not only did Rick pick up on it immediately, but even the Carsons seemed to realize that they had let out more information than they had intended. "You know a David Duncan?"

"No... it's just...." Mrs. Carson began and her husband threw her a glare and hissed, "Shhh!"

"Mrs. Carson?"

"We don't know anyone by either of those two names!" Mr. Carson snapped, giving his wife a murderous look which she returned, but silently.

"Perhaps if we talked alone, Mrs. Carson?" Rick said, his meaning not lost on either of the Carsons despite the politeness of his query.

"She's got nothing to say, Sheriff, not without a lawyer present," Mr. Carson said, his haughty bravado doing a lousy job of masking his uneasiness. His wife hissed, "Shut up!" J.D. stepped forward, holding out his cell phone.

"Perhaps this might jog your memory?" he said quietly. Both Carsons stared in shock, then blanched and the woman covered her mouth with her hand and turned away.

The man licked his lips and tried twice to form a complete sentence. "Is he... is he...?"

"You tell us. Is he Timothy Jenkins? Or David Duncan?" J.D. said.

"I don't know!" the man cried as his wife began sobbing. "I never saw the man! I just heard that name...."

"Which one? Where? When?" Rick shot the words out like bullets from his service weapon and this time Mr. Carson didn't hesitate.

"Some guy was on the phone over by the patio area. He was on a cell phone, talking to someone, and when me and Lisa came out of the store, he said, 'I'll call you back' and hung up."

"What did the man look like?" Rick snapped.

"The man on the phone?" Mr. Carson said, then winced at the stupidity of the question. "Uh... I really don't know, Sheriff. I mean, he was sitting there...."

"Sitting?"

"I think so. In one of the patio chairs. Or maybe he was standing or walking around. I'm not really sure. I wasn't paying attention, I just noticed someone was there on the patio when we came out of the laundry room and I just heard him talking...."

"How did you happen to hear the name?" Rick asked. Mr.

Carson squinted, then he nodded.

"He said 'Duncan is here already' just as we walked out the door."

"That's all you heard?" Corrie couldn't see Rick's face but she was sure that the Carsons were withering under his disbelieving glare. Mr. Carson cleared his throat and stared at the ground.

"Yeah, we were... um... we were talking about something...."

Mrs. Carson turned around and swiped her hands across her tear-streaked face, avoiding looking at the phone in J.D.'s hand. "Oh, for heaven's sake!" she snapped, slapping her hand across her husband's shoulder. "We were fighting, Sheriff! Just like we have been since we came on this stupid vacation!"

Corrie's breath caught in her throat. She remembered the couple now—they were the couple who had been arguing about the best campsite to choose and had finally chosen the one Corrie had NOT recommended. Apparently, they hadn't been able to stop bickering after leaving the camp store and just happened upon someone mentioning the name "David Duncan". Corrie felt herself go numb with the chilling realization that whoever had killed Uncle Bill was already here when Uncle Bill had arrived.

She moved back away from the windows and sat on her stool, listening as Rick gave them his usual assurance that alternate accommodations would be made, at the campground's expense, at a nearby hotel, probably in Ruidoso, since the lodging options in Bonney were tapped out. Neither of the Carsons seemed enthused at the prospect of driving all the way back to Ruidoso. Finally, Deputy Luna spoke up and mentioned that an old hunting cabin, owned by one of his great-uncles, was vacant and conveniently located a mere two miles away and the Carsons would be welcome to stay in it, if they didn't mind roughing it. After assuring Mrs. Carson that roughing it meant simply that there wasn't any TV or Internet, the couple agreed to follow Deputy Luna to their campsite and get a few necessities for what was left of the night and then head to his great-uncle's cabin. Rick and J.D. remained outside until they had departed and Rick had given further instructions to Deputy Ramirez, who remained on watch, before they re-entered the camp store.

Corrie rested her chin on her forearm as she slumped on the counter. Rick's eyes held sympathy. "You okay?"

"As well as can be expected," she said. She straightened up. "I remember them. They were the couple that wouldn't stop bickering."

J.D. laughed shortly. "Bickering? Didn't sound like anything a divorce lawyer couldn't fix!" He caught the sharp glance from Corrie a split-second too late and he winced. "Sorry about that, Sutton."

Rick shrugged off whatever sting J.D.'s words might have carried. "At least they're still speaking to each other," he said dryly. "So, they heard someone talking about David Duncan, or rather Bill Woods, being here already."

"So he was the target of the threat? Why make Corrie shut down the campground then? Whoever did it didn't even wait for Saturday to carry it out," J.D. said, his dark brows knitting in puzzlement.

Rick shook his head. "No, the threat was still meant for Corrie. And whoever sent it had already learned that Bill Woods was here."

"But either he—Uncle Bill, that is—didn't know he was in danger or else knew about it and didn't know or recognize the person who was targeting him," Corrie said and she shrugged off another shiver. "That's just plain scary. But why would they still be threatening me?"

"Apparently, there's more to what Bill Woods was doing here than just trying to mend fences with an old friend... or his family," Rick said, tapping his pen impatiently against the notepad in his hand. "I sure wish people would pay more attention to what's going on around them. I can't believe he didn't see the man who was talking on the phone."

"They admitted they were a little distracted," J.D. pointed out. Rick inclined his head in acknowledgment.

"All right," he said. "At least we have a starting point."

"We do?" Corrie said in surprise. She glanced at J.D. who was nodding.

"Thomas McMillan. He told us himself that he was sitting out on the patio waiting for his wife to finish shopping." He glanced at Rick who gave him a curt nod.

"Yeah, but we don't know if that was at the same time the Carsons, went out the door," Corrie said. "Besides, the McMillans don't look like the type of people who would want to kill someone!"

"Neither did Betty Landry," Rick said quietly.

Chapter 10

Corrie's eyes flew open and the shock of sunlight streaming through the window froze her in place for several seconds. But the sunlight hadn't been what had woke her from a sound sleep; it was the concentrated stares of both Renfro and Oliver, both urgently needing to be let out but too polite to do anything more than stare piteously at their owner, that had finally roused her.

"What the...?" She gasped as she glanced at the clock and flung the covers back, practically falling on the floor in her haste to get out of bed. This time, the dog and cat moved quicker than before and got out of her way and were waiting at the apartment door. They nearly shoved her aside as soon as it opened. She hurried after them as fast as she could without falling and breaking her neck to open the door at the base of the stairs, but it was already open and she stopped short as she heard J.D.'s voice, saying, "Uh, oh."

"Just open the side door. They'll be back after they take care of business." Rick's voice.

"That's not what I meant," J.D. said as he let the two mascots out.

Corrie grabbed the door jamb, holding herself up on shaky knees and trying to bring her racing heart under control. Rick was sitting behind the counter in her usual place with his cell phone in his ear, listening intently and jotting notes in his notepad. J.D. turned from the side door and stopped, his eyes widening at the sight of her.

"We're busted, Sutton," he said, not taking his eyes off Corrie. Rick looked up.

"Thanks. Get back to me as soon as you hear something." He flipped his phone shut and stood up. "Want some coffee? Wilder made some piñon along with...."

"Do you know what time it is? Why didn't you get me up?" she croaked, pushing herself away from the wall and stalking toward the two men. She planted her fists on her hips and glared up at them, only briefly considering how ridiculous she must look as they both towered over her. Their barely-restrained looks of amusement only served to infuriate her more.

"It's eight-thirty. The campground is closed, you had a rough night, and there was no need to get you up. You were exhausted and needed sleep. Any other questions?" Rick asked, moving toward the coffee pot to get her a cup.

"Eight-thirty? Are you out of your minds? How could you let me sleep that long? And your night wasn't any less rough than mine! What gives you the right to decide what time I get up?" she snapped, glaring from Rick to J.D., who had taken up a position by the front counter, leaning against it with his arms folded across his chest. He hadn't said another word, but continued to gaze at her with a half-smile on his face. Rick came back with a cup of coffee for her which she nearly refused, but her will power wasn't as awake as she was. She took the cup from his hand and took a huge gulp.

"Shouldn't have asked," he murmured. Corrie's eyes narrowed and she aimed a punch at Rick's side. For once, he made no move to avoid it, but pain shot through her hand as her knuckles connected with a hard, unyielding surface and she nearly dropped her coffee.

"Ow! What the...?" She shook her hand to try to dispel the sting. She stared at Rick.

"I've been working out a little more," he deadpanned.

"Very funny!" She examined her knuckles. "What are you wearing, a suit of armor?"

"One of the vests I'm considering for the department." He knocked on it, though his blows were nowhere near as hard as the one Corrie had planted. "It's probably way more protection than what we need. It weighs a ton and would probably stop an air-to-ground missile."

"It stopped Corrie's punch," J.D. said with a grin.

"Yeah, but I think I'm the only department member who has to worry about that," Rick said dryly.

Corrie glared at him and plunked her coffee cup down on the counter a little harder than necessary. "This is MY home, MY business, MY life, Sheriff! I have a right to know what's going on, considering that I, my home, my livelihood, and my friends are in potential danger! Any questions?" she shot back and J.D. cleared his throat.

"Yeah. You always sleep in that?" he asked, raising a brow.

With a start, Corrie glanced down at herself. She had started out the night by sleeping in her regular jeans and t-shirt in case something happened and she needed to be dressed quickly, but Rick and J.D.'s insistence that she close and lock her window had made her bedroom stuffy. During the night, after the Carsons had left, she had tossed and turned in discomfort until she finally got up and removed her jeans and t-shirt and changed into her regular sleeping attire—a University of New Mexico replica football jersey, emblazoned with the number 15. Rick's number when he had played quarterback for both the Bonney High School Regulators and the University of New Mexico Lobos. In a fit of nostalgic wishful thinking five years earlier, she'd special ordered the jersey, never intending to let anyone ever see her wearing it. Her thankfulness at not having had Rick's name put on the back of the jersey was currently stalled by the fact that the jersey's length stopped a good six inches above her knees... and both J.D. and Rick were having a hard time keeping their gazes trained on her face.

She folded her arms across her chest until she realized that only hiked the jersey up higher. She dropped her arms to her sides, fists clenched. Fighting the blush that heated her cheeks, she snapped, "No, but my red lace teddy is at the cleaners!" Both mens' startled gazes locked on her face and she felt herself grow even redder than the jersey she was wearing. "I'm going to go get dressed!" She spun and stomped up the stairs to her apartment, well aware of the stares that followed her.

~

"Wish she hadn't said that. I've got a vivid imagination," J.D. muttered as Corrie's door shut a little harder than was necessary.

"Yeah, me, too," Sutton said shortly, as he unbuttoned his uniform shirt and shrugged out of the heavy bullet-resistant vest. "Let's focus on what I've got about our other problem."

J.D. continued to stare at Corrie's door, shaking his head slowly. "I have to wonder about you, Sutton. How did you walk away from that? I don't think I can respect you as a man."

"Yeah, me, neither," the sheriff snapped as he finished putting his shirt back on and J.D. turned to him.

"You're wearing that under your shirt?"

"Just during the trial period. I don't want to create unnecessary concern and gossip by letting everyone in town see me, and no one else in the department, wearing one. That one's off the list," Sutton added, nodding at the cumbersome vest. "Too damn heavy and uncomfortable. This isn't a war zone. Won't do me or the budget any good to invest in gear no one's going to want to wear during the summer. Can we focus on the case now?"

"What'd you get?" J.D. asked, turning his full attention to the note pad in Sutton's hands.

"First off, the lab has an initial report on Bill Woods' autopsy. Stabbed in the heart by a long, thin metal instrument, but they're not sure what. Oddly enough, they found traces of soil around the puncture wound and in the wound itself. No other injuries of any kind, though my deputies found a wrapper from an adhesive bandage in the trash can, along with a few other odds and ends."

"Any prints?"

"Just Bill Woods'. He traveled light, just an overnight bag, and it was hard to tell if his belongings had been searched. The killer was careful not to leave any prints anywhere in the cabin."

"So it looks like the killer went there specifically to take out the victim," J.D. said.

"Unless the killer was already there. Remember, the reservation was for two people. So far, I haven't found any evidence of another person having shared that cabin with Bill Woods. Or that gray Honda, either. The only prints found there are Woods' and Robert Moreno's."

"I don't suppose anyone remembers seeing anyone check in with Woods?"

"They don't even remember checking HIM in," Sutton said, shaking his head.

"You don't suppose Moreno...?"

The sheriff shrugged. "I suppose just about anything. But why would Moreno stick around? To neutralize the threat... or carry it out?"

J.D. breathed an expletive. "He's called an awful lot of attention on himself. Is he that stupid or that smart?"

"I called in a couple of favors from Ruidoso police officers, along with the Bonney police department," Sutton went on. "Fortunately it was a quiet night, although Eldon LaRue gave me some grief as a matter of habit, but I got officers to keep an eye on the Black Horse guests that we relocated."

"And?"

"And... nothing. No one made a move from their accommodations, except a few who went out to dinner. Most actually called out for pizza; here in Bonney, Tony's drivers were running constantly for most of the evening."

"What about our friends at the River's Edge? Moreno and the Mc Millans?" J.D. asked.

"The Kellermans offer a family-style dinner to their guests each night," Sutton said. "The Mc Millans—or rather, Mrs. Mc Millan—wasn't overly enthused about the arrangement, so Vicky Kellerman set them up a private table on the screened-in deck. Doesn't seem like they ran into Moreno, who opted to have both his dinner and breakfast this morning sent to his room."

"So much for seeing if they'd met," J.D. muttered, but then he raised a brow. "Of course, if they HAD met before, they might make it a point not to be seen together." Sutton nodded.

"I wanted to give them the night to relax before I question them again... particularly Thomas Mc Millan. I'm hoping he can give me a better description of the man the Carsons overheard mentioning the name 'Duncan'...."

"Okay, what did I miss?" Corrie interrupted, rejoining the two men. J.D. was equally disappointed and relieved that she had reappeared in a pair of jeans and her customary Black Horse Campground t-shirt. There were still two spots of color in her cheeks, but she had regained her composure. She went to the coffee maker and warmed up the cup she had abandoned earlier.

Sutton watched her for a minute and J.D. could tell that the sheriff was toying with the idea of telling her that she hadn't missed a thing, that the investigation was continuing under his supervision, that she hadn't any business in asking what was going on and he certainly had no obligation to keep her informed, but probably figured she'd already had a stressful enough morning already. "Not a whole lot," he began, and she immediately spun on him, her eyes blazing.

"And that's why you stopped talking the minute I walked in the room?" she snapped and Sutton rolled his eyes.

"No, that's just the truth," he said calmly. "I was just giving Wilder the clinical details of the lab report on Bill Woods—which I'm sure you'd rather not hear—and telling him that it was a quiet night among all your guests and we're going to start a second round of questioning this morning."

"Oh." Corrie seemed at a loss for words. She studied her coffee cup for a few seconds, then went on hopefully, "I don't suppose you have any idea when I might... you know...." Her voice trailed away as the sheriff started shaking his head before she even finished the question.

"No idea yet, Corrie, and I don't know when I'll have one," he added firmly.

"It's Saturday, Rick. No bombs have gone off, everyone

seems to be alive and well...."

"'Seems' is the operative word," he said. "I want to see what, if anything, has changed among your guests and what, if anything, might happen today. After all, it's only been Saturday for a few hours. That note didn't specify what time that danger might come to pass or if it's confined only to this particular day. For all we know, this might just be the first day of a long wait." Corrie groaned.

"Rick, I can't afford this! I managed to hold off the guests scheduled for today, but if I have to call all the ones scheduled for tomorrow...." She stopped, her voice shaking as she blinked back tears.

"Corrie," Sutton said, and J.D. suspected he was using every ounce of self-control to keep his tone even and professional. "I know that. I understand, I really do. But there's still danger. I'll do everything I can to get this case resolved as quickly as possible, but...."

"Then let me help you," Corrie said, swiping her fingers under her eyes and taking a deep breath. "I've been thinking about why Uncle Bill decided to come back after all these years. It's possible he just heard about Billy's passing and decided to come pay his respects. I mean, despite everything that went bad between them, they used to be the best of friends since they were kids, almost like brothers. They trusted each other."

"And he ended up dead," Sutton said bluntly. J.D. winced, but to his surprise, Corrie nodded.

"That's my point, Rick. Why? He didn't come here and kill himself in a fit of remorse over a broken friendship he never had a chance to make right. Someone killed him. Why? What did he do or what did he know that someone felt the need to kill him? And why here? What's the connection?" She stopped to catch her breath and for once, Sutton didn't jump in with an argument. He stood looking at her, chewing on his lower lip, then he glanced at J.D. J.D. shrugged.

"She does have a point, Sutton."

"I know," the sheriff said. "What worries me is what she's planning to do about it."

"I know you guys think I love how you talk about me as if I weren't standing right in front of you," she snapped. Sutton held up a hand.

"Look, Corrie, the thought crossed my mind, but I didn't say anything because I was afraid this was going to be another one of those times when you would interpret me doing my job as me trying to keep you in the dark for no other reason than I'm a jerk."

"So you were planning on keeping me in the dark because it's your job?" she said, folding her arms across her chest. J.D. suspected it was mainly to keep herself from getting arrested for assaulting an officer of the law, although he was sure her knuckles still felt the sting from her earlier attack.

"That's the problem. I can't," the sheriff said. "Because I have no idea what went on between your dad and Bill Woods and what might possibly be the reason he returned. Because I have to get you involved, no matter how much I'd like to keep you out of this for your own protection."

"Well, it's too late for that, Sheriff," J.D. said dryly. "In case you've forgotten, that threat was addressed to Corrie. That automatically involves her."

"I haven't forgotten, Wilder," Sutton said coldly. "But I'm sworn to serve and protect, just as you are. The fact that I need Corrie's help in order to find out how much danger she's in puts her in even more danger. I'm sure that thought doesn't hold a lot of appeal to you as well."

"No, but what choice do we—do you—have?" J.D. said, shaking off a chill. He looked at Corrie and noticed that despite her brave face, the idea made her extremely uneasy. "If we—you—are going to solve this case, Sutton, you don't have a choice but to keep her fully informed of what's going on with the investigation as well as ask her for her help." He waited a few seconds, then, noting that the sheriff still wasn't one hundred percent convinced, added, "It's either that or take a chance that she'll go off and try to investigate it on her own. And you know how that's turned out in the past!" He held up his hands and stepped back as Corrie shot him a withering glare.

"All right, okay," Sutton said. J.D. noted that Corrie was furious with him, but he'd try to make amends later, after the sheriff got the information he needed. "Let's calm down and see what needs to be done. Corrie, who else, besides you and your mother, would have known about your dad's friendship with Bill Woods? What do you remember about it?"

Corrie seemed to have regained control over her temper, although she flashed an irritated look in J.D.'s direction. "I don't remember much, Rick," she said. "I was only ten when Billy and Uncle Bill had their falling out and nothing was ever explained to me about why it happened, other than the fact that he undertook some shady business dealings and got Billy's name involved in it."

"Who else would he have talked to? Surely Billy had other friends besides Bill Woods."

"Toby Willis, but he dropped off the radar before Uncle Bill ever did," she said. "And I have even dimmer memories of him, although he's a distant cousin. Even Billy's family, when I see them, rarely mentions his name." She stopped and her eyes widened and her lips formed an "O".

J.D. raised a brow and glanced at the sheriff. Sutton's eyes had narrowed and he said sharply, "You thought of someone your dad might have confided in?"

"Not my dad," Corrie said slowly, her eyes taking on a faraway look. "But my mother. She used to spend a lot of time with Elsa Kaydahzinne."

"Myra's grandmother?"

Corrie nodded vigorously. "Mom spent a lot of time visiting with her, learning how to make traditional Apache fry bread and other foods my dad liked. Mom didn't have very many friends, and Myra's grandmother was very easy to talk to...." She hesitated for a second, then went on, "It's possible she may have confided something to her. I remember that she was very upset after the blow up between Billy and Uncle Bill and Billy certainly wasn't in any kind of mood to be comforting, not after the shock he'd just had."

"You think she'd tell you what your mother might have told her?" J.D. said, straightening up. Corrie seemed to have forgotten her earlier irritation at him. She shrugged.

"I don't know. It's been twenty years and my mother's been gone for almost as many years, but that doesn't mean Mrs. Kaydahzinne won't feel that she's violating my mother's confidence."

"We'll have to make it clear to her that it's either that or possibly putting her friend's daughter in danger," the sheriff said bluntly. "Let's go talk to her." He turned and headed for the door.

"Wait, Rick, you can't just go barging in like that," Corrie protested, blocking the doorway. He stared at her, his hands on his hips and impatience sparking in his eyes, and she stared right back defiantly. "For one thing, Mrs. Kaydahzinne is almost ninety years old. And she's very much a traditional Apache. There's a certain level of respect and a certain protocol to be followed. I guarantee that if you offend her, she won't give you the time of day, let alone any information that she might have." She sighed and shook her head. "Not every member of the tribe is like Billy. He might not have cared one bit for traditional mores, but Myra's grandmother isn't like that. She's more like my grandmother."

The way Corrie said that intrigued J.D. A tremor of hurt ran through her words and she swallowed hard. He moved toward her, sensing the tension between Corrie and the sheriff. "So what do you suggest?" She licked her lips and took a deep breath.

"The best thing would be to set up a meeting through Myra—if it's a convenient time for her grandmother, if she's up to having visitors...." She looked at the sheriff, her eyes troubled. She knew that time was running out along with the sheriff's patience, but it was obvious that things had to be done a certain way if they were going to be done at all.

The sheriff was chewing on his lip furiously. Apparently he understood the dilemma, even if he didn't like it. "Can you get hold of Myra, ask her if she can arrange for us to see her grandmother?" he asked, his voice tight. She nodded and pushed away from the door.

~

Twenty minutes later, Rick pulled the Tahoe into the dirt driveway of the Kaydahzinne family home. Corrie could sense J.D.'s skepticism; a four-foot high chain link fence bordered the driveway, separating it from the yard, and the old run-down farm house didn't look like it was inhabited by any living creatures, save the numerous scrawny cats that milled about the weed-choked yard. The sagging screen door swung open and Myra came out onto the warped front porch. She hurried down the steps and met them as they got out of the vehicle.

"I appreciate you arranging this for us, Myra," Rick said, as he approached the young woman. Myra forced a wry smile as she tugged open the rusty gate and led them up a cracked cement walkway that sprouted several clumps of grass.

"And I appreciate you calling ahead and giving me a chance to give Grandmother time to get used to the idea of having guests," she said. "It's a good thing she's been having a good day. Not too many aches and pains, so she hasn't needed any pain medication. It makes her drowsy and forgetful and that wouldn't be of any use to you." She paused at the foot of the steps leading up to the porch. "Rick—Sheriff—I think it might be a good idea if Corrie goes in with me and you and Lt. Wilder wait out here.

Grandmother... she's got funny ideas about the police. She might be less inclined to discuss old confidences if you were present. If it's just Corrie...." She let the words trail off and Rick made an heroic effort not to look exasperated.

"Since this isn't an official sheriff's department visit, I guess I can allow that. But," he added, turning to Corrie, "try to get as much detailed information as you can. And remember we don't have much time."

"I'm the last person you have to remind about that, Sheriff," Corrie said dryly. She nodded at Myra who opened the front door and ushered Corrie into a living room that opened directly in from the porch. Unlike the outside of the house, which was run down and in desperate need of paint and maintenance, the inside was meticulously clean although the room was overcrowded with furniture and knick-knacks, no doubt lovingly collected over a long and fruitful lifetime. The room smelled strongly of lavender, no doubt the old lady's favorite fragrance.

Sitting in a wing chair of faded rose-colored velvet sat Myra's grandmother, Elsa Kaydahzinne, the matriarch of the Kaydahzinne family. The tiny old woman seemed like a porcelain doll, covered with a hand-crocheted afghan of many colored flowers. She was nearly invisible in the depths of the chair in front of a brick fireplace which was used to display a large arrangement of silk roses. Her silver hair was pulled back from a surprisingly smooth face and tied in a bun at the nape of her neck. Her dark eyes were lively with curiosity and sparkled with a fierce pride. She straightened up in her chair and fixed her piercing gaze on Corrie. Corrie was suddenly glad she'd insisted on making Rick and J.D. wait until she'd changed out of her jeans and t-shirt; she had chosen to wear her dark blue velvet broomstick skirt and crisp white blouse. She had pinned up her customary braid instead of letting it hang down to her waist. The old woman's eyes widened slightly and her lips moved.

"Gōde." The word came out in a whisper so soft Corrie barely heard it. Myra shook her head.

"No, Grandma. It's Corrie Black, your friend's daughter. See?" She tugged Corrie forward. "She's come to see you, to ask you about her mother."

"Mrs. Kaydahzinne," Corrie said, her voice low and respectful. "It's good to see that you're doing well."

"Corrie." The old woman's voice grew stronger and she nodded, her eyes growing brighter. "My goodness, look at you. I see you at church every Sunday, but it's never struck me before how much you resemble your mother." She murmured something under her breath, in her native Mescalero Apache tongue, but Corrie didn't catch the words; not that she'd ever been fluent in either her father's native tongue nor her mother's. "Come sit down and tell me what you've been doing with yourself these days."

Corrie sat down on the small upholstered love seat next to Mrs. Kaydahzinne's chair. Here, the scent of lavender was even stronger and Corrie shot a glance at the votive candle burning in red glass holder on the table nearby. Despite the small but ornate crystal chandelier that hung from the exact center of the ceiling, the only other light in the room came from the windows and an old-fashioned oil lamp that sat on top of the mantlepiece. Myra discreetly slipped out of the room, probably to give them some privacy but also, Corrie was sure, to prepare some kind of refreshment, lest her grandmother feel that they were being rude to their guest. "I'm sorry that I haven't come to visit in a long time." Elsa Kaydahzinne waved off the apology.

"My girl, you're a busy woman. You've had a business to run almost single-handedly for the last year and you've spent the year before that taking care of your father. You don't need to apologize." She leaned forward, her eyes troubled. "Myra told me that you had some difficulties these last few days... like the last two times."

Corrie felt her cheeks burn. She wondered if people were beginning to think that the Black Horse was cursed or jinxed. She nodded. "That's the reason I came to see you today. The man who died at the campground yesterday was a friend of my father's."

The old woman's brows rose. "Oh? And why would you come see me about that?"

Corrie hesitated; she hoped that Myra's grandmother wouldn't be offended by her questions. She began slowly, "He was a very good friend of my father's, almost like a brother to him. He hasn't been around for many years...." She got no farther as Myra's grandmother nodded once then shook her head.

"Oh, THAT one," she sniffed. "Nothing but trouble; I saw it from the moment he and Billy met. I knew your father since he was a child. He could be so stubborn and blind. He trusted that man, just because he'd known him from childhood, just like he did his cousin, too, but I knew, and so did your mother, that he was only out to take advantage of your father's generosity and friendship."

Corrie stared and then frowned. "My mother knew Bill Woods wasn't to be trusted?" She'd never heard that before. "Did she tell you that?"

Elsa Kaydahzinne studied Corrie for several seconds, her shrewd black eyes glimmering. "What did they tell you about him? Did they tell you why your father ended his friendship with him?"

"Something to do with selling land that didn't belong to him and listing Billy—my father—as a partner. Someone tried to contact him and ended up getting hold of Billy. My father didn't know what the person was talking about, but when he found out what his friend was up to...." She cleared her throat. "I was ten years old, Mrs. Kaydahzinne. I don't remember all the details, just that my father and Uncle Bill had a huge fight over this and we never saw him again."

Myra's grandmother regarded Corrie silently for several seconds. She nodded slowly. "They never said anything to you, did they?"

Corrie stared at the old woman. Had she misunderstood? But then Mrs. Kaydahzinne went on, "They tried to protect you. Your mother, she was afraid of you losing trust at such a young age. I told her it was better for you to know the truth. What if something happened to her and your father and this man were to come back and seek to take advantage of you? To tell you the truth, Corrie, I'm surprised it took him this long to come back." She shook her head. "And you say he's dead? What happened?"

Corrie licked her lips, bewildered by the direction the conversation had taken and not sure exactly how to answer the elderly woman without upsetting her. "He... he was murdered. Someone killed him." She braced herself for the shock and dismay the old woman was sure to experience, but to her surprise, she merely leaned back in her chair and sighed.

"I'm not surprised," she said simply. "He was a man who made enemies very easily." Her gaze narrowed. "Why did he come back? What did he want from you?"

"That's just it," Corrie said, relieved that Mrs. Kaydahzinne was so easy to talk to. "I never had a chance to talk to him. I didn't even recognize him or remember if I spoke to him. He checked into one of my cabins and, the next day, we found him murdered."

Mrs. Kaydahzinne murmured a prayer and quickly crossed herself. "He came to make peace, perhaps, and then...." She shook her head. "There's something else, isn't there?"

"Yes," Corrie said. "Before we found him dead, the night before, someone slid a note under my door at the campground office. It was a threat or a warning, however you want to look at it." She took a deep breath. "It said my life was in danger and that I needed to close the campground down today."

Mrs. Kaydahzinne's brows rose even higher than before. "Bill Woods sent you that note?"

"I don't know," Corrie said helplessly. "It wasn't signed and it didn't say why I was in danger or why I needed to close. He was in the store that day, before the note appeared, but I never recognized him and some of my employees said he was acting strangely." She took a deep breath. "I'm hoping that you might know something that might explain why he came back. And I'm hoping you'll tell me why he and my father had such a falling out after being the best of friends for so many years. I used to call him 'uncle', Mrs. Kaydahzinne," Corrie said softly. "I need to know why my father's trust in this man could disappear so quickly. After so many years...."

Elsa Kaydahzinne studied her for a long time, her eyes alternately gazing sharply and then losing focus as she stared into long lost memories. She patted Corrie's hand. "Your mother wanted to protect you," she repeated. "I'm sure your father did, as well," she said slowly. "But you are no longer a child and what they tried to keep from you is knowledge that might be painful but is necessary to prevent any further danger. Corrie, keep in mind that what your mother told me was told with the understanding that it would go with me to my grave. She never wanted you to hear this; she feared that you would not understand or that you would resent her."

Corrie's heart began pounding as if it would burst from her chest. She leaned forward. "Mrs. Kaydahzinne, I hate to ask you to give up my mother's confidences, but I really need to know. I could be in danger, my friends—"

"I know," the old woman interrupted. "Give me a minute, let me think how to best tell you this."

Myra entered the room at that moment. She set down a tray with two china cups filled with a fragrant herbal tea. She glanced at Corrie and raised a brow. Corrie gave a small shake of her head but Mrs. Kaydahzinne seemed not to notice. Myra left the room, this time closing the door behind her.

Corrie picked up her cup and took a sip, watching Myra's grandmother intently. At long last, the elderly woman leaned forward and took her cup in a frail hand and stared into the golden depths. “Your mother and I,” she said at last, “were kindred spirits, of a sort, despite the fact that I wasn't in complete agreement of her marriage to your father. We old ones, we deplore seeing our culture and traditions diminish. The truth is that your mother wasn't to blame for your father being more of a modernist Apache than a traditionalist; Billy was always the one in his family to buck tradition, always. It was just easier to blame it on an outsider than to accept that one of our own didn't have the fire for keeping the bloodline true. But I understood why it was that way. Your mother and I, we found ourselves out of our 'comfort zone', as they say these days, in order to follow our hearts. Believe me, if it weren't for Myra, I'd be living in a shack on the reservation, waiting out my days. But that girl won't hear of it.” She looked at Corrie with a small, wistful smile. “Your mother was not blind to the challenges she faced in loving your father and making her life with him. She was young, she didn't speak much English, and her family opposed her every step of the way. But your father, he had enough courage and audacity for the two of them. He didn't care that he didn't know more than enough Spanish to get him in trouble, as he used to say. He didn't care that his family was vehemently opposed to his union with your mother—your grandmother had another young woman from the tribe in mind for him, but that didn't matter to Billy. Much as he loved and respected your grandmother, his heart was his master and he followed it.”

Corrie waited a few moments and when it seemed Mrs. Kaydahzinne was content to stop there, she ventured, “I know it was hard on my parents, having their families oppose their marriage....”

“It was harder on your mother than you can imagine,” Elsa Kaydahzinne said. “Billy's family might have estranged themselves from him but they still lived only an hour away, on the reservation. He still saw his family, even if they couldn't quite bring themselves to accept his choice of a wife. But your mother....” She shook her head. “It was so much harder for her. Your mother's family never came here to visit, except one time. Her mother came when you were born.” She smiled and squeezed Corrie's hand. “But it was only a brief visit and it was awkward. They resented Billy having taken her away from them. Fortunately for your mother their love was stronger than their families' bitterness and it gave her courage to live where she knew few people, had few friends, and the people she knew viewed her as an outsider. It made her an easy target." She stopped speaking and pressed her lips together tightly.

Corrie wondered just how impatient Rick was getting. She was also beginning to dread having needed to dig into her parents' past. She knew the basics, but with her mother's characteristic optimism, she had downplayed the cons of having married someone so different from her family's expectations. She shifted in her seat. "Target for what?" she asked when it seemed the old woman was reluctant to resume speaking.

Mrs. Kaydahzinne looked right into Corrie's eyes. "Gossip."

Corrie's mouth dropped open. She could not once remember ever hearing anything bad ever said about her parents, especially her mother. She'd always remembered her friends talking about how sweet and nice her mother was and their parents had always seemed polite and friendly to her as well. If the campground hadn't kept her so busy all the time, then she'd had more of a chance to visit.... "They talked about her because they thought she considered herself above them?" Mrs. Kaydahzinne nodded.

"Your mother took her responsibilities as a wife and mother and business partner very seriously. When your father first decided to build that campground, no one in his own family supported him. They thought he was making a big mistake and all they did was predict failure and make snide comments about his 'pipe dream'. He was determined to make it a success and his dream was your mother's dream as well. She was a hard worker, she knew about hospitality—her family had owned a small inn and cafe in Juarez—and she understood that a small business consumed the lives of the owners until it began to make money. The way she put it was that they had to take care of the business before it could begin to take care of them. So she did work long hours at the campground... twelve, fourteen hour days, and your father worked even longer ones, seven days a week. They couldn't afford to hire help, so they did it all, from cleaning the bathrooms, maintaining the grounds, running the store and office, and of course all the office work. Even when your mother was expecting you, she kept working although Billy insisted she slow down." She grew silent for a moment. "That was when Bill Woods knew that your father was most vulnerable. The campground was struggling, but Billy would not give up and your mother wouldn't let him. His old friend, Bill Woods, came and helped them when your mother could no longer do anything more strenuous than office work. And of course, after you were born, she couldn't neglect you to work."

Corrie felt tears sting her eyes. A sense of pride and a nearly overwhelming rush of love for her parents closed up her throat. She knew that running the campground hadn't been easy for her parents, but she had never realized before how much of a struggle it had been and now she understood just how much faith, love, and determination it had taken to make it as successful as it was. She suddenly felt an even greater debt of gratitude to her parents for her livelihood and a stronger resolution to carry on Billy's and her mother's dream, despite all the obstacles in her way. She swallowed hard and said, "I remember Billy saying that he didn't know how they would have done it without Uncle Bill's help. He said he worked for them without accepting a dime for several months... but then he would have to leave, to take care of his own business, he'd say. Billy said he would come back from time to time and help out for several weeks, never taking any money, just doing what he had to do to keep the campground going and all he'd take was their hospitality." She stopped as Mrs. Kaydahzinne began to shake her head.

"Don't put him on a pedestal, Corrie," the old woman said, her voice as hard as stone. "Your father did, and that was a mistake, probably one of the worst he ever made. Bill Woods wanted more than just your father's hospitality; he wanted your father's good name and reputation. It gave him credibility when he decided to start swindling people out of their money with his shady land deals." She paused and her mouth worked as if she had tasted something incredibly bad and was debating whether she should just swallow it or spit it out. "He wanted something else that belonged to your father," she said at last, giving Corrie a hard look.

At first, Corrie didn't understand what the woman was saying, but when realization dawned, she felt sick to her stomach and she could hardly breathe. "My mother?"

Mrs. Kaydahzinne inclined her head, then sighed. "I don't know how long his interest in your mother had been there. Perhaps from the first time he saw her. Your mother was an extremely beautiful woman, both inside and out. It was no surprise that she had captured Billy's heart and that he was willing to do all he could in his power to make a life with her, despite all the differences and obstacles between them, and it was no surprise that another man would be jealous and desire what your father had. You're very much like your mother," she added unexpectedly.

Corrie felt her cheeks flame and she suddenly remembered that Rick and J.D. were waiting for her to give them some information. She cleared her throat. "Did he...? Did he try to...." She couldn't find the words for what she wanted to say.

"I'm sure he tried," Mrs. Kaydahzinne said brusquely. "He gave her a lot of unwanted attention—not when your father was around, of course—flattered her, hinted things to her. Your mother couldn't bring herself to say anything to your father; she knew Billy regarded Bill Woods as a good man, his best friend, an honorable man. And they needed the help. So she kept quiet, but it was hard on her, especially since Billy trusted that man so much that he often allowed him to take your mother into town to run errands while Billy worked the campground. Your mother never did learn to drive, you know. Well, it gave people ideas. They talked. But they were discreet and Billy, so it seemed, never did hear about it. People in the village respected your father too much to say anything to his face. So your mother carried the brunt of it. She had no friends she could confide in. She talked to me because she had no one else. I told her she had to tell your father, that the longer she put it off, the harder it would be to tell him and the more people would talk. I told her Bill Woods was only waiting for a time when he could use her silence against her."

Corrie gripped the arm of the loveseat so tightly that she was certain her fingerprints would be permanently embedded in the wood trim. "Is that why my father broke off all relations with Uncle Bill? He found out what he was trying to do?" Elsa Kaydahzinne nodded.

"When your father found out about the shady business deals and how his supposed best friend had used his name to make money, he was hurt and outraged. But when this friend tried to use Billy's wife to get back at him... well, there are things that even your father wouldn't forgive, though he was the kindest, most understanding of men."

"He didn't believe Uncle Bill." It was a statement but, to Corrie's ears, her own words sounded like a question. Or worse, a prayer.

Mrs. Kaydahzinne waved a hand dismissively. "Of course not. Your mother may not have been able to bring herself to tell her husband that another man had designs on her or even made a pass at her, but she'd certainly never betray her husband. And your father knew it. He didn't even need to ask her and the thought that Bill Woods' accusations or claims could have a single iota of truth never would have crossed his mind. Perhaps his so-called friend didn't expect that; I'm sure he was hoping that your father would be so upset over his accusations against your mother's virtue that he would forget all about the other things your father discovered about him." She straightened up and fixed a stern look on Corrie. "I'm not a gossip, Maria Inez Corazon Black Horse," she said, using Corrie's full name. "What I told you was to help you discover why your life has been threatened. Nothing about your parents and what they were to each other and to you has changed. Remember that. Billy wouldn't let this Bill Woods destroy them while they were alive. And even though he is dead, don't you let this Bill Woods destroy them now that they are no longer here to speak for themselves. You are their daughter; you know them better than anyone. Billy can't protect you now, so now it's up to you to protect yourself. You're Billy Chee Black Horse's daughter and the keeper of his dream. Don't let him down."

Corrie stood up and bent to give the frail old woman a tender hug. "I won't," she whispered. "I'll be back to visit soon. I promise," she added, feeling a tear trickle down her cheek.

"I'll hold you to that." Elsa Kaydahzinne gave her a firm squeeze. "And next time, don't leave the sheriff and your new gentleman friend out on the porch. I know you don't have time now, but the next time I see you, I want a full report on what's going on!"

Corrie stared at her, dumbfounded, and felt a blush heat her cheeks. "Yes, ma'am," she stammered and backed toward the door. Mrs. Kaydahzinne winked then tapped her cane on the floor and Myra appeared to escort Corrie out.

Once on the porch, Myra turned to Corrie. "Was she able to help you at all?" she asked, keeping her voice to a near whisper. Corrie shrugged.

"I'm not sure. She told me a few things I didn't know, but whether they have anything at all to do with what happened...." She let the words trail off as Rick and J.D., who had gone to wait for her by the Tahoe, approached. Rick raised a brow and Corrie answered the unasked question. "It's a long story and I think we'd best discuss it back at the campground." Rick nodded and he and J.D. stepped back and waited for her to come down the steps. She glanced at Myra and said to them, "Go ahead, I need to talk to Myra for a second."

Both Rick and J.D.'s puzzled looks mirrored Myra's but they turned and went back to the Tahoe. Corrie waited until they were out of earshot and she drew Myra closer. "Listen, this has nothing to do with the case or why I came to see your grandmother, but I think you should know that I believe she won't have as much objections to you and Dudley getting married as you might think."

Myra's brows rose. "You talked to her about that?" she gasped. Corrie shook her head.

"No, no, of course not! I wouldn't do that!" Corrie reassured her friend. "It's what she said about my parents; how the heart was their master and they had to follow where it led and she said she admired them for it...." Myra was shaking her head before Corrie could finish.

"She admired them, Corrie, but that was because it wasn't her own family. And your dad always made his own way. Besides, he didn't care what his family thought. I do," Myra said softly. She took a deep breath. "I love my grandma more than anyone in the world except Dudley. I can't bring myself to hurt either one of them, but if I have to make a choice...." Her voice faltered "Then it will have to be Dudley. Grandma doesn't know about him yet, so it won't hurt her to see me be hurt."

"Myra...."

"No, Corrie, thanks, but it won't work. I'm sorry. And you need to go talk to Rick and J.D. and work on getting the campground open again. I need something to keep me busy," she added, forcing a weak smile before retreating into the house.

"Myra, wait!" Corrie said, stopping her before she shut the door. "There's something I need to ask you." Myra paused and looked at her inquiringly. "When your grandmother saw me when I walked in, she said something in Apache, but I didn't quite catch the word. It almost sounded like 'ghost'...."

Myra shook her head. "No, the word for ghosts or spirits is chidn. What she said was 'gōde'." She looked at Corrie closely. "Do you know what it means?"

"I'm afraid not," Corrie admitted. Myra nodded, her brow puckering.

"It means 'shadow spirit that haunts dreams'," she said, her voice low. She glanced over her shoulder toward the living room. "For the last year, ever since your dad passed away, she's been having restless nights. Every once in a while, when I mention your name, she gets fretful and mutters about 'unfinished business' and then says how hard it is to know whether it's better to know a painful truth or go about your life in blissful ignorance." She cocked her head to one side. "Did what she talked about with you have anything to do with that?"

"Maybe," Corrie said, shaking a small chill off her back. "I just hope I didn't make things more difficult for her."

"She seemed relieved, if that helps," Myra said. She nodded toward the Tahoe in the driveway. "You'd better get going, Corrie. I think Rick's patience is about to run out."

"Wouldn't want that," she said with a grin. "Thanks again, Myra."

She hurried down the steps and out the gate. Rick and J.D. were waiting with identical postures of barely concealed impatience—leaning against the hood with arms folded, fingers tapping impatiently. She suppressed a grin. "Sorry that took so long," she said.

Rick said nothing. He stepped around the front of the Tahoe, but J.D. beat him to Corrie's door. She chose to ignore the look of triumph he shot at Rick. "Get what you were looking for?" he asked as he helped her in.

"Yes... and no," she said. He nodded and climbed in the back after shutting the door. She waited until both men were in the vehicle and Rick had started the engine. "There's a lot more to Billy's falling out with Uncle Bill than I ever suspected."

"Let's hope there's some information there to help us find out why you and the Black Horse are being threatened," Rick said as he backed out of the driveway and turned the Tahoe toward the campground.

Chapter 11

Upon their arrival at the Black Horse, Corrie was forced to wait until Rick had talked to his deputies who had been patrolling the campground and he and J.D. had checked out the entire campground office and store. She drummed her fingers impatiently on the dashboard for what seemed to be an eternity until her safety was assured to both men's satisfaction.

Once inside the store she didn't waste time. “Okay, I found out some things that may or may not have anything to do with the threat to the campground,” she began.

“I'll be the judge of that,” Rick interjected. “That means you tell us—me—everything that Elsa Kaydahzinne told you. Even if YOU don't think it's relevant to the case.”

She felt heat creep up to her ears and hoped that neither Rick nor J.D. noticed. “Rick...,” she said at last, but J.D. spoke up.

“He's not asking because he's trying to be nosy or a jerk, Corrie,” he said, earning a nod from Rick. “If what she told you is that personal or disturbing, then it may just be the key to whatever it was that Bill Woods was doing here and why he's dead and why you've been threatened.”

“She said that Billy and Uncle Bill had a falling out over the fact that Uncle Bill was using Billy's good name to sell land that didn't exist. That's common knowledge,” she hedged, hoping that they'd settle for that.

“So tell us what isn't common knowledge. You remember things from a child's perspective. She had to have told you what she saw or heard,” Rick prodded.

“You said your mother was friends with her. You mean she never confided anything more that what everyone already knew?” J.D. added skeptically.

She leaned against the counter and took a deep breath. “She also said that Billy had a more personal reason for ousting Bill Woods from our lives. And it had to do with my mother.” She stopped because tears clogged her throat, making it hard to breathe and speak, but before the tears could fog her vision, she saw the looks of understanding in the two men's eyes.

Rick said quietly, “He claimed he was having an affair with your mother?”

She gave a quick shrug and swallowed the lump in her throat. "I don't know for sure what he said and Myra's grandmother didn't go into a lot of detail. Just that he was coming on to my mother and pressuring her because they needed his help. The campground was struggling at the time and he took advantage of the fact that my mother didn't want to make things harder on Billy. When Billy discovered his shady deals and confronted him, he lashed back by accusing my mother of having an inappropriate relationship with him. I don't know exactly what he said," she added quickly before the question left their mouths. "I just know that Billy didn't believe him and that was when he issued the ultimatum that Uncle Bill get out of our lives."

"Which he did, for over twenty years," J.D. said, his eyes faraway, shaking his head. "Either he realized he'd underestimated your dad and knew he was in for the whupping of his life or he already had planned to disappear for good and leave your dad holding the bag. But why he came back now...."

"Did he know your mother had passed away a few years later?" Rick asked, his voice gentle despite the seriousness of the question.

"I don't think so," Corrie said, shaking her head. "At least, I don't believe that Billy had any contact with him once he left. He cleaned up the mess Uncle Bill had left him and we all went on as if he'd never existed. Or at least, I think they did. They never talked about him again." After a moment, she went on, "Mrs. Kaydahzinne said she'd told my mother that it was best to let me know what happened, in case something happened to them and he tried to insinuate himself into my life. And then she said something else strange," she went on, her brow furrowing.

"About Bill Woods?" Rick asked, raising a brow.

Corrie nodded. "That he was a man who made enemies very easily. And that she wasn't surprised that he'd been murdered."

J.D. let out a low whistle and Rick looked grim. "She knows more than what she told you. We need to...." The low buzz of his cell phone interrupted him. He flipped it open. "Sutton," he said. For a few seconds he said nothing then he nodded. "Have him come here to talk. I've got some questions of my own for him and I'm not ready to leave the campground yet." He flipped the phone shut. "Robert Moreno says he's got some more information for me."

"Information he's just now conveniently remembered?" J.D. asked dryly. Rick shrugged.

"We'll find out soon. Dudley's bringing him over in a few minutes."

~

Twenty minutes later when Deputy Evans' cruiser pulled into the Black Horse Campground's parking lot, leading another vehicle. Deputy Mike Ramirez stepped down off the porch to converse with Deputy Evans briefly before escorting the private investigator up the steps to the door as Deputy Evans drove off.

Robert Moreno, looking only slightly less polished than the day before, in black jeans and a red polo shirt, got right down to business. "Sheriff, I hope you don't mind, but I took the liberty of making a few calls to some of my colleagues to see if by any chance this Bill Woods, alias David Duncan and Timothy Jenkins, had approached them about securing their services," he began without preamble.

"And?" Sutton said, his curtness not masking his impatience at feeling that he was being yanked around. Corrie sat at her desk behind the counter in an effort to make it easier on herself to follow the sheriff's admonition that she let HIM ask the questions and to keep her own information to herself. J.D. positioned himself where he wouldn't be obtrusive but where he wouldn't miss a thing. Moreno barely acknowledged them both before continuing with his information.

"I understand this man—Bill Woods, to use his legal name—had a connection to this campground at one time. Correct?" The sheriff gave a bare nod and Moreno looked satisfied. "He was a close friend of the owner, Billy Chee Black Horse?" Again, a nod from the sheriff and this time Moreno bowed slightly to Corrie. "Your father and Mr. Woods had a business arrangement." It wasn't a question and J.D. could feel the ire boil up in Corrie.

"If you mean the illegal sale of land that didn't belong to us but to the Forestry Service and the Bureau of Land Management, then you are misinformed!" Corrie snapped, rising from her chair. The sheriff cleared his throat, a warning to Corrie as well as gaining Moreno's attention. J.D. watched Corrie's fists clench until her knuckles were whiter than the papers she had been repeatedly reorganizing and knew it was taking all her self control to keep from coming over the counter.

The sheriff addressed Moreno. "Bill Woods used Billy Black Horse's name to help deflect attention from himself in his illegal dealings. Records show that Mr. Black Horse cooperated with the authorities and cleared his name. Furthermore, and I don't know if this has been relayed to you, but Mr. Black Horse passed away over a year ago." Robert Moreno nodded impatiently.

"Yes, Sheriff, I'm well aware of those facts," he said. "However, it seems that Mr. Woods perhaps came with the intention of presenting proof that he is—or rather, was—entitled to a share of the campground and its profits."

An uneasy silence descended on the camp store. Corrie's eyes widened. She looked from Mr. Moreno, to Rick, to J.D. and back to Mr. Moreno. "What's that supposed to mean?" she said, her voice holding a tremor of emotion that J.D. couldn't quite identify.

Mr. Moreno seemed uncomfortable for the first time and shifted uneasily. "You are the daughter of Billy Black Horse's wife, aren't you?" he asked Corrie.

"I'm the daughter of Billy Chee Black Horse and his wife, Maria Inez Teresa Black Horse de Vargas," Corrie said, drawing herself up to her full height which was equal to that of Robert Moreno. Her dark eyes flashed and she gripped the edge of the counter so hard that J.D. was positive her fingernail marks would be etched into the wood. "What are you suggesting?"

"Well, Miss Black," Moreno said, forcing a sickly smile. "It seems that your father's friend claims that there is a question about your...." He paused, cleared his throat. "family ties."

"There is no question!" Corrie flared, storming around the counter and planting her fists on her hips. "Uncle... I mean, Bill Woods hit on my mother and threatened her with spreading ugly rumors about her faithfulness to my father, but she never gave in to him nor did she betray Billy! And if he claimed that he is my father...." She, paused her chest heaving and unshed tears gleaming in her eyes. "... then he was a liar as well as a thief and I'm glad he's dead!"

"Corrie!" Rick snapped and J.D. fought the urge to cringe. Robert Moreno's expression grew thoughtful.

"That's rather harsh, Miss Black," he said, shooting a sideways glance at the sheriff.

"So is what you suggested!" she hissed through clenched teeth, ignoring Sutton's second "Corrie!" warning. "If you think for one minute that I believe that horrible lie or that anyone else in this community would believe it...."

"Now Miss Black," Mr. Moreno said, holding both hands up as if to ward off anymore outrage, "there are ways to determine whether Bill Woods had a legitimate claim on the campground...."

"Take my word for it; he had NO legitimate claim to anything that belonged to my father! Not his wife, not his home or business, and certainly not me!"

"Easy," J.D. said soothingly, although he himself was seething with rage at what the man was suggesting. "It's all moot anyway, Corrie. Bill Woods is dead. Any 'claim' he might have tried to stake has been forfeited by his death."

Robert Moreno coughed and studiously avoided Corrie's eyes. "Well, actually, someone has come forward with a possibly legitimate claim...."

"Spit it out, Moreno, and stop playing games!" Sutton thundered and Moreno had the grace to blanch. He cleared his throat.

"Sheriff, I just found out through one of my contacts that Bill Woods has one or two surviving family members who are legally entitled to any property or valuables since his death. They are the sole beneficiary of his estate and...."

"'They'?" J.D. interrupted before the sheriff could say anything. "Who are 'they'?"

Moreno actually looked uncomfortable. "It's Bill Woods' wife. His first and only legal wife. She hasn't seen him in over fifteen years, but Bill Woods never divorced her, so she is still his legal heir." He paused. "And her son. Legally, Bill Woods' son." He slid a sideways glance at Corrie. "Putatively, your half-brother."

Before either J.D. or the sheriff could react, Corrie took two steps toward Robert Moreno and slapped him as hard as she could.

Chapter 12

"I know he upset you, Corrie, and you have every right to be upset, but slapping him wasn't a good idea."

Corrie stared at Rick, reflected in the mirror standing behind her. He and J.D. had managed to stop her before she inflicted any further damage to the investigator. Rick had hustled her up the stairs to her apartment while J.D. talked to Robert Moreno and smoothed ruffled feathers. The man had, of course, felt affronted and muttered about the unfairness of the messenger being assaulted. Rick had insisted they take some time to calm down and had ordered Corrie to her room like a defiant teenager.

His eyes, midnight-blue with a mixture of anger and frustration and compassion, met hers in the glass before she turned her attention back to her own reflection. Her eyes were wild, her skin pale, and her jaw was clenched as if to keep her anger and the other roiling emotions that churned in her stomach from erupting out of her. At that moment, she couldn't see the gentle, serene countenance of her mother whom so many people had told her, for so many years, that she resembled.

But what she wanted to see even more, and couldn't find, was her likeness to her father.

Rick came up behind her and gently took her shoulders and turned her to face him. "Stop it," he said. "Stop looking for Billy in your face, Corrie. Your father is in you, maybe in ways that can't be seen on the surface, but you're Billy Chee's daughter. Make no mistake about that. I knew the man just as well as I know you." He caught the tears trickling down her cheeks with his thumbs and swiped them away. "I don't know what proof this guy thinks he has, or what he thinks he's going to get out of you, but he'll have to come up with something pretty rock-solid to convince me that anyone but you has a claim on the Black Horse Campground."

"Rick, you don't believe... I mean, you don't think that it's... that it's possible...," she stammered, not able to bring herself to say what she was thinking.

"No, I don't," he growled, releasing her shoulders and stepping back into being Sheriff Sutton rather than her friend Rick. "For one thing, why wait until after Billy died? My guess is Bill

Woods was hoping he could just spring this on you and you'd be so rattled you'd give in, just because he was once someone you considered your 'uncle'. He would have known that Billy would have demanded proof—DNA testing or whatever—before he let him have so much as a free night at the Black Horse."

"But Rick, he's dead," she whispered. "Someone killed him before he had a chance to make any claim. Why would they do that? And who?"

Rick looked grim and he chewed his lower lip. "There are two people, according to Moreno, who would have had a claim on anything Bill Woods stood to gain. His wife and son. He hadn't seen his wife for fifteen years, supposedly. I assume he hasn't seen his son in all that time, either." His eyes bored into Corrie's and along with the official consternation of a dedicated law enforcement officer determined to bring a criminal to justice, she also saw the fear of a man who had a close friend's life in danger. "It's possible, Corrie, that either Bill Woods' wife or son, or both of them, were here, checking in, waiting for him."

She wrapped her arms around herself, unable to stop shaking. Rick stepped forward and reached to steady her and somehow she found herself clutching at his shirt and his arms went around her. She burrowed into his embrace, wishing that all the fear, confusion, and hurt whirling in her mind would just go away. "But why, Rick? What were they after? And why track him down here?"

"If they thought he had something to gain from this, they might have wanted to get in on it and if he refused...."

"You mean someone would actually kill for the Black Horse Campground?" Corrie stared up at Rick, into the hard grimness of his face, and started shaking her head in disbelief. "Rick, that's crazy! Who would do such a thing?"

The apartment door opened and J.D. walked in and stopped short, his eyes registering momentary surprise at seeing Corrie in Rick's arms, but his face remained impassive as she moved away and cleared her throat. Rick straightened up. "What's Moreno got to say?"

J.D. nodded at Corrie. "That he's got an answer for Corrie's question... and I don't think either of you is going to like it."

~

"You want me to what? Are you out of your damn mind?"

J.D. had never seen the sheriff lose his cool, but he wasn't surprised, considering the curve Robert Moreno had just thrown him. It had been all he could do not to lose his own temper earlier when Moreno had dropped the bombshell on him.

Now Moreno looked slightly pained, though more aggrieved and self-righteous than he had earlier. “Look, I know I have no jurisdiction of any kind in this case, not even in Texas, because I'm not a law enforcement officer. However, Sheriff, it seems to me that if you're serious about trying to discover who murdered Bill Woods, who happens to be—or rather, was—my client, then it would be remiss of you to exclude any possible suspects, simply because they happen to be....” He paused and cleared his throat, sliding a sideways glance at Corrie. “... personal friends of yours.”

Corrie's face had gone white when Robert Moreno had first put forth his theory that Corrie should be treated as a potential suspect in the murder of Bill Woods, but now her cheeks had two burning spots of red in them and fire blazed in her dark eyes as well. Whether she wasn't saying anything because she was speechless from shock and indignation or because both he and the sheriff had shot her warning looks, J.D. couldn't say, but he could tell that it was all she could do to keep from hauling off and slapping Robert Moreno once more. She had her arms folded across her chest and her hands balled into fists. So did J.D. And so did the sheriff.

“Mr. Moreno, you have also just given me two other possible suspects: Bill Woods' wife and son, whom he abandoned years ago. Do you happen to know their names and where they might be? Isn't it possible that they followed him here and killed him?”

“Anything's possible,” Moreno countered, with a slight stress on the word “anything”, though he didn't look at Corrie. J.D. cleared his throat, keeping a tight rein on his temper.

“Let's assume, for one ridiculous moment, that Corrie did have an axe to grind with Bill Woods. Why would she commit the crime on her own property?”

“Well,” Moreno said, before J.D. could continue, “for the simple reason that it doesn't make sense, so of course, law enforcement would be less likely to consider her a viable suspect.”

“Mr. Moreno, I don't know if you've just flattered me or insulted me!” Corrie snapped, unable to keep silent any longer. “Just what reason, in your wildly imaginative scenario, would I have for murdering Bill Woods?”

Robert Moreno actually smirked. “As I mentioned before,

although you didn't like hearing it, there is a possibility that you are, er, related to him. Therefore, he would have had a legal claim on the property or the business itself. If you weren't so concerned about the possibility of having to share the wealth, you wouldn't have reacted so strongly to that news."

"You think I'd kill someone—a family member—just to keep from sharing the 'wealth'?" She shook her head. "Mr. Moreno, you don't know me at all and my business even less. There is no 'wealth' to be shared. In fact, this threat against the campground has crimped me financially to the point that I don't know if I'll be recovering any time soon!" Her voice shook slightly, the tremor reminding J.D. that Corrie could ill afford what this threat was costing her. Sutton cleared his throat.

"Moreno, if you have information about Bill Woods' family, especially their current whereabouts, I need to know it immediately. Because while you are focusing on someone who has a very shaky motive and almost no opportunity...."

"And you know this how, Sheriff?" Moreno asked coolly.

"I have several witnesses who can verify Miss Black's whereabouts the day that Bill Woods was killed, as well as her movements the day before when Bill Woods was casing the campground store."

"Are you one of those witnesses?" the investigator asked with a sneer.

"No, but I am," J.D. said, straightening up. Moreno shot him a wary glance and J.D. went on, "I happen to work here and I was working the day that Woods was seen casing the campground office. I was also here the day he was discovered dead. Rest assured, Miss Black never approached Bill Woods or his cabin at any time."

"Of course, she didn't have to, herself," Moreno said, shaking his head as if he couldn't believe the idiocy of J.D.'s statement. "She could have had someone do the dirty work for her. I get the feeling she inspires a great deal of loyalty among her employees. Any of them would have done it for her, if she paid them well enough." He gave J.D. an appraising look up and down. "Someone for whom it would have been natural and normal to be approaching a guest or their lodging."

"That's enough, Moreno!" Sutton thundered as J.D. made a slight move toward the investigator. He didn't look at J.D. but his warning to remain calm came through loud and clear. "Unless you have some kind of evidence or a real motive to link anyone to

Woods' murder, then your speculations are unfounded. And you still haven't told me where Bill Woods' wife and son might be or, for that matter, who hired you and why you're here in the first place." Robert Moreno tried not to blanch too obviously, but both J.D. and the sheriff noticed the hesitation. "They hired you, didn't they?" Sutton shot out. "Your contacts are Bill Woods' wife and son. Where are they, Moreno? Are they here?"

Moreno took a step back, holding up his hands as if to fend off the sheriff's questions, and cleared his throat. "Okay, yes, they hired me but it was all done over the phone, payment was sent via direct deposit, and I've never seen either one of them or spoken to them face to face."

"You've got to be kidding," J.D. said while Sutton glared daggers at Moreno. "You're a hell of a lousy investigator, Moreno, or else you're just desperate for money!"

"Or you're lying," Sutton put in.

Moreno looked pained and gathered up his tattered bravado. "Look, it's true, times are hard and I took the job because I needed it. Thanks to the internet, everyone is their own private investigator," he added bitterly. "All I was told was that Bill Woods was a bigamist and deadbeat dad and that my clients feared that he was taking advantage of someone else with whom he'd once had close ties."

"You never checked up on the legitimacy of those claims?" Sutton asked, his voice edged with ice. Moreno looked at him uneasily.

"I didn't see the need to, Sheriff. I wasn't asked to do anything more than see if Bill Woods had actually checked into the Black Horse and was staying here. My clients did mention the fact that Woods might be mentally unstable, that there was a possibility that he might make some kind of threat, but I was given to understand that the threat would be mainly against himself and should I feel the need to report it to law enforcement, then I should, but that they simply wanted to know if he was, indeed, hiding out in his former stomping grounds."

"It never occurred to you that your clients might be a source of danger to the man you were asked to find? That maybe YOU might be putting Bill Woods in danger by reporting his whereabouts to your clients?" the sheriff said scathingly.

Moreno shrugged, regaining his former attitude. "Sheriff, for all you know, my clients DO have a legitimate claim to this place and Bill Woods was swindling them out of it. That does seem to have been his specialty. I assumed that my clients merely wanted to ascertain Bill Woods' current location in order to be able to take legal action against him. I'm neither a lawyer nor a law enforcement officer. I did my job, a job for which I was well paid, and that's all I did."

"Yes, you did," Sutton said, nodding slowly. "You got your money and your clients ended up with a dead body on their hands. Or rather, YOUR hands," he added as Moreno's face paled. "Because, as of right now, you, Mr. Moreno, are the only person who's admitting to have come here specifically to find Bill Woods."

"Now wait just a minute, Sheriff!" Moreno spluttered. "I had a legitimate reason for being here and looking for Bill Woods. It's not my fault that he turned out to be a lot more trouble than a deadbeat dad and a bigamist and it's certainly not my fault that he ended up dead, for whatever reason!"

The office phone rang before anyone else could say anything and Corrie answered it. "Black Horse Campground," she said tersely, then rolled her eyes. "Hi, Buster, look, this isn't a good time to talk. If you want to know when to come back to work, you'll have to wait till I call you and... what?" She frowned and listened, her eyes narrowing slightly. "Are you sure?" She glanced at the sheriff, who was looking more and more impatient. "He's here right now, Buster. Come over as soon as you can."

"Corrie," Sutton said as she hung up the phone, not bothering to mask his exasperation, "I don't have time to waste chasing down figments of Buster's overactive imagination. Whatever he has to say can wait until later."

She shook her head. "I don't think so, Rick. This is one of Noreen's figments and I'm pretty sure it's going to be well worth your time."

Chapter 13

Buster and Noreen arrived within twenty minutes and J.D. enjoyed seeing the look of confusion and consternation on the face of Robert Moreno when Noreen Adler rode her customized Harley-Davidson motorcycle into the parking lot with Buster riding on the back seat. When Noreen removed her helmet to reveal a glorious cascade of shining blond hair, Moreno's mouth actually dropped open.

Buster gallantly held the door open and ushered his beloved into the campground store. The sheriff stepped forward and held out his hand, his previous annoyance dissolving into professional courtesy and, though it wasn't apparent to anyone but J.D. and Corrie, curiosity. "Noreen, thanks for coming over. You've got some information we could use?"

Noreen nodded, flashing a smile at Corrie and J.D. and giving a polite nod to Robert Moreno. "I hope so, Sheriff," she said, her husky voice capable of raising the temperature of every male in the room... or at least those not aware of her ardent, though inexplicable, fidelity to Buster. "Oscar told me that one of the guests here had a problem with another guest and that she was gone all day visiting a relative near Alamogordo?"

It took J.D. a minute to realize that Noreen might be the only person who ever referred to Buster by his given name. The sheriff nodded. "Marjorie and Thomas McMillan. They have a niece stationed at Holloman."

"Judy Marshall," Noreen said promptly. "She's an old college friend of mine. We were supposed to leave this morning to go up to Red River on our bikes for a girls' weekend away, but then this aunt of hers called yesterday and changed her vacation schedule and showed up a week early."

"You're sure her aunt is Marjorie McMillan?" Sutton asked, raising a brow. Noreen gave him a ghost of a smile.

"Oh, yeah, I'm positive. Judy was praying for a surprise deployment to Afghanistan before her aunt showed up."

"Yep, that's her aunt," J.D. said dryly.

"All right," Sutton said. "So what do you have for us?"

Noreen pulled a slip of paper out of her jeans pocket. "It was something Judy said about her aunt, this Marjorie McMillan, asking about someone that Judy is pretty sure her aunt's never met. It made an impression on her because, one, her aunt is the type that makes plans well in advance and hates to deviate from them, so her showing up a week earlier than originally planned seemed weird. Two, her aunt seemed to be fishing for information about this friend—more like an acquaintance—of Judy's and after she thought about it, she couldn't remember her aunt ever meeting this friend before... and Judy's pretty sure she's never mentioned her, either."

"Who's this friend?" Sutton asked, flipping open his notepad. Out of the corner of his eye, J.D. could see that Corrie was avidly curious about the whole thing while Robert Moreno, though unable to stop glancing appreciatively at Noreen, started to shift his weight and check his watch as though bored or irritated. Or nervous.

"Layla Woodson. She's someone Judy met briefly at the bike rally in Ruidoso this spring. She was having trouble with her bike, so Judy recommended a place for her to take it near Alamogordo. She told me about it because I was having the same trouble...."

Robert Moreno interrupted with an impatient snort. "And just what trouble were you ladies having with your bikes, ma'am?" he asked. "You get a scratch on your paint job?" he added, as if asking if their nail polish had gotten chipped.

Noreen turned to him, widening her baby-blue eyes and said in her most innocent voice, "The cam chain adjusters were so bad that the oil pump, support plate, and lifters were all shot. So they replaced the cam chain tensioners with gear-driven cams, along with a new oil pump and support plate. Talk about an improvement in performance! Made all the difference in the world."

J.D. bit back a grin as Moreno's mouth dropped open and he sputtered, "Well, what's that got to do with anything? So she had trouble with her bike. So what?"

"The name 'Woodson' doesn't set off any alarms, Moreno?" Sutton asked, eyeing the investigator closely. J.D. knew quite well that the sheriff didn't believe in or like coincidences, and this woman's last name, so closely resembling the deceased's, being mentioned by a possible suspect was nothing if not coincidental.

"I'll take it into consideration, but really, Sheriff, there's no way that woman, McMillan, could possibly have anything to do with Woods' death."

"And you know this...?" J.D. interjected. Moreno shrugged.

“Well, she lacks any discretion, for one thing,” the investigator said. “I'd think someone about to commit murder would do their utmost NOT to stand out in people's minds, don't you agree?”

Neither J.D. nor the sheriff commented, although J.D. was positive that Sutton was also thinking what J.D. was thinking: Marjorie McMillan didn't necessarily have to be thinking about murder to be considered a person of interest.

“Well, Noreen, thank you for bringing us this information,” Sutton said, extending his hand which Noreen took with a quizzical expression, probably wondering why she was being dismissed so quickly. Moreno gave a smug smile which faded when his cell phone rang. He glanced at the screen and mumbled a quick “Excuse me,” before heading to the TV room to take the call. Sutton added, “Wilder, you have anything else you want to say or ask?”

J.D. nodded, picking up on Sutton's cue. “Yeah. What's the name of this place, Noreen? I think I might be having the same kind of trouble with my bike.”

She smiled with understanding; she was one sharp lady. “I'm not surprised, Lieutenant. Lots of Twin Cams have that problem. It's Desert Eagle Motorcycles, on La Luz Gate Road, just before you get to Alamogordo. Tell Mike I sent you and tell him to tell Patty that Buster and I are still waiting for that chile rellenos dinner she promised us.”

“Will do.” J.D. straightened up, nodded to the group, and headed for the door before Moreno returned or anyone said another word.

~

It was after two o'clock when J.D. returned to the Black Horse. Corrie tried not to let her relief show too obviously in front of Rick, but part of her had feared that the campground threat had followed J.D. and something had happened to him.

“Find out anything?” Rick said the minute J.D. walked in. J.D. cocked a brow.

“Geez, not even dinner and a movie, Sutton?” He shook his head as Rick glared at him. “Where's Moreno?”

“He asked to be excused. That was supposedly another client of his who called and he informed us that he had a business to run, so I let him go back to the River's Edge. Dudley's keeping a close eye on him, to make sure he doesn't decide to go handle this other client's business in person." Rick's patience was evaporating quickly and J.D. got to the point.

"All right, here's what I got. Seems like this Layla Woodson raised a few red flags to Mike, the fellow who owns the shop. He remembered her immediately. She refused to give him any personal information, insisted that she would pay cash, so no need to send a bill, or give a credit card or driver's license. Mike said he told her he needed to order a part and would need some way to contact her and that it would be far easier for her to give him a phone number than to have her go all the way out to his shop to see if the part was in. She finally gave him a cell phone number with an 806 area code."

Rick's brows rose. "That's a Texas area code."

"Lubbock, to be exact," J.D. said. "Turns out Mike never did have to call her. Says he'd swear she was stalking the UPS guy to see when he delivered the part and then she practically camped outside his gate while he worked on her bike. No surprise she stuck in his memory."

"Wonder if she was meant to," Rick said.

"It also occurred to me that Noreen might be able to get me a picture of this woman. Her friend sent her a picture from her phone—blurry as hell, but she sent it on to me." He flipped his phone open and brought up the message. "Not much help," he added, holding the phone out to Rick.

Corrie craned her neck to look. Rick angled it so they could all see it. The picture showed three women in Harley-Davidson t-shirts, blue jeans, and black leather jackets. One wore a black ball cap, one had short, spiky black hair, and.... "That's Noreen in the middle," she said.

"The woman with the cap is Noreen's friend, Judy Marshall. The one with the black hair is Layla Woodson," J.D. said. "But other than black hair and a petite frame, you can't make out any other defining features. She's wearing shades so you can't even see her eye color." Corrie cleared her throat.

"So what's the connection with Mrs. McMillan? Is this Layla Woodson really related to Bill Woods or is Mrs. McMillan one of Uncle Bill's 'wives'? And why would either of them want to kill Uncle Bill now? I mean, if he was hoping to get something out of me, why kill him before he gets it?"

"That's assuming that they knew the reason he was here, or cared. It could be they had an axe to grind that had absolutely nothing to do with you or the Black Horse. They might not even know there is a connection." Rick was chewing his lip and Corrie groaned.

"Now that's adding insult to injury!" She rubbed her temples. "Do you really believe someone had it in for Uncle Bill and it had nothing to do with me or Billy but still this is where they decide to exact their revenge or whatever?"

Before either J.D. or Rick could respond, they heard a noise from upstairs.

J.D. looked up and grimaced. "How long's it been since you let those poor guys out?"

"I haven't let them back in since this morning," Corrie said in a near-whisper, feeling herself go cold. Rick slipped his gun out of its holster, releasing the safety as he moved toward the stairs.

~

J.D. didn't wait for an invitation. Motioning to Corrie to stay put, he moved on swift, silent steps alongside the sheriff and waited at the foot of the stairs, listening intently. Sutton glanced at him and J.D. nodded without hesitation; this wouldn't be the first time he'd backed the sheriff without a weapon in his hands.

They took the stairs slowly, the carpet deadening the sound of their steps. They were halfway up the stairwell when the sound of some heavy object striking the wooden floor above them froze everything for a second before the sound of hurried footsteps propelled them up the stairs.

"Sheriff's department!" Sutton barked, as he burst through the half-opened door at the top of the stairs, his gun leading the way. J.D. slipped in right behind him as Sutton quickly checked the closet, bathroom, kitchen, and spare room. The only movement in the room came from the curtains billowing in from the open window. "Clear," Sutton said as J.D. went to the window and looked out, careful not to touch the sill. No one was visible on the roof and he heard the sheriff delivering curt orders to his deputies stationed on the grounds to be on the lookout for anyone around the building. J.D. hoisted himself out the window onto the roof of the camp store. He moved to the fire escape that was secured to the side of the building that faced the storage shed and the RVs belonging to the Myers and the Pages. Beyond them was the forest. He shook his head.

"See anything?" Sutton asked as J.D. carefully let himself

back into Corrie's apartment.

"Just that whoever broke in had it planned out well. If they hadn't made a sound...." He watched as Corrie, wearing latex gloves that the sheriff must have provided for her, picked up various items scattered on the floor around the nightstand next to her bed. The nightstand was actually a two-drawer wooden file cabinet that was covered by a white cloth embroidered with red roses that hung askew. The top drawer was pulled out almost all the way.

"When they pulled out the drawer, it tipped the cabinet and everything fell off," Sutton said. "That's the crash we heard." J.D. grimaced; a small bedside lamp lay beside the cabinet, its base broken in two. Several picture frames had also fallen and shards of glass mixed with scattered photographs on the floor along with various manila folders and papers.

"Did they take anything?" J.D. asked, edging closer. Corrie looked up at him, gingerly holding an 8 x 10 photograph that was partially still in its frame, her face devoid of any emotion.

"Nothing that matters," she said, her voice trembling slightly. Sutton had bent down and, with gloved hands, picked up one of the folders that lay opened. He looked at the title written on the flap and threw Corrie a sharp glance.

"This doesn't matter?" he said, flipping the folder shut and handing it to her. J.D. saw the words "Birth and Marriage Certificates and Legal Documents" written in dark ink on the flap. "It's empty. Whoever broke in here must have taken those documents!"

Corrie sat back on her heels, still holding the photograph, and shook her head. "No, Rick. They took two sealed manila envelopes that Billy put in that folder. He labeled one 'Birth and Marriage Certificates' and the other 'Legal Documents'. But they were both empty." She half-smiled at the look of confusion on the sheriff's face. J.D. was certain he looked equally perplexed when she looked at him and nodded. "My dad was a cautious man. He would have kept his personal documents in a safety deposit box, except that he wanted to have access to them on his time, not the bank's. And he didn't keep them in a safe because he worried about losing the key or forgetting the combination or that a safe would indicate that there WAS something valuable to be found."

"Someone was looking for these papers," Sutton said, gesturing at the empty folder. "They took those envelopes, thinking they had what they were looking for. Do you know why those papers would matter to anyone?" Corrie shrugged.

"Some people have gotten the impression that Billy wasn't my father. Maybe they think that my birth certificate reflects that. Or else they were looking for the deed to the campground, or Billy's will." She took a deep breath. "They're going to be in for a big disappointment."

J.D. asked, "So where did he keep his personal papers?"

Corrie smiled and held up the photograph. "Right in plain sight." She carefully removed the staples that held the cardboard backing in place. Once the backing came off, the cracked glass fell to the floor with a soft tinkling sound and the photograph slipped loose from the frame. She took the photo in one hand and held the cardboard backing toward them. A five by seven manila envelope was taped to the backing. J.D. glanced at Sutton and shook his head.

"I'd have never looked there," he commented. Sutton grunted his agreement and took the backing, carefully peeling the tape off the envelope.

"This is where your dad kept his personal papers?" He didn't remove his gloves. He nodded at the envelope. "All right if I open it?"

"Sure," Corrie said, holding the photo against her heart. "Believe me, there's nothing in there that's going to shock me."

J.D. hoped fervently that that was true. He watched as the sheriff carefully straightened the prongs of the envelope and opened it. He reached in and his expression changed. "What is it?" J.D. asked.

Sutton didn't answer. He slid a three by five index card out of the envelope that had only five words printed on it: "Papers are with Elsa Kaydahzinne".

Chapter 14

“'Shocked' doesn't even begin to describe how I feel right now.”

Corrie shook her head and stared at the index card in her hand. Nothing made sense and her brain was a whirlwind of confusing thoughts. She looked up and caught the attentive gazes of Rick and J.D. and shook her head again but couldn't find any words to say.

Rick cleared his throat. “You mean you never looked at the contents of this envelope since Billy passed away?”

“There was no need to,” Corrie said. “Dad took care of everything practically up to the moment he stopped breathing. He made sure that the Black Horse was signed over to me as soon as he got his prognosis, along with a power-of-attorney, so there was no need to go to probate or any other legal action. All the 't's were crossed, all the 'i's dotted, and the only thing I needed to keep everything going was his death certificate and once that was filed, the campground was mine. That was the way he wanted it and that was what he planned. I remember watching him tape that envelope to the backing behind this photo and teasing him about his high-tech security measures.” She took a deep breath that felt like it was going to burst her chest open. “I thought those documents were in there but I never looked myself. I can't imagine why he felt he had to secure these papers somewhere else.”

“Maybe he wanted to make sure that no one would find them, in the event of....” J.D. gestured to the break-in evidence. “Which means....”

“No, J.D.!” Corrie snapped, struggling to her feet and clutching the photo even tighter against her heart. It was the last family photo taken just two weeks before Corrie's mother had succumbed to her heart aneurysm. She wiped away the tears that threatened to drip onto the two-decades-old photograph, angry at herself for allowing them to surface. “It means nothing like what you're suggesting! Billy didn't hide my birth certificate because it listed someone besides himself as my father!”

“Easy,” he said softly, holding his hands up and taking a step back. Corrie swallowed hard and, through tear-glazed eyes, she could see that Rick, though prudently keeping quiet, appeared to share J.D.'s opinion.

"All right," Rick said. "Let's go downstairs. I need to get this place dusted for prints before we disturb anything else." He held his hand out toward Corrie. It took her a second or two to realize that he wanted her to hand the photograph over.

She almost protested; after all, the photo was in the frame, between the glass and backing. It wasn't likely that whoever had broken in had left any fingerprints on it. But she knew that Rick was only being thorough and he didn't want any potential evidence handled more than was necessary.

"I'm going to get it back, right?" she said, hanging on after Rick's fingers closed on it.

"Of course," he said, and she released her grip on it. She glanced around the room at the disarray and took a deep breath.

"All right, let's go see what our next step is."

Neither Rick nor J.D. questioned her use of the word "our".

~

J.D. took a quick look around the grounds, noting that the deputies probably didn't need his help, but not sure he was welcome in Corrie's apartment while it was being processed. And he wasn't sure that Corrie wanted his company while all that was going on. He returned to the office just as Sutton was coming down the stairs.

"Anything?" he asked and the sheriff blew out his breath in frustration.

"No, and it seems that whoever was in there knew exactly where to look... no sign of them having searched anywhere else. They went directly to that file cabinet."

J.D. raised a brow. "They knew it was there?"

"Must have," Sutton muttered. "And what bothers me is how they knew to look for it in Corrie's apartment instead of the campground office. That's where she keeps her important papers pertaining to the business." J.D. felt a chill spiral down his back.

"Who would know something like that?" He glanced around the store and, not seeing Corrie, raised a brow at the sheriff.

"She's cleaning up the apartment, said she wanted some time alone," Sutton said. "I think this shook her up more than she'd like to admit."

"So what's next?" J.D. fought the urge to head for the stairs and offer Corrie help, knowing she wouldn't accept. But standing around was making him antsy.

"I've already called Myra and asked to speak to her grandmother. She said that now wasn't a good time... her grandmother had taken some medication and was quite drowsy. She asked what it was all about and seemed a bit irritable when I told her that it was something that I couldn't discuss with anyone but her grandmother."

Something in the sheriff's tone mirrored the suspicion that churned in J.D.'s gut, despite his best efforts to squelch it. "How long has Corrie known Myra?" he asked, cringing inwardly in anticipation of the sheriff's response.

To his surprise, Sutton didn't snap his head off. In fact, he looked as if J.D. had brought up something that the sheriff had thought of himself but hadn't wanted to voice. "There is not a snowball's chance in hell that I'm even going to suggest that to Corrie, Wilder. For one thing, she's going through enough as it is and, for another, she'd never believe that Myra could have had a hand in this."

"If we're talking opportunity and forget about motive...."

"Myra's the only person who regularly goes into Corrie's apartment alone," Sutton said shortly. "She cleans in there once a week and she has a key to the building and the apartment. I don't want to even think that she might have some connection to this," he said, rubbing the back of his neck. "But who else would know Corrie doesn't keep her personal papers in the office downstairs?"

"But why would she wait until the entire sheriff's department attention is focused on the campground and break in through the upstairs window to get my personal papers instead of grabbing them on one of her regular cleaning days, where it's not likely I'd notice they were missing for weeks or even months?" Corrie's dry words were the first indication that the two men had that she had rejoined them. J.D. wondered how long she'd been listening to them before announcing her presence.

Sutton nodded, not seeming the least bit surprised. "That's why I don't seriously consider Myra a suspect, Corrie."

"At least, not a suspect in this break-in," she said, her dark eyes challenging him.

The sheriff said nothing for a moment. "Who else knows where you keep your personal papers?"

"Besides you two, now? Jerry and Jackie and probably Shelli." Corrie shook her head. "Please don't even suggest...."

"Give me some credit," Sutton said dryly. "Even if I hadn't known them for years and trust them with my own life, it doesn't make sense for them to take part in some kind of hostile takeover of the Black Horse." He tapped his pen against his notebook. "Who does stand to gain in the event of your death?" he shot out.

Corrie blanched and J.D. felt a hitch in his gut. She cleared her throat. "I guess the only ones are Jackie and Jerry. I mean, I have family on both my mom's side and my dad's side, but no one that I keep in regular contact with." She bit her lip. "I suppose that legally...."

"You have a will?" J.D. asked. Corrie's face paled even more and even the sheriff raised a brow.

"You don't have a will?" Sutton asked, disbelief evident in both his expression and tone.

Corrie shook her head. "Come on, guys, what do I have besides the campground? A pile of debts, that's all. If anything happened to me, the Pages would probably do well to just sell the Black Horse to the highest bidder and retire for real!"

"If it were theirs to sell," J.D. said and the sheriff nodded in agreement. Corrie's face reddened.

"Billy's family thought he'd lost his mind when he decided to take this piece of land and turn it into a campground. Why would their attitude have changed now?"

"Because it's developed and might be in the red on paper, but it's successful enough to keep going," the sheriff said. "And didn't your dad acquire this land from his family in the first place?"

"Yes," Corrie admitted. "His grandparents gave it to him when he turned twenty-one. It was the least desirable tract they owned and the furthest from the reservation. It was their way of letting him know they weren't happy about his marriage."

"And then he turned it into a relatively successful business. People have killed for less," J.D. commented. Corrie shook her head, her irritation at them both evident before she said a word.

"So now the whole Black Horse side of my family makes the list of possible suspects. Why not throw my mom's family in as well? Maybe you can implicate them in the Kennedy assassination while you're at it!" she snapped.

"Corrie," Sutton said quietly and she blew her breath out.

"I know," she said, her voice subdued. "I'm sorry. I know you're doing your job... both of you," she added, giving J.D. a look of such contrition and gratitude that he nearly blushed. He cleared his throat, preparing to argue that, technically, it wasn't HIS job to investigate but Corrie went on as if reading his mind. "Neither of you wants to see me get hurt and if it were anyone but me, I'd be demanding you be just as thorough and annoying as you're being right now." She gave them a slight smile and J.D. couldn't help but grin back at her. Even Sutton seemed to relax. "So okay, then," she went on. "What opportunity could anyone else have had?"

Sutton shook his head. "Before we look at opportunity, let's look at who might have had some connection with Bill Woods. He was your dad's childhood friend. Is there a chance that someone in your dad's family still had contact with him even after he and Billy had their falling out? What about Toby Willis's family?"

"I don't know." Corrie shrugged helplessly. "I rarely ever talked to my cousins about stuff like that when we were kids and I hardly ever see or speak to any of them today. Even after my mom died, we all remained kind of distant. I haven't seen any of them since Billy's funeral."

"Who would know about that? Someone you or the sheriff could talk to," J.D. persisted.

Both Corrie and the sheriff looked at him and responded, "Elsa Kaydahzinne."

Chapter 15

"I have no idea," Myra said flatly. "And I'm positive my grandmother wouldn't either."

Corrie was thankful that Myra couldn't see her roll her eyes over the phone. She glanced at Rick and J.D. and shrugged as she shook her head. "Myra, I know you don't want to upset her, but this is really important. If I could come over and talk to her again...." She ignored Rick's glare and emphatic head shake, but Myra was equally adamant.

"Corrie, I know this is important, but I don't want anyone else coming by and demanding to speak to her, she's already been through enough—"

"Wait, hold it, Myra," Corrie said, motioning Rick and J.D. closer as she hit the speaker button on the phone and held a finger to her lips to signal the men to keep quiet. "What do you mean 'anyone else'? Did somebody besides me come and talk to your grandmother today?"

"Some man," Myra said, her indignation coming over the speaker loud and clear. Rick was scribbling furiously on his pad and he thrust a note at Corrie, as Myra went on, "He claimed he was working with the sheriff's department, and scared Grandmother into speaking with him. Wouldn't you know I had just run over to my sister's place down the road to borrow some eggs...."

He had to have been watching to see when Mrs. Kaydahzinne was alone. She didn't have to glance at Rick's note to know what to ask Myra. "What did he look like, Myra? Rick needs to know if anyone was impersonating a deputy."

"Well, he didn't claim to be a deputy," Myra said with a sniff. "And I know it wasn't any Bonney County deputy. It was probably just some nosy person, a reporter or something, looking for a story."

"What did he look like?" Corrie repeated, not as urgently as Rick or J.D. would have preferred.

"I never saw him, myself," Myra clarified and Corrie stifled a groan as both Rick and J.D. let out various silent expressions of exasperation. "I asked Grandmother if she could describe him and she said he was just a young man, probably about my age."

"He was young? Was he dark? Fair? Did she notice his eye color?" Corrie tried to ignore the gestures Rick and J.D. were using to suggest questions, for fear she might let out an inappropriate snort or giggle, and focused her attention on Myra's answers.

"I'd have to ask, but she seemed perturbed about what he was asking her. She said something like, 'That young man has no business asking such personal questions'."

"Did she say what those questions were?" Corrie asked, feeling her throat close up, wondering what Mrs. Kaydahzinne might have said to Myra.

She could almost see Myra give a shake of her head. "Oh, no, she never repeated what he asked her. She was just indignant that he would even ask her, being he was a stranger to her."

"So she's never seen him before," Corrie said, running through her mind what young men might have been involved in this case. The only one she could think of was Jamie Carson, the young man who, along with his wife, had overheard someone mention the name of the murdered man. Unless, of course, to a nearly-ninety-year-old woman, Robert Moreno, would be considered young, but Corrie dismissed that immediately; Elsa Kaydahzinne had said that the man was about Myra's age, not nearly twenty years older.

"No, she hasn't," Myra was saying as Corrie reined in her thoughts. "Corrie, I don't want my grandmother getting involved any further in this mess. I don't want her being harassed by strangers in her own home. Whatever it is this man, or whoever else is threatening the campground, is looking for is putting her in danger. I can't be with her every single minute. Can't Rick do something to keep her safe?"

Corrie glanced at Rick. His face had reddened slightly and she knew Myra's question had touched a nerve. "I'm not sure how much manpower he can spare for that," Corrie said carefully. "He's got his deputies spread thin, following up on leads in this case and...."

"I know," Myra sighed and went on in a subdued voice, "I understand that. It's just frustrating that it doesn't seem like we're any closer to finding out who threatened the campground and killed that man than we were yesterday."

Corrie was touched to hear Myra accept ownership of the problem instead of focusing all the blame and responsibility on the police—or on Corrie. She hesitated a second, then went on slowly,

"Myra, I know it's difficult, but I really think if your grandmother would just speak to me once more...." She let the words trail away and mentally crossed her fingers as Myra's silence went on.

Finally Myra said, "All right, let me see what she says about talking to you, Corrie. I know she'll do it if it's going to help keep you safe; I just want her to be safe as well."

"So do we, Myra," Corrie said, blinking back tears. She was about to ask if she should call back to give Myra a chance to talk to her grandmother when a torrent of half-Apache, half-English suddenly welled up in the background and she waited while Myra's voice, muffled by her hand over the mouthpiece, sorted out the confusion.

"Well, Grandmother is insisting you and the sheriff come over as soon as you can," Myra said, her voice a mixture of exasperation and affectionate humor. "Apparently all those admonitions about eavesdropping on phone conversations don't apply to her."

"That's great, Myra. We'll be over as soon as we can!" Corrie stood and hung up the phone only to be met by a stony glare from both Rick and J.D. "What?"

"Why do you insist on putting yourself in harm's way?" Rick snapped. "There's no need for you to go over to the Kaydahzinne place. Mrs. Kaydahzinne has already agreed to talk to me; you don't have to be the go-between."

"Mrs. Kaydahzinne agreed to speak to BOTH of us," Corrie said. "You heard Myra," she added, aiming a sharp gaze at J.D. who half-heartedly shrugged in agreement. "Besides, what harm am I putting myself in?"

"Did you already forget that someone broke into your apartment looking for information and someone—perhaps the same person—showed up to try to get information from Elsa Kaydahzinne?" J.D. folded his arms over his chest as if to brace himself against Corrie bulldozing her way past him. "I don't want to scare you, Corrie, but it could be possible that the intruder heard us say something about Elsa Kaydahzinne being your mother's confidant and that's how they knew to go to her."

"They might have even followed us there earlier," Rick added and Corrie fought back a shiver.

"If you're trying to scare me, it's working," she said, fighting back the tears and the trembling in her voice. "But I'm still going with you. I have a right to know what Mrs. Kaydahzinne knows and why it's affecting me and my home."

“And you don't trust us to tell you everything?” Rick said, but he didn't sound offended. He sounded as if he were admitting it. Corrie gave him a tight smile.

“The thought hadn't even occurred to me, but since YOU brought it up, Sheriff.... Besides, how much safer can I possibly be than going with the sheriff and another police officer?”

~

J.D. tried to relax, but he felt on edge as they once more pulled into the Kaydahzinne driveway. As they got out of the sheriff's Tahoe, both he and Sutton scanned the area. Two deputies had been left at the Black Horse Campground to keep watch, while two others had been sent to check out the area around the Kaydahzinne home. So far, no suspicious person or persons had been seen but J.D. knew that whoever had visited Elsa Kaydahzinne would have been very careful to stay out of sight, just as they had at Corrie's place. He didn't doubt Mrs. Kaydahzinne's visitor and the person who had broken into Corrie's apartment were one and the same and he was sure that the sheriff shared his opinion.

This time, Elsa Kaydahzinne herself stood on the porch, waving them in, despite Myra's feeble attempts to get the old woman to stay inside the house. She brushed off Myra's fussing as she beckoned Corrie and the two men to follow her inside, then shooed Myra out of the room. She shook her head as she seated herself in her wing chair. The flame in the votive candle holder danced in the breeze she created by her movements and the chandelier crystals tinkled softly. The scent of lavender hit J.D. like a two-by-four; Trish, his deceased wife, had been enamored of the scent. J.D. could have done without it. He tried not to let it distract him from the purpose of their visit.

“I should have known it wasn't going to be enough to simply tell Corrie what I knew. I should have known someone was going to search for proof.”

“Proof of what, Mrs. Kaydahzinne?” Sutton asked. He had removed his hat as a sign of respect to the elderly woman, but it was plain that he was there on official business.

Mrs. Kaydahzinne's brows rose. “Proof that doesn't exist,” she said sharply. “They are looking for some way to prove that they have some legal claim to Billy Chee's property and they aren't going to find it. There is none.”

"Who are 'they', ma'am?" the sheriff asked. "Myra said only one person came to see you." Elsa Kaydahzinne nodded and frowned.

"Yes, I only saw one person. A man, a young man. My eyesight isn't too good," she added, inclining her head in apology. "So I can't tell you what he looked like or what kind of car he was driving. I just know it was a white one, rather small. But he slipped up when he spoke to me. He said, 'It's important for us to know the truth.' He caught himself afterward, went on to say, 'I really need to know', but I heard what he said."

"Did you see anyone else waiting in the car?" Sutton asked. Mrs. Kaydahzinne shook her head.

"It was too far away and it was dark inside the car. If someone was in there, they kept still; I'm sure I would have seen movement."

"Do you think you might recognize the person if I showed you a photo of him?" the sheriff said. She shook her head and shrugged.

"Perhaps, perhaps not. I kept the screen door latched and told him not to come too close and he stayed by the gate." She gestured out toward the yard and J.D. calculated that the man had to have been a good thirty feet away. Still.... "And he was wearing sunglasses and a baseball cap, Sheriff," she added and J.D. knew that scratched out any chance of a positive identification.

"What else was he wearing?" Sutton asked, his pen out, taking notes.

"Jeans, a white t-shirt, sneakers. His cap was blue and I couldn't make out any kind of emblem on it." She seemed perturbed and J.D. guessed it was because her description was so vague that it could be applied to almost anyone. He glanced up when Corrie slipped in a question of her own.

"You said he was young, Mrs. Kaydahzinne, about Myra's age. How could you tell if you couldn't see him clearly?"

"Well, my eyes aren't all that great, but my ears work perfectly fine," the old lady said with a sly smile. "This man sounded young and strong, except his voice was a little hoarse... raspy. Maybe he had a cold or was a smoker."

J.D.'s head jerked around and his gaze met Sutton's. The sheriff cleared his throat. "Do you think you'd recognize his voice if you heard it again, ma'am?"

"I might," Elsa Kaydahzinne said, frowning. "Do you think you know who it might have been?"

The sheriff skirted the question. “What information was he asking you for, ma'am?”

She shot a glance at Corrie, her brow puckering with concern. Corrie nodded and squeezed the old woman's hand. “Go ahead, Mrs. Kaydahzinne. It'll be fine.”

“Well,” she said, returning the squeeze, “he said he wanted to know the truth about... about Corrie's family. That the reason this man was murdered had to do with the legal ownership of the Black Horse Campground.” Her voice trembled and her scowl deepened. “He insinuated that he knew the truth and he just wanted the proof. That was all he wanted and if I would give it to him, he would leave me alone.”

“What proof was he asking you for, ma'am?” Sutton said.

“He kept saying 'the package',” Mrs. Kaydahzinne said, shaking her head. “I kept asking him 'What package?', but that's all he said, over and over, 'I know you have the package'.”

“What 'package' do you have, ma'am?” the sheriff asked. Corrie flinched and Mrs. Kaydahzinne shifted uneasily, sliding a sideways look at J.D. “It's all right, ma'am,” Sutton said quietly. “All of us know that Billy Black Horse left you his important papers. We found where he had supposedly hidden them. That's how we knew to come ask you.”

“He told me what he'd done,” she said shortly. “He thought he was being so clever, got a laugh over Corrie's reaction,” she added, nodding toward Corrie. “But I'm not sure that the papers he left with me are the ones you're looking for.”

The stunned look on Corrie's face mirrored the expression on the sheriff's although he recovered quickly. “What exactly do you mean?”

“You want Corrie's birth certificate, don't you?” the old woman said. She went on before any of them could say anything, “But why should Billy hide that? It's easy enough to get a copy from the county or the vital statistics office or whatever it's called.”

“If it wasn't the original... I mean, if information on the original had been altered....” J.D.'s voice trailed away as Corrie threw him a furious glance. Sutton held up a hand before she could respond.

“Lt. Wilder has a point, ma'am.” He paused when Elsa Kaydahzinne nodded.

“I understand what you're both saying, Sheriff,” she said. “But there wasn't any need to alter the information on Corrie's birth certificate. Go ahead, look for yourself." She nodded toward a china cabinet in the corner, its three shelves crowded with various knick-knacks. A painted glass image of the Virgin of Guadalupe in an eight-by-ten frame provided a backdrop to the religious figurines that populated the top shelf. "There's an envelope behind the picture of La Virgen. Be careful you don't break any of my things," she warned as the sheriff stepped over to the cabinet. He moved a few items before reaching behind the picture and removing a five-by-seven manila folder. The irony wasn't lost on J.D. and Mrs. Kaydahzinne caught his eye, her own eyes twinkling.

"Yes, we old ones enjoy being clever, and perhaps we lack imagination or originality," she said and J.D. allowed a smile. She smiled back and then looked at Corrie with an expression of deep affection. "I couldn't tell you now whose idea it was originally, but both Billy and I agreed that it would be one of the last places anyone would look for an envelope."

Sutton held the envelope out to Corrie. "Do you want to do this here?" he asked. J.D. wondered if Sutton was hoping Corrie would say "yes" and they would have their answers immediately, but she straightened up and nearly snatched the envelope from him.

"It won't make a difference about anything that matters," she said stiffly. "It's only going to prove what I already know!"

"Then why is someone willing to break into your home, not to mention murder someone, for it?" the sheriff shot back. He glanced at the elderly woman who was watching the entire interaction with an expression of doubt. "Do you have any idea, Mrs. Kaydahzinne?"

"It makes no sense," she said slowly. "But there must be something in that information that means more to this person and to Bill Woods than what appears obvious to us. But I have no idea what it could be." Sutton nodded.

"All right, Mrs. Kaydahzinne. We appreciate your time and I'll keep a deputy stationed nearby in case anyone bothers you again."

"Thank you, Sheriff." She glanced toward the door leading into the kitchen and frowned. "Myra will be glad for that. She worries too much about me, that girl. She should be dating and having fun, finding herself a good husband instead of looking after an old woman. I feel I'm taking advantage of her generous and kind nature, but she insists on bothering about me...."

"Myra doesn't consider you a bother, Mrs. Kaydahzinne, and she'd be horrified to think you'd consider yourself one," Corrie scolded her gently, giving her a hug. "She loves you dearly and would do anything for you and not just out of a sense of duty either!"

"That's why you two get along so well, Corrie," the old lady said, patting Corrie's hand. "You felt the same way about Billy. Now it's time you go," she said, pulling her shawl closer about herself. "The sheriff and this other gentleman are getting impatient but they're both too kind to rush you!"

J.D. cleared his throat as both Corrie and the sheriff headed for the door. "Excuse me, ma'am, but if you and the sheriff don't mind, I have a question for you." He paused. Corrie gave him a curious glance and Sutton responded with a lifted brow. Mrs. Kaydahzinne tilted her head and gestured for him to continue. "Did you ever look inside that envelope that the sheriff found behind that picture?"

Mrs. Kaydahzinne frowned. "No. I had no reason to do so. Billy just told me that it was important that these papers remain in a safe place with someone he trusted." Apparently she anticipated J.D.'s next question. "I never asked what the papers were and he never told me. I assumed they were legal documents of some kind—birth certificates, deeds, that sort of thing." She stopped and looked a question at all three of them. J.D. looked at Corrie.

Her face reddened. "I don't know what papers my father gave you," she said stiffly. "He never told me, I just assumed...." She cleared her throat and shot a glare at J.D. "And, yes, I know what 'assume' means!"

"I never said anything," J.D. protested, holding up his hands. Sutton moved toward Corrie.

"All right, enough. Corrie, you have to open that envelope right now. We need to know what it is that we're dealing with."

There was no room for discussion. Corrie hesitated for a second before thrusting the envelope at the sheriff. Sutton took it and ripped it open and pulled out two pieces of paper. The silence in the room stretched for what seemed like an agonizing hour but was really no more than a few seconds. To J.D.'s surprise, Sutton handed the papers to him.

"I want you to verify what's on these documents Billy hid," he said.

J.D. said nothing and, avoiding Corrie's eyes, scanned the papers. The first one was simply Corrie's birth certificate, stating that Maria Inez Corazon Black Horse was born to Maria Inez Teresa Black Horse (nee Vargas) and William Chee Black Horse on the seventeenth of September. He mentally filed away Corrie's birthday while looking at the other paper which was merely a deed to the Black Horse Campground, listing both Corrie and her father as co-owners. It was signed and notarized almost two years earlier—around the time, J.D. surmised, that Corrie's father had been given his prognosis. J.D. looked up at Corrie and the sheriff and shrugged, handing the papers to Corrie. “Just what you said. No surprises.” He noted, however, that Corrie visibly relaxed after glancing at both papers. “So what, exactly, is the big deal about this information?”

“That's what puzzles me,” Sutton said. “If the information in that envelope was so crucial to Bill Woods, why was someone willing to kill him for it? It only proves he didn't have any kind of legitimate claim to the Black Horse Campground.”

Chapter 16

“Someone had to believe that they were going to find some other information on those papers.”

Corrie, Rick, and J.D. had returned to the Black Horse in relative silence. The silence stretched as they returned to Corrie's apartment where, without asking, she prepared them each a plate of migas, her favorite comfort food that Billy had often prepared for her during her teen years. Rick's words echoed as she cut up the corn tortilla strips, jalapeños, and onions and scrambled the eggs. She could tell, as she laid the food in front of them, that their hunger for answers was almost stronger than their eagerness to attack the food.

J.D. took a long swallow of iced tea and Corrie wondered if he'd found the jalapeños too hot for his taste. “They had to have a real good reason to think so. Would they have been so willing to kill for information that might not be the truth or even exist?” he asked.

“Bill Woods must have believed the information was true,” Rick said. “That was the reason he came and someone close to him must have found out about it.”

“That young man,” Corrie said, her stomach twisting into knots. “That young man who visited Mrs. Kaydahzinne had to have some knowledge. If he killed Bill Woods to get it and he knows Mrs. Kaydahzinne knows about it....”

“She's safe, Corrie,” Rick said. “Deputy Andy Luna is stationed there and he won't let anyone get near her again.” She nodded, not fully convinced. “You should eat,” Rick prodded her but she shook her head.

“I'm not hungry. You guys finish it,” she said, pushing her plate toward them. Neither man argued although she noted with amusement that they were careful to make sure that they weren't stinted on their portions. She waited until the feeding frenzy had abated before she went on. “Why was Bill Woods so positive that the information in that envelope proves something that would be to his benefit? I mean, surely, of all people, he knows that we're not related. He had to know there isn't any proof that he has any claim on my property.”

J.D. paused with his tea glass halfway to his mouth then he

set it down slowly. Rick stared at him.

"Want to share with us, Wilder?" Rick asked and J.D. shook himself.

"Woods knew he didn't have a legitimate claim. But what if whoever killed him believed he did?"

"We've already been over that." Rick frowned. "The person who killed him...."

"Either didn't know that his claim wasn't legit or else killed him for leading him, or her, or them, to believe that it was." JD. looked at Corrie. "Bill Woods swindled people out of money by making false or misleading claims, right?"

Corrie nodded. "He sold property he didn't own. That's what led to his falling out with Billy. And he also married women without telling them he was already married...." She stopped and her mouth dropped open.

"I'll bet they were wealthy," Rick muttered, jumping up from the table and punching in the number on his cell phone for the sheriff's department. He barked an order to the deputy on duty to look up the financial records of the women who had been married to Bill Woods. He listened for several seconds then he flipped the phone shut, looking grim.

"Let me guess. They WERE wealthy when they married Bill Woods, then he left them all after clearing out their bank accounts," J.D. said, tilting his chair back. Rick gave him a humorless smile.

"That widens the field considerably," Rick said. "Now we're not looking for potential heirs to the Black Horse family fortune," he said, with a nod to Corrie. "Now we've got to consider how many disgruntled heirs to his wives' money might have been out for his blood."

"I thought he didn't have any children," Corrie said.

"No, but a couple of his wives did have children before he married them," Rick said. "And if he swindled his wives out of their life savings, he swindled those children out of whatever inheritance they might have had coming to them. Corrie, let's go down to your desk and check your computer. I'm having photos of those 'children' sent to your e-mail, along with those of the many Mrs. Woods. The printouts will be easier to examine than having them on my phone."

J.D. let the chair legs hit the floor. "Would one of those children be a son about the age of Jamie Carson?"

"Who happens to be about Myra's age," Rick finished as he

snatched his hat off the hook near the door. "I'll bet he has a blue baseball cap and dark glasses as well!"

"Wait a minute!" Corrie cried as J.D. also headed for the door. "You're going to confront Jamie Carson without a shred of proof?"

"No, I'm going to take a look at those photos and see if any of them look like Jamie or Lisa Carson. However, it was a man who approached Elsa Kaydahzinne about the papers and I'm going to see exactly where Jamie and Lisa Carson were during the course of this morning!"

"And then what?" Corrie asked, her heart pounding. Rick gave her a grim shake of his head.

"We'll look at the pictures first. Then it all depends on what I find out from them."

They made their way down the stairs and there were several files waiting in Corrie's inbox on her computer. She opened them after casting a nervous glance out the front window of the store, as if afraid that someone might look in and see what they were doing.

It appeared that none of Bill Woods' wives' children would be mistaken for siblings, even the two that were blood related. The only thing they had in common were light-colored eyes, either blue or green. "None of them look familiar," Corrie muttered. "What a surprise," she added under her breath, remembering the crowd that had populated the now-deserted store just a couple days earlier.

Rick shook his head. "Print them out, Corrie. It's just possible that one of them might trigger Mrs. Kaydahzinne's memory. I've got someone checking up on their whereabouts. They live in different cities in Texas...."

"... like most of Corrie's guests," J.D. interjected.

"It's the best we can do!" Rick snapped and Corrie blew out her breath in frustration.

"Okay, okay, let's not lose our cool," she said, waving her hands in their faces to distract them from glowering at each other. The printer hummed and spit out three color photos which she gathered up and handed to Rick. "It's hard to say whether the man in the photos resembles Jamie Carson. He's clean-shaven and the guy in the picture has a full beard and mustache."

"The eye and hair color are similar," J.D. said. The animosity between him and Rick seemed to have dissipated and he was allowed to look at the pictures as well. "Height and weight are pretty close, too," he added as he read the fine print under the image.

"It's a start," Rick said. "Dudley will take these over to Mrs. Kaydahzinne, while we go talk to the Carsons." He headed for the door, J.D. right behind him.

"We?" Corrie said in surprise as she jumped up and followed them. Rick turned and fixed a hard stare at her.

"Wilder and I are 'we'," he clarified. He pointed at her computer screen. "Print out the photos of Bill Woods' wives' as well. I want you to study them carefully and see if you even remotely recognize any of them. I'll have copies taken over to the Pages and the Myers and anyone else who might have come in contact with any of your guests. One or more of these people have been here and someone had to have seen them." He strode out the door without another word, J.D. close on his heels.

"Never heard of the guy," Jamie Carson said flatly. "In fact, we never heard of the Black Horse Campground, either, until some friends recommended it to us a few weeks ago."

The sheriff had driven over to the cabin owned by Deputy Andy Luna's great-uncle and J.D. had to admit he was a bit surprised to find that the Carsons were actually at the cabin. In fact, neither seemed to be particularly surprised to see law enforcement show up. They were sitting in a couple of folding camp chairs on the cabin's porch and almost seemed to be expecting them.

"And what made you decide to come to Bonney County for your camping trip?" Sutton asked, leaning casually against the porch railing, his voice almost friendly. It didn't seem to make Mr. Carson any more willing to share information, but his formerly aggressive attitude was noticeably absent.

"I don't know," Jamie Carson said with a shrug. He glanced at his wife and nodded at her. "Lisa found it online. It was near Ruidoso, the price was good, we'd never been to this area before...."

"You're from Texas?" Sutton slipped the question in. Lisa Carson spoke up.

"From near Wichita Falls. We go camping about three times a year, usually in Colorado. The people we carpool with got us into camping and they're always giving us ideas for places to go." Despite her earlier hostility, she was doing everything she could to cooperate. Her husband shot her a scowl which was hard to miss... and neither Sutton nor J.D. missed it.

"They suggested you come to the Black Horse?" the sheriff asked. Mrs. Carson shook her head.

"Not exactly. I mean, not this campground, specifically," she explained. "They had been in the area before and...."

"Can you tell me the names of the people who suggested this trip to you?"

It was as if Sutton had pulled a plug on the couple in front of him. Silence greeted his question and the Carsons went rigid. His eyes met J.D.'s and he gave a slight nod. J.D. cleared his throat.

"Where do you and these folks who give you camping advice work? You did say you're co-workers, right?" More silence. Lisa Carson stared at the floor. Jamie Carson stared straight ahead. J.D. looked at Sutton and the sheriff leaned forward.

"Is there a problem, Mr. and Mrs. Carson?" he asked. "Is there a reason you won't tell us where you and these co-workers are employed?"

"What's it matter?" Jamie Carson said suddenly, his formerly defensive attitude returning in full force. His wife started to say something, but pressed her lips shut when he glared at her. "Besides, we just carpool together; we don't all work at the same business, just the same office building. We just share driving costs, that's all."

"And this office building you all work at is in Wichita Falls?" Sutton prodded, not raising his voice or indicating that his patience was evaporating. J.D. could see that the Carsons were growing more and more uneasy the calmer that Sutton seemed to be. "Would it happen to be at an agency that deals in real estate, vacation rentals, maybe a travel agency?" Lisa Carson opened her eyes wide and her lips parted, but a swift glare from her husband caused her to look away and swallow hard. Sutton's voice took on a slight edge. "I have to say that your refusal to answer a simple question about where you work is starting to make me very suspicious." He waited a few beats before adding, "Especially since you're well aware that I am investigating the murder of a man you admitted to recognizing...."

"We told you we didn't do anything to that guy!" Jamie Carson exploded, jumping to his feet and almost knocking over the camp chair in which he'd been rocking nervously. Lisa Carson twisted her hands in her lap and stared at the sheriff and J.D. with eyes brimming with tears. "I swear, all we did was check in like we were told to...."

"By whom?" both J.D. and Sutton barked immediately. Jamie

Carson stepped back, nearly falling over his chair. By the time he had regained his balance, it was apparent that he had lost all his other equilibrium. His shoulders sagged and he gave his wife a look of defeat that allowed her tears to start flowing. The sheriff pressed his advantage. "Who asked you to check in at the Black Horse and why?"

Jamie Carson blew his breath out and raked his fingers through his hair. "Some guy. Not the one who was found dead," he added quickly. He glanced at his wife and nodded toward her. "Look, I better let Lisa explain. She's the one who carpools with the guy's secretary and she's the one who asked."

"Asked what?" Sutton repeated, his jaw tight and his eyes hard on the young woman. One look at his face was enough to convince her to spill her guts.

"One of the girls I carpool with, she worked for this guy, I'm not sure he's a travel agent, but he's some kind of businessman. I'm not sure what business," she added quickly. "He works out of Lubbock, but he's got a couple of other offices and she worked in the one in Wichita Falls." She took a deep breath. "She said he was looking for someone to check out this campground. She wasn't interested. She and her husband are more into 'roughing it' type of camping, you know, wilderness-type without any kind of facilities. She thought Jamie and I might want to do it. He was offering to pay for everything and we figured, 'why not?'" She sniffled and dragged the sleeve of her lightweight windbreaker under her nose. "We were cool with it, but then she said he wanted us to keep an eye on some guy who would be staying here. The guy who ended up dead...." She swallowed hard. "I didn't tell Jamie that part, about keeping an eye on someone. Not until we got here. I thought he'd be upset that we would be spying on someone. And he was," she added as her husband nodded grimly. "But I figured if we were only supposed to watch the guy, just text or e-mail back a report on what he was doing or going or who he was talking to, what was the big deal? We weren't supposed to ask him anything or approach him. But then we were in the camp store that day and I saw him and Jamie wanted to leave, but I thought the guy was acting kind of weird and so I wanted to hang around and see what he was up to. Jamie was starting to get irate so I had to tell him why I wanted to hang around...."

"And I told you that you should have never agreed to this!" he snapped. "You should have told me and now the police think we killed this guy and—" J.D. cut in before his voice rose any further.

"What you both need to do now is tell the sheriff who paid you to come here and keep an eye on the man who was killed." The Carsons looked at each other, then Jamie Carson shrugged.

"We figured you all were already wise to whatever was going on. You were talking to the guy, weren't they, Lisa?"

J.D. and the sheriff exchanged an alarmed glance. "Robert Moreno?" J.D. blurted.

The Carsons' eyes widened and Jamie Carson shot a look at his wife. She bit her lip and looked away and gave a faint nod. Her husband straightened up. "But we didn't take any money from him! He just paid for the campground site and sent us a prepaid credit card for gas. That's all!"

"Well, Mr. Carson, that's pretty much the same as taking money from him," Sutton said coldly. "What information did you pass on to him? Besides the whereabouts of the man you were supposed to be keeping an eye on?"

"Nothing! I mean, well...." Jamie Carson looked pained, as if he'd had a sudden attack of kidney stones... or conscience. "Lisa did say he wanted to know about the campground owner."

"What, exactly, did he want to know about her?" the sheriff said, his voice tightly controlled. J.D. tensed, wondering how Sutton would react to whatever the Carsons were about to say. And wondering if he would be able to stop the sheriff or join him instead.

"Just... he just wanted me to let him know what she looked like. So I took a picture of her with my phone and sent it to him. That's all!" Lisa Carson stammered when Sutton made a slight move in her direction. Her husband stood up, weariness battling with what was left of his bravado.

"Look, Sheriff, we messed up, okay? We should have known this deal was too good to be true and we should have bailed when this guy started asking us to spy on people. But we didn't mean any harm to anyone, honest. If any of what we did hurt someone...." He let the words trail and his face registered alarm and despair when Sutton removed the cuffs from his belt.

"Someone is dead and someone else was threatened, Mr. Carson. And it appears that you and your wife are accessories to both. What happens next depends on your willingness to cooperate with us."

~

Corrie stared and stared at the photos of the three women to whom Uncle Bill had been married during the course of the last twenty years. She kept going back to one of a woman with curly dark hair, narrow light-colored eyes, and a pale complexion. The woman was easily in her early fifties but she didn't look like anyone Corrie had ever seen before. And yet she almost looked familiar. Corrie shook her head, wondering if all the stress was making her suffer from wishful thinking. The other two pictures didn't ring any bells but Corrie knew that photos of any of the dozens of women who had walked through the door of the campground store in the last couple of weeks probably wouldn't either.

She looked up with a gasp when the front door flew open and J.D. walked in. “Why didn't you lock this?” he demanded in greeting.

She slumped back in her seat, her heart thudding. “Why didn't you knock?” she managed to sputter. “You nearly scared me to death!”

“If you'd locked the door, then I would have had to knock! Lucky for you it was me who scared you!” He took a deep breath as Corrie's heart rhythm slowed down to normal. “Sorry, the sheriff and I just had an interesting interview with the Carsons,” he said and Corrie's heart began pounding again.

“What happened? What did they say? Is Jamie Carson the man who went to Elsa Kaydahzinne?”

J.D. held up a hand to stop the flow of questions and filled her in on his and Rick's visit with the Carsons.

~

“So that's that?”

“Looks like it,” J.D. answered, watching the lines of tension in Corrie's face ease for the first time since the nightmare had begun Thursday night. He didn't want to let on that he was still feeling as if his stomach were tied in knots; the idea that Corrie had been in such close proximity to danger, even with him and the sheriff and the entire Bonney County sheriff's department at hand still unnerved him. The sheriff hadn't allowed him to be present when he had taken the Carsons down to the county lock up, nor did he invite him along to pick up Robert Moreno. J.D. figured Sutton was going to do everything by the book to make sure that no one who had threatened Corrie would be walking on a technicality. Deep down, J.D. was in total agreement though the cop in him wanted to be there when Sutton threw the book at the Carsons and Moreno. And he was impatient to hear what it was these people had wanted from Corrie.

It was as if she'd read his mind. "Did they say what it was that Uncle Bill was after?" she asked, her voice trembling, probably from relief rather than fear. He shrugged.

"Not in front of me. I'm willing to bet that the sheriff is working on getting that out of them, along with finding out what Moreno's stake in the matter was."

"I can't believe he had us cooperating with him." She shook her head and wrapped her arms around herself. J.D. allowed himself to draw her into his arms and was rewarded by her body relaxing.

"It's okay, Corrie. There are still a lot of questions to be answered and there's a chance that...."

He felt her hands ball into fists, clutching at the front of his shirt, her tension returning. "A chance that what? That there's still danger?"

He could have kicked himself for bringing that up. His arms tightened and he gave her a small shake. "You know it's best to be safe than sorry. We're still trying to find out the reason that Bill Woods came here, why he was killed, and who wanted him dead. For now, we have suspects in custody and we're not going to stop until we figure out what this is all about." The last thing he wanted to do was let her go, but he figured it would be best for them both to stay focused on the investigation, so he forced himself to release her. "Did those pictures of Bill Woods' wives ring any bells?"

"Sort of," she said, letting go and stepping away. J.D. wondered if her apparent reluctance was real or a product of his imagination. "Although I think it might be my nerves making me think I really might recognize any of these women. Especially this one," she added, indicating a picture of a dark-haired, pale-eyed woman. J.D. glanced at it and frowned.

"She looks like she'd be hard to forget if you'd seen her," he said, shaking his head and pushing the paper away. He almost immediately pulled it back toward him and stared at it again.

"See what I mean?" Corrie said. "You think you've seen her before, too, don't you?"

"Something about her looks familiar, but I can't put my finger on it. And she sure doesn't resemble any pictures of those 'children'," he said. He shrugged. "Could be our imaginations or could be a coincidence. But you know how the sheriff feels about coincidences," he added.

"Right," Corrie said with a nod. "But if he thinks he's got the main suspects in custody...."

"Still doesn't mean you can sleep with your windows open," J.D. said with a grin. "Not until we're sure that all the loose ends are tied up and all the bad guys are locked up." Corrie smiled wistfully.

"I can dream, can't I?" She straightened up. "I don't suppose Rick said anything about possibly re-opening the campground any time soon?"

"Not to me. But I know that's one of his priorities, after making sure you and your friends and staff are safe. If it's any consolation, he did release cabin A-6, now that his team is done going over it." He captured her gaze with his and he hoped she could find reassurance in his eyes. "It's almost over, Corrie. It's going to be okay."

She smiled and it was like watching a rose bloom. He could feel her anxiety slip away and for a moment, he felt a stirring of alarm, a sense of uneasiness creep over him. Was he being overly optimistic in relieving her fears? He wondered if maybe he'd jumped the gun in telling her that it was almost over. Before he could speak up, Corrie said, "Just to be safe, I'm going to keep on as if things were still unresolved. I assume the sheriff is keeping at least one deputy on guard here at the campground tonight?"

"Deputy Ramirez is sticking around tonight. The sheriff sent Deputy Evans to go make sure the rest of the county hasn't gone to hell in a handbasket while he's been keeping most of his people here at the campground."

"I figured as much. Well, I don't want to end up disappointed if this whole mess isn't completely wrapped up, but I know Rick. If he's got a case, he'll make it stick."

"Unless the Carsons and Moreno lawyer up," J.D. muttered, hating to be so negative, but knowing how THAT usually turned out. To his surprise, Corrie shook her head, smiling with confidence.

"Rick will know what to expect and he'll be ready for it. Studying law is a big help in knowing what law enforcement needs to do to make a case stick."

"Wait, 'studying law'?" J.D. said. Corrie's smile vanished and her face reddened. "You're telling me that the sheriff is a lawyer, too?" He couldn't help but sound shocked. Corrie sighed.

"No, actually, he's not, but don't tell Rick I told you this. He doesn't talk about it." She rubbed her temples. "He studied criminal justice at New Mexico State before transferring to UNM for pre-law. After the first year, he decided he had to see for himself how law enforcement really worked if he was going to be prosecuting criminals, so he joined the Albuquerque PD. He liked police work so much, he decided to stick with it instead of...." She cleared her throat. "Instead of going to law school back east."

J.D.'s jaw had dropped. "Don't tell me. Harvard?"

"Yale."

J.D. slumped against the counter, dazed. "How the hell does a hot-shot law student end up as sheriff in Small Town U.S.A.? Tell me he flunked out...."

"Rick? Flunk out? Are you kidding?" Corrie smirked. "He already had a scholarship to UNM and he was being offered free rides to Columbia University, Cornell, and Stanford for law school. His mother was set to send him to Yale, but...." She took a deep breath. "There was a change of plans. It's a long story," she finished abruptly.

From the look on Corrie's face, J.D. could see that the "change of plans" hadn't included her, but some other woman. "I'm sorry," was all that came out of J.D.'s mouth. She shot him a dark look.

"It's ancient history, J.D." she said briskly. "Rick might have become a great lawyer, but Bonney County would be out an even better law enforcement officer. He's doing what he loves and what he does best. Oh, by the way, whatever happened to that job application he gave you for the village police department?" she asked. It was one of the most obvious subject changes J.D. had ever heard, but he pretended to believe it was just as casual as Corrie was acting.

"Still thinking about it," he drawled. "Not sure if I really want Eldon LaRue to be my new boss. And I'm not thrilled about going back to being in uniform all the time." Corrie laughed.

"Well, if you're going to keep doing police work, you might as well get paid for it," she said. "I'm sure you can work something out with Eldon about the uniform."

"Yeah? You still have that blue dress you wore on your last date with him? Maybe you can go put in a good word for me with him," he said, giving her a sly grin.

"You're hilarious, Lieutenant Wilder," she said, rolling her eyes as she blushed. She glanced out the window and her smile turned to a grimace. "Looks like the wind's picking up. We might end up with a rainstorm again tonight."

J.D. detected a note of anxiety in her voice. "Nervous about the weather?"

"I love the rain, but I hate thunder and lightning. Always have since I was a kid," she said, shrugging as she folded her arms across her chest. "You'd think I'd have outgrown it by now."

For a moment, J.D. debated asking her if she wanted him to stick around until the storm had blown over, but he knew that idea was probably not going to be accepted. There was something about being in close proximity to Corrie with a storm brewing that stirred up feelings in him that were probably not going to be reciprocated. He'd seen her face when she had talked about the sheriff and let slip a few of his secrets. There was no sense in setting himself up for disappointment.

"Well, maybe in that case, I'd best get to my tent and batten down the hatches. You going to be okay?" he asked.

"Oh, sure," she said but her smile didn't quite reach her eyes. "Thanks for everything, J.D. And I do mean everything. You have no idea how much it means to me to know you care and you're in my corner." She looked into his eyes and her smile became real.

Damn. It was all J.D. could do to reach for the door handle. He took a deep breath. "Be sure you lock up tight. I'll see you in the morning." He managed to tear his gaze from hers and let himself out of the camp store.

Chapter 17

Corrie sighed with relief as she shut and locked the door behind J.D. All was well; the Carsons were behind bars and Robert Moreno would be facing charges of fraud, intent to commit fraud, and who knew what else Rick would be able to pin on him. And the best part was that soon she would be able to reopen her campground and hopefully recover from this setback as quickly as possible.

Thunder rumbled in the distance as Corrie turned out the lights in the camp store. It was getting late. Through the closed blinds she could see flashes of lightning and she grimaced. Rain was always welcome but thunder and lightning always made her jumpy and nervous, and judging from the way the wind was gusting hard, they were in for a real storm. For a brief second, she let herself wonder if she shouldn't have let J.D. stay for a while, but she shook her head and scolded herself. That would have been a mistake. The events of the last few days and her phobia about lightning and thunder made her too vulnerable. Not that she didn't trust J.D....

She let herself into the apartment and went about getting ready for bed as rain began thudding on the roof. As she pulled up the blankets she allowed herself a moment of gratitude that she didn't have to worry about any of her tent-camping guests having to ride out a torrential downpour that could flood their tents, if not completely destroy them, or be exposed to dangerous lightning strikes. All her tent guests were safely in a motel room for the night.

All but one.

She sat bolt upright in bed as a tremendous thunderclap shook the entire building and the storm let loose, rain lashing against her windows as if to shatter the glass. Renfro whined and burrowed his head under Corrie's quilt. Oliver let out a hissing yowl, his back arched and his fur standing on end. Corrie pushed them aside and ran to the window facing J.D.'s campsite. It was too dark to see until a flash of lightning gave her a brief glimpse of J.D.'s tent, nearly flattened by the howling wind. Raindrops ran down the panes, distorting the view, and her heart leaped into her throat.

Thunder cracked like a whip and she jumped, barely stifling a shriek. She hit the light switch and made a dash for her clothes. Another bolt of lightning lit up the night. All the lights blinked and went out, plunging the campground into complete darkness.

She gasped and waited for a second, hoping that the lights would come back on. She hated thunderstorms almost as much as her pets did, but concern for J.D. galvanized her into action. In the dark, she pulled on her jeans, t-shirt, and sneakers. She groped her way to the kitchen and found a large, heavy-duty trash bag. She stumbled to the linen closet and took a blanket, a spare set of sheets, a pillow, and a couple of bath towels and stuffed them into the trash bag.

From Renfro came a questioning whine. "It's okay, boy. I'll be back soon," she reassured him. He burrowed his head under the blankets as lightning lit up the room again. She used the momentary illumination to grab a hooded windbreaker off the coat rack.

Taking hold of her courage and the bag as tightly as she could, Corrie made her way down the darkened stairs then over to her desk. She scrabbled in the darkness for the master key to the cabins and then stumbled to the side door. She paused, hoping for a break in the storm, but the rain only came down harder. She took a deep breath, pulled up her hood, and opened the door.

The wind nearly forced her back into the store. She pulled the door shut behind her and, shielding her face against the stinging raindrops, moved in the direction of J.D.'s tent. She missed the step off the walkway and her foot sank into a puddle up to the ankle, nearly causing her to drop the bag and fall on her face. Too late, she realized she should have brought a flashlight. She flinched when another flash of lightning illuminated the campground, but it helped her get her bearings and she made a splashing run for J.D.'s tent.

"J.D.!" she screamed, not sure if he could hear her over the noise of nylon flapping in the wind. She gasped when he suddenly materialized in front of her.

"What the hell are you doing out here?" he shouted. "You're soaked to the skin!"

Corrie resisted the temptation to get into an argument right there in the rain. "Come on!" she yelled, running toward the cabins. He caught up to her and grabbed the bag out of her hands and followed her onto the porch of A-6. She fumbled the key out of her pocket and opened the door.

The darkness in the cabin was immediately dispelled by a

beam of light. Corrie turned to J.D., who was holding a small, powerful flashlight, and swiped the wet strands of hair out of her eyes. He pushed the door shut and turned to her, his eyes and mouth grim in the shadowy light. She took a deep breath and forced a smile. "Glad one of us brought a flashlight," she said, her smile weakening.

Streams of water trickled down his face and puddled at their feet. He ran his hand over his soaking wet hair. "Are you out of your mind, Corrie? What possessed you to pull a stunt like that?"

"I was worried about you," she said, trying to keep the hurt out of her voice. She was glad that the dim light prevented him from seeing the tears in her eyes. "Your tent is a total loss and you're soaked as well. I thought the least I could do was open up the cabin for you and bring you some towels and a blanket," she said, indicating the bag he still held. "You can't sleep out in the rain."

He took a deep breath and rubbed the raindrops off his face. "I took shelter on the back patio, under the awning."

"Why didn't you come to the camp store?"

"I didn't want to wake you."

"So you'd rather drown out on the patio? Now who's out of their mind?" she snapped.

He shook his head. "Okay, I'm sorry," he said, his voice subdued. "I guess if you'd done the same, I'd be a little irate, too."

"A little?" Corrie said, raising her brows. J.D. laughed.

"Right," he said and swept a hand toward the bag and around the cabin. "Thanks. I appreciate this, Corrie. You didn't have to do this."

She was going to argue, but another crash of thunder made her shriek and jump. He dropped the bag and reached for her and she clutched at him with trembling fingers.

"It's okay," he said, pulling her into his arms. "You're safe. We're both safe. Everything's okay." She couldn't stop shaking; the realization that she had actually gone out into a thunderstorm, exposing herself to the terrors and dangers of lightning, wind, and rain, had suddenly sunk in. Despite the blush heating her cheeks at being held in J.D.'s muscular arms, she couldn't make herself let go. And it didn't seem like J.D. minded at all.

"The rain... flooding... the wind... I saw your tent...," she stammered, not sure if J.D. would understand. Her teeth were chattering, but not from the weather, and she buried her face in his chest.

"I know," he said softly, rubbing her back to soothe her. It only succeeded in heightening her embarrassment and her reluctance to step away. "It's okay, Corrie. I just wish you hadn't come out in the storm to help me. Now you're all wet, you might catch cold...."

"Nah," she said, forcing herself to pull back although J.D.'s arms still remained around her. She smiled, despite the fact that he couldn't see her face in the darkness. "As warm as the weather has been lately, I doubt my health is in any danger."

He brought the flashlight up to where their faces were illuminated. His face was still grim though the lines had softened. "I think you need to dry off as soon as possible before you catch a chill."

"What's the point?" Corrie stepped out of his embrace and wrapped her own arms around herself. She was glad the semi-darkness hid the blush that heated her face as she fought off a shiver. "I'm just going to get wet again when I go back to the camp store."

"You're not going back out into that storm!" J.D. growled, his eyes narrowing. He took a step toward her and she backed up till the backs of her knees hit the edge of the double bed, almost throwing her off balance. Her cabins didn't have much furniture; one double bed and a set of twin bunk beds, a mini fridge, a small table, and two chairs which most guests moved out to the porch upon arrival to allow more walking room inside the cabin. Corrie had reached the limit of where she could move inside the ten-foot by twelve-foot space that made up the cabin's floor plan and she half-hoped J.D. wasn't going to move any closer into her personal space.

"I can't stay here, J.D.," she said as firmly as she could. His scowl deepened.

"You don't trust me?" His voice had a thin thread of hurt running through it, and Corrie fought the urge to reach out to touch his arm.

"Of course I do," she said, not sure if she was being completely honest about trusting or not trusting him—or herself. "But it wouldn't be proper." That was what her parents and Jackie would say, and that was what came to her mind immediately. J.D.'s brows rose.

"Under the circumstances, propriety seems to be a pretty minor concern," he said mildly. "If the weather is bad enough for you to risk coming out here to make sure I have shelter, then it's wrong of me to expect you to go back out into that same weather when you're already under shelter. You're safe here. In every way," he added pointedly.

"I know." A flash of lightning heralded another clap of thunder and she flinched, but this time it was more of a low rumble. She took a deep breath. "I think the storm is breaking up. I should head back."

"I'll walk you," J.D. said, his tone leaving no room for argument. He was soaked to the skin already anyway, so she just nodded.

The wind had calmed to a stiff breeze that slapped raindrops against their faces, preventing them from talking. They walked quickly, J.D.'s flashlight beam helping them to avoid the worst of the puddles. They reached the side door and J.D. opened it up for her. "Thanks," she said, as she stepped inside and shrugged out of her jacket. He shook his head.

"You didn't lock the door when you left?"

"It didn't occur to me that I had to," she said mildly. "The 'perps', as you cops call them, are all in custody and I was only gone a few minutes. And if the rain hadn't let up, I'd be standing out there in a downpour trying to get the key into the lock. But you're welcome to check the place out, if it'll make you feel better," she added, thinking they were right back to where they were before.

J.D. accepted the invitation and quickly walked through the camp store, checking for any signs of anyone entering since he'd left earlier. "Are your two buddies upstairs?"

"Yep. Renfro, boy! You okay?" she called and the old dog answered with a "woof" that sounded both happy and relieved. Oliver added an affirmative "meow" and Corrie grinned. "The upstairs is clear." J.D. nodded, apparently satisfied.

"Okay, well, I guess I'll head back to the cabin now."

"Thanks, J.D.," she said. "You really didn't have to walk me back."

"And you didn't have to come out in the first place," he said with a grin. "But I have to admit I'm glad you did." He stopped, his gaze intensifying, and Corrie wondered if inviting him in had been a bad idea. He stepped back before she said anything. "I'd better let you go get out of those wet clothes and I should go back to the cabin," he said. "Sure you're all right?"

"Now that I know you're not drowning in your tent, I'm fine," she said lightly, her smile feeling forced. She wondered why she felt a lump in her throat and if she was just imagining the look of disappointment in J.D.'s eyes. Maybe he had been expecting an invitation to stay. She wiped the raindrops off her cheeks, hoping to hide the heat and color she felt rising in her face. "Thanks for walking me back. Good night," she blurted and he stiffened.

"Good night," he said, then turned and disappeared into the rain-soaked darkness.

Chapter 18

J.D. let himself into the cabin and shut the door behind him a little harder than necessary. He hadn't intended to make Corrie feel like she was backed into a corner by his offer to let her stay in the cabin till the storm ended. Her response was probably justified, but his feelings were a bit raw—by her implication that he wasn't trustworthy, and by the fact that she hadn't seemed thrilled at the prospect of being in the cabin alone with him on a rainy night.

He automatically hit the light switch, his momentary confusion at the darkness irritating him as he remembered the power outage. He shook his head and rubbed his eyes to wipe away the raindrops as well as the image of Corrie with her rain-soaked hair cascading down her shoulders like a black velvet waterfall. Funny what seeing her with her hair loose did to him; he had to admit it was probably best that she had turned down his invitation. Maybe she was a better judge of his will power than he was.

Gloomily, he set the flashlight down on the table and set about stripping off his clothes and drying off. He pulled the sheets, blanket, and pillow out of the bag and made up the double bed. He crumpled up the bag, instead of his usual habit of smoothing it out and folding it, and flung it in the direction of the trash can near the door. It hit the flashlight as squarely as if he'd aimed at it and sent it rolling off the table. He lunged toward it but missed and it went out as it hit the floor.

He groaned in frustration as he dropped to the floor and began groping in the darkness for the flashlight. His forehead came into sharp contact with the wooden table leg and he muttered a curse as he continued to inch forward. His hand closed around the slim metal handle and he pressed the switch. A soft "click" and nothing else. The room remained pitch black.

He sighed and rolled onto his back, still under the table, and slapped the flashlight into his palm, hoping to jar it back to life. With his luck he knew that if he tried to take the batteries out, he'd end up having to search for them next. Come on, give me a break.

The lights in the cabin flickered and came on. He blinked then realized that he'd left the switch on earlier. Thank you! He began to inch out from under the table when he caught sight of a small envelope, stuck haphazardly on the underside of the tabletop near the edge. He reached up and tugged on it. It took a little effort to peel away whatever was holding it in place but then he crawled out and laid it on the table. He frowned at what was holding the envelope in place—an adhesive bandage. A faint alarm went off in his head which urged him to handle the envelope by the edges and he managed to open it with a minimum of damage. A folded sheet of paper slid out and popped partially open... just enough for him to see the words "Dear Corrie" scrawled at the top.

He snatched up his wet clothes and pulled them on, his heart hammering. He grabbed his cell phone and punched in Corrie's personal number as he fastened his belt one-handed. "J.D.?" Corrie sounded wide-awake.

"Are you okay?" J.D. barked, flicking off the cabin's light switch and scanning the campground. The security lights had come back on and he could see that the light in Corrie's apartment was on.

"Yes. What's wrong?" she asked, her voice tense.

"Shut your lights off and lock the door to the apartment. Don't open it until the sheriff or I get there, understood?"

"What...?" He cut her off before she could ask anything else and, as he punched in the number to Sutton's personal cell phone, he nodded grimly as the light in her apartment went out.

"What's up, Wilder?" Sutton answered on the first ring despite the late hour. Did the man ever sleep?

"Sutton, get over here to the campground. I found something in the cabin." He didn't bother to explain what he was doing in the cabin; the sheriff would have it figured out before he finished talking.

"Already on my way. Did you call Mike?"

"Mike?" J.D. said, his mind blank.

"Deputy Ramirez. He's still there, isn't he?" Sutton's voice became sharp as a razor and J.D. let out an expletive.

"I forgot all about him!" Dimly he heard the sheriff put in a call to his deputy.

"He's not answering his radio. Corrie?" Sutton said tersely.

"I just talked to her. She's fine. I'm on my way there now," J.D. said as he slipped out the door and ran for the campground store.

~

Corrie stood by the door, the phone still clutched in her hand, and stared at the locked knob, as if afraid it would suddenly take on a life of its own and start to turn or rattle. Following J.D.'s orders, she had switched off the overhead light but the plug-in nightlight near the bathroom door still gave off a faint illumination. She wondered if she should shut it off as well, but she didn't dare step away from the door. She hoped J.D. would call her when he and Rick were at the door. How else would she know, locked up safe in the apartment? He hadn't said so, but surely that was the plan, he'd call her and....

The nightlight went out, plunging the apartment into total darkness once more.

Corrie gasped and jumped, her heart hammering. She couldn't see a thing; the power had gone off once again. She wasn't going to wait for J.D. to call her first. Her fingers shaking, she hit the "on" button on the phone and waited for a dial tone. The phone remained silent.

Frantically, she fumbled with different buttons until the realization hit her that the cordless phone wouldn't work if the power was out. That meant J.D. couldn't call her, either. Which meant she wouldn't know if he and Rick were at the door downstairs. Should she go down and wait? But J.D. had told her not to leave the apartment, not until he and Rick had arrived. But how would she know? He'd knock, of course, but how would she know it was them? Because there was a chance it wouldn't be them or else J.D. wouldn't have warned her to lock the doors....

Renfro let out a low growl and she jumped again. She groped in the darkness near her side, but couldn't feel her old dog's comforting bulk. Where was he? "It's okay, Ren," she whispered and then gasped when she heard the sound of fists pounding on the side door down below.

"Corrie!" Both Rick's and J.D.'s voices came to her dimly through the building and she unlocked the apartment door and hurried down the stairwell as quickly as she could. The headlights of Rick's Tahoe silhouetted the two men in the doorway; there was no mistaking their distinctive shadows. She made her way to the side door and unlocked it.

"You all right?" J.D. asked as he and Rick slipped into the camp store. J.D. was still soaked to the skin. Rick was wearing a dark blue windbreaker, slick with raindrops, and his gun was in his hand, down by his side, and he reached for the light switch.

"I'm fine, but the power's out again," she said. She held up the phone. “I tried to call you....”

“That explains why you wouldn't answer your phone,” J.D. said as Rick turned on his flashlight.

“Doesn't explain why the safety lights are on in the campground,” he said in a low voice and Corrie felt a chill slip down her back. Rick's headlights had kept her from noticing that the lights around the pool and on the poles near each cabin were on. From upstairs, Renfro let out another growl that ended in a sharp bark. The sheriff keyed his radio and called Deputy Ramirez. She'd forgotten he was supposed to still be on guard. Silence answered Rick's call.

Corrie sucked in a sharp breath and she heard Rick release the safety on his firearm. “Wilder?”

“I got the upstairs, you go around outside,” J.D.'s voice was a barely audible whisper and Corrie felt terror twist her stomach.

“Corrie, stay out of sight,” Rick instructed, taking her arm and urging her toward her desk behind the counter. She grabbed for his hand as he released her arm.

“Rick, you can't go out there! And J.D.'s unarmed! If someone hurt Mike, they're probably still out there... up there....”

“Backup is on the way,” Rick said quietly. “We can't just sit here and wait. They might get away.”

“You ready?” J.D.'s voice came across the room, as low as a rumble of thunder. Rick squeezed Corrie's hand.

“Let's move,” he said. He released her hand and moved back to the side door. Corrie listened to the rustle of his windbreaker and was relieved to hear only the faintest tinkle as he stilled the bells over the door as he opened it and slipped outside. She watched his shadow pass the windows, moving swiftly but cautiously, the wind and occasional splashes of rain silencing any sound he might have made. She sensed, rather than saw or heard, J.D. making his way up the stairs and she once again felt dread settle in her stomach like a boulder at the thought of him facing danger unarmed.

She waited in the silent darkness, wondering what was happening, when she heard the faint creak of hinges as a door opened. She tensed; the sound hadn't come from the stairwell. She glanced in the direction of the laundry room; the alarm buzzer on that door was electronic and was probably out along with the lights. But why was the door unlocked in the first place? She usually unlocked it first thing in the morning. It was a habit, but surely, she had locked it at the end of the day... or thought she had.

It was the first night Rick and J.D. hadn't checked her locks. With all that had happened today, she must have forgotten. Why had she even unlocked it in the first place? The campground was closed! How stupid.... Hoping she couldn't be seen in the darkness, she edged toward the side door.

"Going somewhere, little sister?" Corrie froze as a high-powered flashlight clicked on, the beam aimed directly at her eyes, and her heart nearly stopped. The voice, rough and hoarse, could have belonged to a man, but the figure that moved out of the shadows in the camp store was petite and slim, nearly a foot shorter than Corrie, with cropped black hair and a face that seemed to be all hard angles. Her brows were drawn together over eyes that were mere slits of fury. Her lips were stretched in a tight smile that was almost a smirk. But what made Corrie take a step back was the gun in the woman's hand, pointed straight at her. "What's the matter, Corrie? I thought you were all about family. You don't seem happy to see me."

"Who are you?" Corrie managed to keep her voice from trembling even though her mouth was dry and her knees were shaking. She wondered if she could make a dash for the door, but it seemed like the woman could read her mind.

"Don't think about running for it," she said. "You'll be sorry if you make a move I don't tell you to make. Don't make me pull the trigger. Come over here, in front of the counter, and make sure your hands are where I can see them and that there's nothing in them. Move slowly."

Corrie noted that the woman's voice was only slightly less steadier than the hand that held the gun. Swallowing hard, she made herself follow the woman's directions; in spite of her initial fear, she hated being ordered around and whoever this was, the gun in her hand was the only thing keeping Corrie from defying the woman's commands.

That and the knowledge that Rick and J.D. would be putting themselves in danger if she did anything to provoke the intruder.

Praying that the woman wasn't aware that J.D. was in the stairwell, she moved slowly, keeping her hands palms out at shoulder height. She moved slowly, the light shining in her eyes causing her to squint and blinding her to what might be in her way.

"All right, that's close enough," the woman snapped, dropping the light beam to just above Corrie's waist. Corrie blinked away the wateriness in her eyes and gasped when she saw that the woman was not much more than a few feet away and had raised the gun until it was practically in Corrie's face. “No more fooling around,” the woman said, her voice and the gun both wavering dangerously. “Let's finish this. Where is it?”

“Where is what?” Corrie asked, hoping the woman wouldn't think she was just buying time. “What are you looking for?”

“Quit playing games, little sister!” the woman said, stamping her foot. Corrie smothered a gasp, hoping the gun wouldn't go off accidentally... or on purpose, either. “You know what I'm looking for!” Corrie didn't answer immediately; she had no idea what she could say. The woman went on, “I'm looking for what rightfully belongs to me!”

“And... and that is...?” Corrie said, struggling to keep her own voice strong and steady. She wondered what had happened to Rick and J.D. and while a more noble, heroic part of her was glad that they were, for the moment, out of harm's way, another rapidly growing and decidedly less altruistic part of her was wondering why the hell the cavalry hadn't arrived yet.

“Don't pretend, Corrie.” The woman's voice sounded choked with tears and Corrie found herself swallowing hard and frantically searching her mind for an answer. “You know perfectly well what I'm talking about. The fact that our dad favored one daughter over the other, just because he favored the one's mother over the other!”

Corrie's mouth went dry. “You're Bill Woods' daughter?”

“Supposedly,” the woman snorted. She gave a shaky laugh. “We're sisters, aren't we?”

“I don't know what you're talking about,” Corrie said sharply. Out of the corner of her eye, she detected a slight movement of shadow in the stairwell. J.D. Her heart began to pound harder and she forced herself to keep her focus on the person in front of her and not give away J.D.'s presence. “Bill Woods wasn't my father!”

“So you've said, over and over,” the woman sneered. In the dim light, Corrie could make out the woman's lips twisted in an expression of cynicism or rage... or both. “You've got the police and a couple of other people convinced of that. You've even got them convinced that I'm the villain!”

“I don't even know who you are!” Corrie said, trying to keep the surge of anger out of her voice. “I've never seen you before and whatever it is you think I have that belongs to you, I wish you'd quit playing games and just say what it is!”

“You know what it is!” The woman's screech made Corrie jump and her heart lodge in her throat again. Before she could say anything, Rick's voice came from the darkness behind the woman.

"Sheriff's department. Put down your weapon."

The gun wavered dangerously and Corrie sucked in a deep breath. The woman cleared her throat. "You put YOUR weapon down, Sheriff, or I'll pull the trigger. If you shoot me in retaliation, so what? What have I got to lose? She's already taken everything that should have belonged to me." A soft click indicated that the safety had been released on the gun in the woman's hands. "Don't push me, Sheriff."

"Put your weapon down." Rick's voice, calm and authoritative, was closer. "No one needs to get hurt." The woman laughed.

"Too late for that," she said in a tear-choked voice. "There's nothing left to be done but for my dear little sister to admit to our relationship and accept me as her family. That includes the family business and any inheritance my father—our father—left!"

"What are you talking about?" Corrie couldn't keep the frustration and bewilderment that was whirling through her mind from making her voice break. Rick's shadow, approaching the woman from the side closest the front door, morphed into a recognizable form, his eyes and gun trained grimly on the woman.

"Layla Woodson," Rick said and the woman's eyes flicked toward him for an instant before she refocused her glare and aim back on Corrie. "Put the gun down and step back."

"I'm not going to play games, Sheriff," she said. "None of this 'I'm going to count to three and pull the trigger' crap. You'd better put YOUR gun down and step back, or I'll blow my little sister away without warning! NOW!" she yelled suddenly and Corrie gasped and squeezed her eyes shut.

"Okay," Rick said and Corrie's eyes popped open in surprise. Perhaps no one else could detect the change in Rick's tone, but she knew something was up.... "All right, there's my gun." Corrie heard a "thunk" and the sound of metal skidding across tile as Rick's weapon landed somewhere between her and the agitated woman and became one with the darkness. She hoped to heaven that Rick was bluffing and had another weapon—anything—on him. "I'm unarmed now," he said slowly and calmly, "so you can put the gun down, Ms. Woodson...."

"DON'T call me that!" she snapped and Corrie's heart somersaulted as the gun shook even more violently. "I never want to hear that name or the name Bill Woods again! Pay attention, Sheriff! I've been robbed, okay? All my life, everything went to my dear little sister, Daddy's little princess... everything! Not a day went by that I wasn't reminded who was really important in my father's life... and it sure as hell wasn't me!"

"Stop it!" Corrie cried, forgetting the gun wavering a few feet away. She could hear sirens approaching though they still seemed to be miles away. "Bill Woods was NOT my father! He was nothing to me and neither are you! I don't have anything that belongs to you or to Bill Woods!"

"I'm not talking about Bill Woods!" Layla Woodson shrieked, forgetting about the gun and the flashlight as she reached up as if to cover her ears.

Rick lunged out of the shadows toward the young woman.

"Rick!" Corrie's scream was drowned out by the roar of gunfire. Rick let out a sound that was part grunt, part cry of pain, and he staggered backward towards Corrie, clutching his side, before he fell heavily to the floor.

"Rick! NO!" She dropped to her knees and scrambled across the floor to where he lay. Dimly, she saw J.D.'s dark form engulf the stock-still form of Layla Woodson and grab the gun from her hand. He twisted her arm behind her back and snatched the flashlight out of her grip and aimed the beam at Rick's gasping form. "Rick! Oh, my God, Rick, no, NO!" Corrie cried as she threw herself at him, pulling his head and shoulders onto her lap.

"It was loaded," Layla Woodson's husky voice was a shaky whisper, thick with incredulity. "Oh, God, it was loaded. They told me it wasn't. Oh, dear God, I shot him. I killed the sheriff."

"No," J.D. hissed through gritted teeth. The lights suddenly came on, their harsh, flourescent glare flooding the campground store. Corrie glanced up at J.D.; his face was twisted with rage and disbelief as he shook his head. Layla Woodson winced and Corrie knew that J.D.'s grip had tightened painfully on the woman's arm. Flashing red and blue lights shot through the windows, turning the room into a horrific parody of a fun house. She heard one deputy coming in through the laundry room door and another opening the front door as she cradled Rick in her arms. His face was twisted in pain and he was clutching his side. Gingerly, she pried his fingers away from the torn fabric of his windbreaker, hoping she wasn't going to make the wound worse....

To her shock, there was no blood. None on the windbreaker, on the floor beneath Rick, nor on his or her fingers. She stared numbly for a second before she looked at Rick's face.

His eyes met hers as he fumbled for the zipper on his

windbreaker and pulled it open, revealing the black neoprene cover of his bullet-proof vest. The bullet was imbedded firmly at the very edge, at the bottom of his ribcage.

"I think we'll go with this one," he muttered, closing his eyes and laying his head back as Corrie burst into tears.

Chapter 19

“That wasn't funny, Rick.”

“Believe me, I know,” Sutton muttered, giving Corrie a half smile before turning his attention to J.D. “Layla Woodson safely locked away?”

“Didn't take much. She let the deputies take her away without a fight,” J.D. said. “She kept saying she didn't know the gun was loaded. In fact, she kept insisting that the gun wasn't supposed to be loaded at all.”

“One bullet?” The sheriff winced, doing his best to maintain an official demeanor despite the EMS worker who was tightly taping up his side. Sutton had, predictably, declined a trip to the ER but had to give in to both Corrie's and J.D.'s insistence that he allow the emergency medical workers to check him over. The preliminary findings were a possible cracked rib and some deep bruising. Considering that the bullet could have caused a great deal of damage if the vest had failed to do its job, he was in great shape, including his characteristic impatience. He waved off the offer of a painkiller or sedative and thanked the workers as they left the camp store, then he eased his undershirt down over his bandages and slipped his uniform shirt back on.

“Just the one. Presumably meant for Corrie,” J.D. added, suppressing a shudder as he glanced at her. She looked like she could use a sedative herself. He knew he sure could. “I guess it's possible she didn't know that the gun had a bullet in the chamber, but she keeps insisting that 'they' told her it wasn't loaded and she didn't even know how to check if it was loaded or not. She claims she only knew how to release the safety and that she never intended to pull the trigger. And 'they' told her to throw the breaker in the laundry room to shut off the power in the campground store.”

“How's Mike?” the sheriff said, his expression growing stonier for a second.

“Got a whopper of a headache, but no lasting damage. He was shoved under a picnic table at the far end of the patio. Says he was patrolling around the patio when he saw the lights in the building go out and the last thing he remembers is reaching for his gun. Miss Woodson swears she didn't take him out, says she didn't even know there was a deputy on duty. That was something else that 'they' must have done."

"And who are 'they'?" Corrie demanded, crossing her arms in front of her. J.D. didn't think she felt a chill from the abating wind and rain, but neither he nor Sutton tried to stop her as she headed for the coffee maker and started a pot of coffee. "It sounds like someone or more than one person sent her after me to find out... what?"

"She's not saying who 'they' are," J.D. said, shaking his head, as he and the sheriff moved to join her at the courtesy table. "But she insists that 'they' told her that she could get all the information she wanted from Corrie with a little, ah, persuasion," he added.

"And what information are 'they' so sure that I have?" Corrie snapped, blinking rapidly to hide her tears. J.D. stopped and looked at the sheriff. Sutton was chewing his lower lip. Corrie noticed. "What?" she said, giving them each a sharp glance.

"Wilder found something in the cabin," the sheriff said without hesitation, knowing there was no easy way to bring it out. "We were coming over to show you when we got distracted." He picked up his windbreaker from the counter, reached into the pocket, and pulled out a plastic evidence bag with the envelope in it. "I haven't had a chance to process it for prints or any other evidence, but it's addressed to you and it's signed by Bill Woods."

She seemed to freeze as she stared at the bag that Sutton held out to her. She looked at J.D., her eyes wide with disbelief and shock. She reached for the bag as if afraid it would explode or catch fire when she touched it. "I can open it?" she asked. She sounded as if she wanted the answer to be "no".

The sheriff shrugged. "It's yours," he said quietly.

She took the bag and removed the envelope. She looked at J.D. "My name's not on this," she said.

"I found it taped under the table in the cabin," he said. "I opened it to see what was inside."

"You read it?" Her voice cracked and her face turned white.

He didn't hesitate. "Yes. And you need to read it, too."

She glanced from him to the sheriff. "He told me what it said," Sutton confirmed, and she took a deep breath and drew out the paper that was inside, her hands shaking slightly. The note was rather lengthy; the handwriting was small and the whole front of the sheet was filled. Corrie was a fast reader. It only took a few seconds before she let an incredulous "WHAT?!" burst from her lips.

"Easy," Sutton said, reaching for her shoulder. She gulped and her breath came in heaves as she finished reading the letter.

"This is insane! This can't be true!" she cried, looking wildly from J.D. to Sutton. She held the paper away from her as if it were contaminated.

"Can't it?" Sutton said, his voice gentle and his grip on her shoulder tightened. "Are you sure?"

"I... Rick... no... no...." She slumped against the counter and tears rolled down her cheeks. Her body shook with sobs for a few seconds then she rallied. "Uncle Bill is mistaken. He's wrong, dead wrong!" She flinched at her own words. "There's no way that Layla Woodson is Billy's daughter!"

The sheriff sighed and looked at J.D. with a shrug. "Corrie, I don't want to believe it either, but it explains a lot of things. It explains how someone else might feel entitled to a share of the Black Horse or any inheritance Billy might have left...."

"If Billy had any other children," Corrie said, her voice colder than J.D. had ever heard it, "he would have never cut them out of his will. He was far too generous and fair-minded to pretend that they didn't exist. No matter how much it would have hurt me, he wouldn't have kept this a secret from me... or my mother! For that matter, there's no way they wouldn't have been a part of our lives all along!"

"If," Sutton said, raising his voice over Corrie's, "if Billy had known about them, Corrie. Think about it. Is it possible that Bill Woods knew something about this that Billy didn't? That maybe he kept it secret until he could use it? Now with Billy gone...."

Corrie shook her head and J.D. cleared his throat.

"He claims that back in the day, he and Billy and another friend of theirs...."

"Toby Willis," Corrie said stiffly. "I told you about him. He's a distant cousin. My family's known his family for years. They still live on the rez."

"...in their younger days, just after your parents got married, went on a trip to go look at a piece of land that Bill Woods had found near Lubbock. He and Toby Willis were thinking of buying it and Billy had offered to help them develop it into a campground, much like the Black Horse." J.D. gestured to the letter. "They were young, they were stupid, Billy was a newlywed and the stress of starting a business and married life without the support of his family was taking its toll. It was part business, part pleasure trip and this friend, Willis, knew a guy who owned a bar. You know it could be true, Corrie," he finished quietly.

"Billy was always warning us about the dangers of mixing alcohol with stupid friends," the sheriff commented. Corrie shot him a look that J.D. couldn't decipher, and she shook her head.

"This is just as impossible for me to believe as it was to believe that Bill Woods was my father," she said, her face blank, her voice numb with pain. She sounded as if she were trying to convince herself. Sutton shifted restlessly.

"It opens up more possibilities as to who wanted to kill Bill Woods and who threatened you and the Black Horse," he said, his voice returning to its authoritative crispness. He nodded at the note. "Toby Willis. You said you know his family and they live on the reservation. When was the last time you saw Toby Willis himself?"

She shook her head. "Who knows, Rick? I mean, I know who he is and I know his family, but that doesn't mean we see each other regularly or that we're close friends, even though we're related. I think I've seen his mother or sister a few times in the last several years, but it was by chance. I mean, Toby Willis was Billy's age and even Billy didn't spend a lot of time with him, not that I remember. You don't think he...."

"Would you recognize him if you saw him?" J.D. asked. She started to answer, then hesitated.

"I'm not sure," she admitted at last. "I have an idea, but it's vague." Her eyes narrowed as if trying to look deep into her memory. "Wait a minute, I think there's some old pictures in a box of things that belonged to my dad." The sheriff raised a brow.

"You have that upstairs in your apartment?" he asked. She nodded.

"It's in the bedside filing cabinet, the one that—" Her eyes went wide and her mouth dropped open.

"Maybe it WASN'T personal papers that intruder was after!" the sheriff muttered as the three of them ran for the stairs.

~

Corrie's heart hammered in her throat as she pulled aside the embroidered table cover and reached for the handle on the bottom drawer.

"Did the person who broke in open the bottom drawer?" J.D. asked. Corrie shook her head.

"No, they just opened the top one and it tipped the cabinet

over before they had a chance to look in the bottom one." She pulled the drawer open, a split-second before it occurred to her that maybe she should be careful of preserving fingerprints. She pushed back a few empty hanging files. In the bottom of the drawer was a flat, sturdy cardboard box decorated with faded pastel pink and blue teddy bears. She looked up into the confused faces of the two men and allowed a small smile. "It's the box my baby book came in. Mom never threw anything away."

She opened the lid and sifted through old greeting cards, postcards, prayer cards, and photos. She fished out an old Polaroid picture and nodded before handing it to Rick. He took it and frowned.

"Billy kept a picture of the man who tried to involve him in illegal activities and made a pass at his wife?" he asked, disbelief tinging his voice.

"No," Corrie said. "He kept a picture of the man whom he believed to be his best friend. Billy wasn't one to hold grudges, Rick, and you know that; the only reason he cut Uncle Bill out of our lives was to protect me and my mother."

J.D. leaned closer to look at the picture. The colors were washed-out and there were cracks around the edges. It showed three young men leaning against the hood of a pickup truck. They appeared to be in their early twenties and, from the grins on their faces, it was evident that they were at some kind of party. Bill Woods was clearly the one in the middle; his blond hair and light-colored eyes set him apart from the other two. The men flanking him almost appeared to be brothers. One wore a black cowboy hat with a large feather tucked into the band, the other wore a blue baseball cap and dark sunglasses. "My dad's the one in the cowboy hat," Corrie said for J.D.'s benefit.

"You look like him," J.D. said, glancing at her and back at the picture. "But his friend, Toby Willis, sort of resembles him, too."

"What, all Indians look alike?" Corrie said with a wry smile. Before J.D. could say anything, she added, "He's a distant cousin of my dad's, so I guess that explains any similarities. But our families haven't been close since...." She stopped as a thought occurred to her.

Rick looked up. "Since...?"

Corrie shook her head. "Since before Billy and Uncle Bill had their falling out." She took a deep breath. "I don't know why I never thought of it before... maybe because he wasn't such a big part of our lives. I mean, Billy and Uncle Bill would mention him from time to time, but always as a 'remember when' type of story. Billy used to change the subject quickly whenever Toby Willis came up," she added. "I wonder if Uncle Bill kept in touch with him after he and Billy ended their friendship." Rick cleared his throat.

"Can you tell me how to get in touch with Toby Willis or his family?" Corrie grimaced.

"I'm sure I can, Rick, but you know how touchy relations are between me and Billy's family. My family," she corrected. "My grandmother has always hated any hint of scandal and if she thinks I'm throwing another family member under the bus to protect Billy...."

"You're not throwing anyone under the bus. You're assisting in an official sheriff's department investigation into a murder committed on your property... a murder which happens to be of someone you know and which occurred in conjunction with a written threat that was directed at you," J.D. said dryly. "Surely your grandmother would understand that."

"Maybe YOUR grandmother would," Corrie snapped and felt guilty when J.D. stiffened and his face turned red. She sighed. "I'm sorry, J.D.," she said. "It's just that my grandmother... she's got a way of making you second-guess everything you do, no matter how right it is. She's always looking at the worst of every situation."

"I'd like to see her find a 'best' of this situation," Rick grumbled. Corrie nodded, pulling an old black address book out of the drawer.

"You're right," she said as she flipped through the pages. "But you'd probably have better luck checking the Mescalero phone directory. The last number I have listed has a notation in red next to it—'not in service'—and, judging from how faded the ink is, it was probably made over ten years ago."

Rick was shaking his head as he scanned his phone screen. "There's only one Willis listed in Mescalero, first initial 'C', and no street address given. I'll have to have someone make inquiries and...."

"Meaning Toby Willis is a person of interest and you're going to have to bring him in for questioning," Corrie interrupted. "No need to sugar-coat it for me, Rick."

He gave her a grim smile. "I didn't think that's what I was doing, but you're right. We need to know where Toby Willis is and where he's been and just how close in touch he's kept with Bill Woods all these years." He grimaced as he turned toward the stairs.

"Any chance on convincing you to take it easy, Sheriff?" J.D. asked as Rick unconsciously gripped his side.

"I'll take it easy after we find Bill Woods' murderer and find out who sent Layla Woodson to threaten Corrie. In the meantime, Wilder, I'd appreciate some help."

"Name it," J.D. said, straightening up, his eyes alert.

"I need to find out what, if anything, Robert Moreno knew about Toby Willis. I had to let him go; I didn't have anything positive to pin on him. He claims he's never heard of the Carsons and he didn't hire them to spy on anyone. And suddenly they claimed they'd never seen or heard of him before, either. Moreno said he's had enough of all this and he'd be leaving for Lubbock in the morning, but he'd be at the River's Edge for tonight. He's not a huge fan of mine and he's not going to want to share info with me, but maybe if you approach him, unofficially, with the news that the I've been shot...."

J.D. grinned. "No need to tell him you're alive and well, right?"

"Don't lie, but don't give him too much good news," Rick said. J.D. nodded.

"In the meantime, what are you going to do, Sheriff?" he asked. Rick looked at Corrie.

"We're going to go talk to Elsa Kaydahzinne again. And, no, this time we're not giving fair warning that we're coming over," he said, giving Corrie a hard glare. After what had transpired in her own home, she wasn't going to argue with him; she nodded. "I think it's a little odd that not once in any conversation that we've had with her did the name Toby Willis ever come up."

"I agree," she said, fighting to keep the trembling out of her voice. She wrapped her arms around herself. "If she knew so much about what went on between Billy and Uncle Bill, she had to have known there was another person who might have been involved." Rick and J.D. exchanged a glance.

"Any chance that there's a connection between Elsa Kaydahzinne and Toby Willis?" Rick asked.

Corrie felt her face go white. "I don't know," she said, feeling tears sting her eyes. "On the rez, there are so many distant family connections... for all I know, I'm related to the Kaydahzinnes and don't even know it!"

“Terrific,” J.D. muttered. “You want me to see if Layla Woodson knew anything about this Toby Willis? Or if Moreno knew about her?”

“Find out everything you can and call me as soon as you know,” Rick said. A low rumble of thunder, like the growl of an angry animal, reached them from outside; the storm wasn't over yet. As if by instinct, the three of them moved closer together, the two men flanking Corrie. She took a deep breath and straightened her shoulders.

“Okay, let's go find out what we can before the storm starts up again and makes things harder on us all. I don't know if Mrs. Kaydahzinne stays up late or not, but the sooner we get over there, the better.”

Chapter 20

J.D. stopped long enough to put on his rain gear before mounting his Harley and heading for the River's Edge Bed and Breakfast. Raindrops splashed the helmet visor, forcing him to go slower than he would have liked, as the darkness and rain-slicked roads made travel dangerous. It was well after nine o'clock. He slowed even more as he passed by the sheriff's department building and the county jail. The thought occurred to him that perhaps Layla Woodson might have some knowledge about Robert Moreno. He was certain that the sheriff shared his distrust of the slick investigator and Miss Woodson might be rattled enough from having shot the sheriff to tell them a few things she might know about him.

He pulled into the parking lot and coasted to a spot near the door. The doors were locked and only the dispatcher and one deputy were on duty in the building. He rapped on the door and was greeted by Deputy Bobby Fletcher who had his gun drawn and a nervous look on his face. His brow furrowed when he saw J.D. and punched the button on the wall speaker.

"Lt. Wilder? What are you doing here?" he asked. J.D. tried not to flinch at the fact that Deputy Fletcher had chosen to use the hand holding the gun to activate the intercom button.

"Can you let me in, Deputy? I need to speak to someone you're holding." J.D. said. He didn't want to raise his voice, but Deputy Fletcher seemed to not understand him over the sound of the rising wind and he had to repeat himself before comprehension showed on the deputy's face.

"You want to speak to a prisoner, Lt. Wilder? That Layla Woodson that was brought in earlier?" J.D. groaned; Deputy Fletcher had no clue as to what "discretion" meant. "The sheriff say you could talk to her?"

"Yes," J.D. said as loudly as he dared, not feeling one bit guilty for ignoring Suttons' directive not to lie. Besides, he was talking about Robert Moreno, not Deputy Fletcher. He just wanted to get out of the rain, out of earshot of anyone who might be listening, and in to talk to Layla Woodson as soon as possible. To his relief, Deputy Fletcher unlocked the door and ushered J.D. into the building. He cleared his throat and adjusted his utility belt.

"It'll take a few minutes to prepare an interrogation room...," Deputy Fletcher began, but J.D. cut him off.

"That's not necessary," J.D. began, then a thought occurred to him. "On the other hand... where is the sheriff holding the Carsons?"

"The Carsons?" Fletcher frowned. "Oh, that couple he brought in earlier? He had them transferred to the Bonney police station. Chief LaRue came himself and got them."

"Really?" Sutton hadn't told him that. J.D. realized that the sheriff was deliberately keeping the Carsons, Moreno, and Layla Woodson apart from each other. "In that case, I'd like to see Ms. Woodson in her holding cell."

"Why's that, Lieutenant?"

"Because," J.D. said, hoping he could talk fast enough to discourage further questions. "I'm not an official county employee and I'm just trying to get some information for the sheriff because he's got other, more important, business to tend to. And he needs the information as soon as possible!" he added. "There's no need to waste time taking her to another room. He's trying to keep it quiet, so he won't want everyone in the county to know I'm here talking to Ms. Woodson. You know how impatient he can get when things don't go smoothly," he finished. He was rewarded by a look of alarm and instant cooperation from Deputy Fletcher.

"Right this way, Lieutenant," he stammered, leading J.D. past the dispatcher's desk. J.D. glanced at the dispatcher, Laura Mays, who gave J.D. a knowing wink and pointed at the desk phone; apparently Sutton had already greased the skids for J.D. should Fletcher give him any trouble.

They made their way down the hallway and Deputy Fletcher unlocked the door leading to the holding cells. J.D. stopped in the doorway and blocked him from coming in any further.

"Thanks, Deputy, but I've got it from here. Remember, the fewer people know about it, the happier the sheriff will be."

Deputy Fletcher almost saluted. "Yes, sir, Lieutenant!" he said and quickly stepped back, shutting the door firmly.

J.D. sighed with relief; he'd worry about Sutton's reaction later. He stopped in front of the cell furthest from the door. Layla Woodson sat on the bed with her knees drawn up under her chin. She rocked back and forth, sniffling. J.D. cleared his throat. "Miss Woodson?"

"I didn't do it," she moaned, her voice deep and raspy. "I mean, I didn't mean to do it. Oh, my God, is he dead? Did I kill him? I didn't mean to... they said it wasn't loaded...."

"That's enough," J.D. said, his voice stern but not loud. She stopped speaking and whimpered. "The sheriff is alive and if you're telling the truth about not meaning to kill him...."

"I didn't mean to kill anybody! Not even Corrie!" she cried, sitting up straight and rubbing her hands over her face. J.D. kept his expression passive though he grimaced inwardly at the sight of Layla Woodson's blotchy, tear-stained face. Her mascara had smeared so much she appeared to have two black eyes. He realized that she wasn't much older than Corrie, but right now, her fear made her seem so much younger. "They told me it wasn't loaded!"

"WHO told you the gun wasn't loaded? Who sent you after Corrie?" J.D. barked. She shrank back, covering her mouth with her hands. She stared down at the floor. "Look, you're in more trouble than you even realize. You have any idea what the penalty is for trying to murder a law enforcement officer?"

"But I didn't...."

"Prove it! Who sent you? Bill Woods? Robert Moreno?" J.D. paused then threw caution to the wind. "Toby Willis?"

Her head jerked up and her coffee-brown eyes were like saucers. "No, no, he didn't... I mean, I don't know any Toby Willis!" she cried, but J.D. nodded.

"Is he the one who came here to find Bill Woods? Is he the one who threatened Corrie and the campground?" Layla Woodson kept shaking her head.

"I... I don't know what you're talking about!" she stammered. J.D. gritted his teeth in frustration.

"Miss Woodson, you're not helping yourself," he said, trying not to lose his temper. He gripped the bars of the cell and forced himself to use a calm tone. "What did you think Corrie had that belonged to you? You were pretty adamant that she hand it over. What was it you were expecting?" He paused and then went on, "You were told that she's related to you, weren't you? That's what this is about. Family inheritance. Bill Woods heard Billy Black Horse had died. Did he tell you Corrie had something that belonged to you?"

"She... she's my sister," Layla said through hiccuping sobs. "She's my sister and didn't even know who I was! How do you think that made me feel!" she cried, her eyes blazing with anger.

J.D. raised a brow. "What makes you think she's your sister? Who told you that?"

"Because we have the same father! That's what my...." She

clamped her lips shut and looked away from J.D.'s penetrating gaze.

"That's what your mother told you?" She barely nodded but didn't turn her head. "Who is your mother, Miss Woodson?"

"What's it matter? She's got nothing to do with any of this," the woman said stiffly, keeping her eyes trained on the wall beside her.

"Obviously, she does, if she's the one who told you that you and Corrie have the same father," J.D. countered, folding his arms across his chest. "She told you Billy was your father, but who was the man you believed to be your father all your life? Was it Bill Woods?"

She threw J.D. a hateful glare. "Who cares? He didn't want me, either, or my mom! He took off when I was five. He came back, from time to time, played Santa Claus whenever he did, as if a new bike or clothes or toys were gonna make up for not being around!" She swiped her hand under her nose, sniffling, and J.D. reached through the bars and handed her his handkerchief. She eyed it suspiciously before taking it and nodding her thanks. He waited until she blew her nose and pulled herself together before he went on.

"Did your mom remarry after Bill Woods left?" he asked.

"When I was thirteen," Layla said dully. "Nice guy, but he wasn't my dad and he didn't even try. Didn't matter if I was doing good or getting into trouble. He always said he didn't know anything about kids and he'd shove some money into my hands. I guess that's all he had to offer." She took a deep shuddering breath and fixed a stony glare on J.D. "But I'm not telling you his name or my mom's name. She changed hers after Bill Woods left. Leave them out of it. I split when I was eighteen and neither of them cared enough to try to stop me or find me, which is fine by me. I changed my name, too. All I want is a chance to be part of the family that really was mine. I know my real dad is dead, but I've got a sister and a family business he left behind. That's good enough. Corrie owes me," she finished. She stood up. "Maybe I shouldn't have tried to... to scare her into giving me my share, but I was told that if I could prove our relationship, I would get my fair share without any trouble. Except I couldn't find the proof he told me Corrie had," she muttered.

J.D. waited a few seconds. "He knew where Billy would have hidden it in the apartment," he said.

"It wasn't there. The envelopes in the files were empty...."

She gasped and clamped her lips shut, staring at J.D. with fear in her eyes. He nodded.

"Bill Woods knew Billy and the business well enough to know Billy's office operations were unconventional. So after you killed Bill Woods...."

"I didn't kill him! Even though I wanted to, after he promised me he'd bring me here and make everything right and fair with me and Corrie and then he backed out...."

"But you know who killed him, don't you? You were there when...."

She was shaking her head, tears streaming down her face. "I wasn't there... I mean, I saw what happened, but I didn't realize at first... I had gone to the bathroom and when I was walking back to the cabin, I saw him and I wondered what he was doing here, then I saw him stop and pull that metal stake out of the ground, from that tent near the cabins, and I couldn't imagine why he wanted it. Then my dad—Bill Woods, that is—opened the door when he knocked and he looked so shocked, Woods did, and then he stumbled backwards and... and I knew something bad had happened and I just... I just left," she said in a whisper. "I had my backpack with me when I went to the bathroom. All my stuff was in it. I just left. I was afraid I would be next."

She was shaking as she covered her eyes with her hands and J.D. felt a twinge of sympathy for the young woman... though not enough to make him forget that she had threatened Corrie with a gun. "Why would Toby Willis want to kill you?" he asked.

"Because he was already upset that Bill Woods wanted to come back and stir things up again! Oh, my God...." Her hands had moved down her face to cover her mouth, but there was no calling back the words. She stared at J.D. and the look of dawning comprehension he knew his face was showing.

"They were in on it together... all the scams that Bill Woods was involved in, Toby Willis was there along with him. But he kept his distance from Billy and the Black Horse Campground...." He waited for Layla Woodson to fill in the blanks. And she did.

"He didn't want my 'dad'—Bill Woods—to stay close to Billy—my real dad," she added defiantly, "because he didn't want what eventually happened to happen... he was afraid Billy Black Horse would find out about their scams and put an end to them." She sighed and rubbed her temples. "He was pretty upset, Toby Willis, that is," she added. "He and Bill Woods had a good thing going. They were making pretty good money, so I heard." She laughed, a sour, brittle sound. “The funny thing is, a lot of times, Toby Willis would pretend to be Billy... I mean, none of the people they were scamming would know who he was anyway, but Toby did kind of resemble Billy, especially when they were younger. They were related somehow, cousins, or something, and lots of people think all Natives look alike anyway.” J.D. shook his head.

“You're saying that Toby Willis resembled Billy Black Horse that much? And no one seemed to notice Billy's 'twin' around the campground?”

Layla Woodson seemed to have given up the fight. She shrugged, looking weary. “He used to look more Indian than he does now. His dad was Hispanic, but he always looked more like his mother. He was furious when Billy messed up their scam. Bill Woods said Toby threatened to get back at Billy someday, somehow....” She jumped when J.D. slammed his fists against the bars.

“Damn it! It's Moreno, isn't it? He's Toby Willis! He's been playing us all along! Am I right?” he barked at the frightened woman. Despite the bars between them, she moved back until she was flat against the back of the cell. She nodded, her eyes wide and brimming with tears.

“He heard Bill Woods was coming to make things right... he told me it was my chance to get what was mine. He told me that Bill Woods was going to mess everything up again if I didn't stick close to him and keep an eye on him.”

“Mess what up? What was Bill Woods coming to do? I found the note,” he added when it seemed Layla was going to clam up again. She shook her head.

“Toby was right,” she said in a whisper. “He said that Bill had a guilty conscience and that he was going to spill his guts to Corrie about... about everything,” she said with a bitter laugh. “Toby said I had to get to Corrie before Bill did, but then... Bill said it was all a mistake, that things weren't the way he had thought and that it was best that we leave well enough alone. He said we were going to leave, right away, without even checking out. I went to the bathroom to call Toby, tell him what was going on, what Bill said and then....”

“He was already here, at the campground, and when you called to tell him that Bill Woods wasn't going to follow through on his original plan, he stopped him. What WAS the original plan, Miss Woodson? What was it that Bill Woods came here to do?”

J.D. fought to keep the panic out of his voice. He was distressed that Sutton had released Moreno and he was wild with fear about Corrie.... "You have to tell me, Miss Woodson. Maybe you didn't intend to hurt Corrie...."

"I didn't! Really, I didn't! They said it wasn't loaded!"

"Well, THEY lied to you! THEY intended to kill Corrie and planned to have you take the fall! Who are THEY, Miss Woodson?" J.D. yelled, slamming his fists against the bars once again. "Who are they and what are they after?"

She let out a little shriek and her face turned white. Behind him, J.D. heard the door rattle open and Deputy Fletcher burst into the cell block. "Lieutenant? Something wrong?" he asked. J.D. shook his head as Layla Woodson licked her lips.

"It's my... my mother. And her husband. They said the Black Horse should be half mine... ours. Because Billy Black Horse was my dad. She said he... he promised. He promised to take care of her. And me. But she said he had another wife and daughter he loved more. She said she'd make sure we'd get what was ours someday. When he died, she said it was time...."

"Who is your mother?" J.D. demanded. Tears pooled in her eyes and spilled down her cheeks. All the fight was gone out of her.

"Marjorie McMillan," she whispered.

~

Corrie said nothing on the drive to the Kaydahzinne home. Part of the reason was because Rick was stonily silent and she knew that conversation would not be appreciated. The other part had to do with the lump in her throat, a dam that was on the verge of bursting open and releasing a deluge of tears. Something else she knew Rick wouldn't appreciate.

At least not right now.

Lightning flashed, lighting up the dark road leading to the Kaydahzinne home. Corrie noticed that the trees were swaying in the gusty wind as if executing deep bows in response to the thunder's applause. She wrapped her arms around herself and shook her head.

Rick broke the silence. "It's going to be okay, Corrie." She nodded stiffly and he went on, "There has to be an explanation for all this. There's a reason why Elsa Kaydahzinne never mentioned Toby Willis and we're going to find out what it is."

"Do you think Layla Woodson is my sister? Do you think she's Billy's daughter?" Corrie kept her gaze fixed out the windshield, afraid to see the sympathy in Rick's eyes. Part of her was afraid to hear what Rick was going to say, but she could accept his honest answers as long as he wasn't feeling sorry for her. He cleared his throat.

"What if she is? Does that change your relationship with Billy? Or your mother's relationship with him? Your dad was an honest, fair, and compassionate man. If, and that's a mighty big if, Layla Woodson is your sister then I have to believe that Billy didn't know about her. I don't believe he would have kept it a secret from anyone, least of all your mother or you." Corrie allowed her shoulders to relax. She realized that she was tensed as if Rick were about to deliver a physical blow. "And not that it proves or disproves anything, but I don't see any kind of resemblance between Layla Woodson and you or your dad." He stopped as Corrie glanced at him and noticed him chewing his lower lip.

"But she does remind you of someone. Am I right?" Corrie asked. "J.D. saw a picture of one of Uncle Bill's wives and he thought she looked like someone he'd seen before. Their names didn't match but maybe they're related?"

Rick shrugged. "Yes, but damned if I can think of who she reminded me of." He stopped as they turned up the dirt road leading to the Kaydahzinne driveway. He frowned. "It's awful dark. I know they probably turn off the porch light at bedtime, but there isn't even a safety light on anywhere."

"The storm took out the power earlier. Maybe it's still not restored out here," Corrie said, trying to convince herself, even as she and Rick looked out through the rain-splattered windows and noted the gleam of a light at the nearest neighbor's house.

"Or someone else made sure the power stayed off," Rick said, keeping his voice low and killing the Tahoe's lights as he drove by.

"Where are you going?" Corrie asked, keeping her voice down. Her question came out as a squeak and she wasn't sure Rick heard her when he didn't answer right away.

He stopped halfway between the Kaydahzinne home and the next house on the street. He keyed his radio and, in a low rumble called the deputy who was guarding the Kaydahzinne residence. Silence greeted his radio call and he muttered an expletive followed by, "Not again." Corrie felt her heart leap into her throat.

"Who's supposed to be out here?" she whispered.

"Andy Luna," Rick whispered back as he checked his sidearm and retrieved the shotgun from the rack in the Tahoe. He slipped his cell phone out of its holster and hit a speed dial number.

"Yes, Sheriff?" Dudley's voice echoed inside the interior of the Tahoe, louder than the raindrops that were thudding on the roof and windshield.

"Dudley, get to the Kaydahzinne house. No lights, no sirens. Andy isn't answering his radio." His voice, despite its tight control, betrayed his anger and fear for his deputy's safety. Corrie squeezed her hands together in her lap and tried not to let her own terror escape in tears. "You know a way in from the river where you can't be seen?"

"Yes, sir. ETA five minutes." He hesitated a second, then, "Sir? The residents...?"

"I don't know, Dudley," Rick said shortly. "The lights are off in the house. I see Myra's minivan in the driveway. I don't know what we're walking into," he added.

"Yes, sir," Dudley answered and hung up. Rick turned off the dome light before opening the door. Corrie reached for the handle on her side and Rick grabbed her arm.

"No, you don't," he growled. "You're staying here. And no arguments! I don't have time for it and I don't need you putting yourself in danger."

"What about you?" she snapped. "I know it's your job, Rick, but you don't have any help...."

"Backup's on the way. You stay here."

"And do what?" she cried. Rick shoved his cell phone into her hands.

"Dispatch is speed dial 3. Wilder is speed dial 6. If you see or hear anything suspicious, call dispatch and tell Laura to get hold of Eldon and the village police for more backup. Call Wilder, find out what he's learned and let him know what's going on." He took a deep breath. She could barely make out his profile in the rainy, windy night. "If I'm not back in ten minutes, drive to the nearest house and stay put until help arrives. I mean it," he added, his shadow turning in her direction. She couldn't see his eyes, but she could feel his gaze boring into her in the darkness. "I mean it, Corrie."

She swallowed hard. "Okay," she choked out. The door shut softly and he was gone.

No tears, stay calm, she ordered herself as she fumbled with Rick's phone and managed to dial J.D.... only briefly wondering when Rick had put J.D. on speed dial. He answered after only one ring.

"Sheriff, glad you called, there's something you need to know...."

"J.D., it's Corrie," she hissed, afraid to raise her voice and hoping J.D. could hear her.

"What's wrong? Where are you?"

"At the Kaydahzinne house. The power's off. Deputy Luna isn't answering his radio. Rick called for backup...."

"And he's going in like Rambo, by himself. I'm on my way. Stay put. Keep the line open unless I tell you to call for help." She heard him gun the Harley's motor and the scream of the tires on the wet asphalt drowned out her reply.

Chapter 21

J.D. tried to organize his thoughts as he roared through the rain and darkness toward the Kaydahzinne house. Whatever it was that Billy Black Horse had left with Elsa Kaydahzinne, it was something that was important enough to kill for. And it seemed that Bill Woods and Toby Willis had both been aware of it.

He'd made a quick call to the River's Edge Bed and Breakfast and asked Vicky Kellerman about her tenant. He hadn't been surprised when she'd told him that Robert Moreno had left earlier in the evening and hadn't returned yet.

J.D. had an idea where he might.

He flinched as lightning crackled overhead. The rain was coming in spurts, hard drops then blowing wind and light sprinkles. He hoped that the sounds of the storm would keep anyone from hearing the Harley as he approached the Kaydahzinne house.

He turned onto the dark street. A flash of lightning gave him a glimpse of the house, looming ahead. The only lights were from neighboring houses, too far away to illuminate anything around Myra's grandmother's place. He parked the Harley under a tree on the curve before the driveway to the house and dismounted. He didn't see the sheriff's Tahoe or any other vehicle except for a white minivan which was parked in the driveway. He crouched near the gate behind a bush and pulled out his cell phone. “Corrie, you there?”

“Where are you?” He was grateful she was whispering; he knew how far sound carried out in the open.

“By the Kaydahzinne gate. Where's Sutton?”

“He was heading that way a few minutes ago. Don't get shot,” she warned him. He smiled grimly.

“I'll do my best. Stay on the line.” He shoved the phone back in his jacket pocket and wondered for a minute about the wisdom of approaching the house without a weapon, but realized that there was nothing he could do about it. He crept toward the house on the far side of the minivan and slipped into the shadows alongside the carport.

There was a dim light showing through the curtains in the front room. He didn't go onto the porch; he knew the squeaking boards would give him away immediately. He went to the back of the house, near the kitchen door, and found the window over the kitchen sink. It was open a few inches. He waited a few seconds, giving his pounding heart a chance to settle down, and he raised his head to look inside.

It was too dark to see anything, but he heard footsteps, slow and measured, moving inside. He flattened himself back against the wall next to the window and waited. The footsteps moved closer until they stopped at the window. He held his breath, trying to melt into the shadows of the overhang. He heard the blinds being parted....

“See anything yet?” Moreno's voice, a cold whisper, reached J.D.'s ears and it was all he could do not to move any closer.

“Nothing. But don't think that means there isn't anyone out there. I'm telling you, I saw a vehicle go down the road and then the lights vanished. I don't think it was one of the neighbors. I think it was the police and they're out there somewhere.”

“The sheriff would've come screaming in with lights and sirens the minute his deputy didn't answer his radio. You're getting paranoid.” Moreno was getting impatient with his partner in crime, but the other man continued in a worried tone.

“This was a mistake. We should have cut our losses and just left town.” The voice sounded familiar, but J.D. couldn't put a face to it.

“What have we got to lose? Layla's going to spill her guts. She thinks this is all about family and the business. She doesn't know about the money. All she cares about is Corrie, her 'little sister', and her fairy-tale happy ending,” Moreno sneered. From deeper inside the house, J.D. heard a woman's voice being raised in anger and frustration.

“I'm through fooling around!” The nasal twang, not as pronounced as before, hit J.D. and his gut hitched. Marjorie McMillan. Layla Woodson was right. The other man had to be Mr. McMillan... and he didn't sound as meek and henpecked as he had earlier. “You better tell me where you hid the papers Billy Black Horse gave you and the package Bill Woods brought you or you're both going to join that deputy when the house goes up in flames!”

J.D.'s blood ran cold when Elsa Kaydahzinne's voice, strong despite its years, responded. “Why do you pretend? You know you're going to kill me as well. But you'd better not hurt my granddaughter. She knows nothing about all this. You gain nothing by keeping her here. Let her go.”

"I'm not leaving you, Grandmother!" Myra cried, her voice cracking with tears.

"You'll tell me what I want to know or your granddaughter WILL be the one to pay for the injustice that we've suffered. Billy Black Horse robbed us in the past and now Bill Woods robbed us as well... and you're helping him! You helped them both!"

"Billy never cheated anyone and he certainly never lied. He knew what your 'husband' was up to... he knew that his so-called friends were setting him up to take the blame for their scams. If Bill Woods chose to make past wrongs right, then good for him. Billy never wanted anything from his old friend, except for his name to be kept clean."

"Stop arguing with the old hag and just get what we came for!" Moreno snapped. "I'm sick of this! We should have been gone a long time ago! If she won't tell us where to find it, then let's go before we get caught!"

"We're not leaving without our money!" Marjorie McMillan screeched.

J.D. froze. Money? What were they talking about? What about the papers they were so intent on getting earlier? He shook his head, then glanced around as lightning lit up the sky again. At the corner of the house, his eyes met those of the sheriff. He caught the flash of recognition in Sutton's eyes as he silently scooted toward him and they slipped around the corner of the house.

"Where the hell did you come from?" Sutton hissed.

"Layla Woodson's mother is Marjorie McMillan. Moreno is Toby Willis. They're in the house, the McMillans and Moreno, and they're holding the Kaydahzinnes hostage," J.D. answered in a whispered rush, even as his mind tried to untangle the meaning of what he'd heard.

"Andy?" Sutton asked in a strangled voice. J.D. grimaced but he knew the sheriff couldn't see it.

"I don't know. They're threatening to torch the house but they're trying to get information from Elsa Kaydahzinne about money that Woods stole from them."

"What?"

Another flash of lightning and suddenly everything started to make sense. "Woods came here to make amends. He tried to convince Moreno—that is, Willis—that it was time to make peace with Billy's family. Willis wouldn't hear of it. He and Marjorie McMillan, Layla Woodson's parents, had been planning all along to use Layla Woodson to try to get close to Corrie." He took a deep breath. "They panicked when Woods had an attack of conscience, so they convinced her to approach Bill Woods and give him the sob story that she was Billy's long-lost daughter, something that they had told her for years, in order to keep tabs on what he was up to. All Layla Woodson ever wanted was a family. She jumped at the invitation, thought the plan was to get Corrie to accept the relationship and it was... I think Toby Willis is Layla Woodson's real father," J.D. blurted. "And I think Billy knew it and had proof of that and that's what they're trying to get from Elsa Kaydahzinne."

"Why, for God's sake?" Sutton muttered. J.D. shook his head.

"Because that would prove they had no claim to the Black Horse. Their plan was to convince Corrie that Billy had other children, that there was at least one other person who should have inherited when Billy died. They had Bill Woods convinced of that or he wouldn't have let Layla Woodson come with him. As for McMillan and Willis, I doubt they wanted a share of the campground. I think their plan was to work on Corrie's sympathetic and generous nature—so much like her dad's—and demand their fair share."

"They didn't know Billy as well as they thought... or Corrie, for that matter," the sheriff said. "She might give someone the shirt off her back, but she's going to make damn sure it fits first." He blew out his breath in frustration. "I wonder if they saw the Tahoe go down the road. Corrie's in it."

"Not anymore."

The voice came from J.D.'s pocket as well as from behind them and both men jumped. J.D. had forgotten he still had Corrie on the line. He yanked the phone out, stifling a curse. "Where the hell are you?" he hissed.

"Don't shoot, I'm right behind you, by the fence."

They spun around and saw movement by an old tree near the fence line. In an instant, Corrie was beside them. J.D. could feel the sheriff's fury vibrating in the air. "Weren't you listening? I told you to stay put!" he snapped.

"I know you did, and I was also listening while those jerks in there were talking about seeing a vehicle go down the road. If they decided to go investigate, the fat would be in the fire for sure." She spoke in a soothing whisper, but it wasn't having much effect on J.D. and the sheriff. "Look, guys, I know you're not going to like this, but I have an idea how to rescue the Kaydahzinnes and

Deputy Luna, but you're going to have to trust me...."

~

Corrie took a deep breath and willed her hands to stop shaking as she made her way through the darkness to the Kaydahzinne front gate. Even knowing that Rick and J.D. were nearby and armed—Rick had hurriedly deputized J.D. and handed over his shotgun—did little to dispel the wobbliness in her knees. Deputy Dudley Evans had arrived just as their plan was about to be executed and his assistance was immediately put to use. Corrie licked her lips and fought the urge to look anywhere but at the front of the house, lest she give away the fact that she wasn't alone. In case anyone was watching.

She pulled J.D.'s phone out of her pocket and punched in Myra's number, grimly reminding herself that it would probably be better if she had her own phone at times like these. She listened, pressing the phone tightly to her ear and blocking out the sound of the intensifying storm in her other ear. After three rings, Myra answered, her voice curt, "Yes?"

"Hey, Myra, it's Corrie!" She winced at how fake-happy she sounded, but she wasn't sure who else might be listening. "Uh, listen, I know it's kind of late and all, but I was wondering if I could stop in and talk to your grandmother...."

"Uh, Corrie, hold on, I have to put you on speaker." Great, Corrie groaned to herself, thinking fast about how to proceed. Rick and J.D. had both warned her this might happen, so she had to be careful....

"Okay, um, go ahead, Corrie, what were you saying?" Myra's voice sounded subdued and far away, almost like an echo. Corrie forced herself to keep her nervousness out of her voice.

"Yeah, well, as I was saying, I know it's late but... I, uh, I've been thinking a lot about, you know, what's been happening and...." Stop stammering! she ordered herself, and suddenly she decided how to handle herself. "Look, the truth is, I'm outside your house and Rick would kill me if he knew I was here, but there's a few things I need to talk to your grandmother about...."

She was rewarded by a dim light appearing at the front window. She decided to capitalize on it as she opened the gate and started up the walk. "Hey, is your power out or something? Your house is awfully dark...."

"What do you need to talk to my grandmother about?" Myra

asked, her voice betraying fear despite its steadiness. Corrie wondered if the intruders had guns and were threatening to shoot Myra—or her grandmother—if she didn't cooperate. Corrie decided it was time to get serious.

"Listen, Myra, it's about... about my dad. And something I found out. I need to know if it's true."

She cringed as she listened to Myra's heaving breaths. "Corrie, I don't know what you're talking about and I'm sure my grandmother doesn't either! You have to leave...." Scuffling sounds, then muffled voices as if someone had covered the phone receiver so Corrie couldn't hear. Her heart was pounding so loud she doubted she could have heard anything anyway, then Myra's subdued voice, a bit shakier than before, came back on the line. "All right, if you really need to talk to her...."

"Yes, thanks, Myra!" Corrie drew a deep breath for the first time all evening. "Um, I'm parked down the road, but I'm actually outside your house right now so...."

Lights blazed from the front porch light, the front windows, and a powerful flashlight that shone right into Corrie's face. She blinked and took a step back, her hand flying up to shield her eyes, and collided with someone standing behind her. She whirled around and caught a glimpse of Robert Moreno, aka Toby Willis, scowling at her before a hand grabbed her arm and yanked her in the direction of the front porch. "About time you got here, Miss Black. For your sake, let's hope you didn't come empty-handed," snarled Thomas McMillan.

Chapter 22

It was all J.D., Deputy Evans, and the sheriff could do to hold their positions as Corrie was being hauled into the Kaydahzinne home. J.D. couldn't see if either man was armed. With Corrie between the two men, he couldn't risk any kind of shot, even if their plan had called for it, and he knew that the sheriff was equally frustrated. Through Deputy Evans, they had been able to acquire a third cell phone. He was stationed near the back door, the sheriff around the corner by the carport, and J.D. just beyond the bushes by the front gate. All they could do was hope that, with Corrie in the house now, with Deputy Evans' cell phone on and the line open to the sheriff's phone, they could hear what was going on in the house.

It would have been so easy for one of them to have grabbed Moreno/Willis when he slipped out through the carport and sneaked up behind Corrie, but they needed Corrie in the house to find out what was going on with the Kaydahzinnes and Deputy Luna. And hopefully get an answer to all their questions once and for all.

~

Corrie tried not to stumble as Thomas McMillan pulled her into the house. She fought the urge to look around for her backup and concentrated on keeping her wits about her. She found herself in the sitting room where she had talked with Elsa Kaydahzinne... was that only yesterday? Earlier today? The last few days since the threat had been slipped under her door had become a blur. She blinked in the dim light of the sitting room. To her surprise, Myra sat in the rose wingchair. Marjorie McMillan stood over her, gripping the girl's shoulder with a claw-like hand, the other hand holding a gun aimed at Myra's head. Mrs. Kaydahzinne was nowhere to be seen. The smell of lavender was overwhelming. Corrie's heart plummeted and she reminded herself to keep Rick in the loop. "Myra, what's going on? Where's your grandmother?" She tried not to over-emphasize any particular words. "Mrs. McMillan, why are you holding a gun on Myra?" She cringed inwardly. Was that too obvious? Marjorie McMillan smiled tightly.

"Will you two take that phone away from her before she passes all kinds of information on to the sheriff?" she snapped. Both Moreno and Thomas McMillan stepped forward and McMillan snatched J.D.'s cell phone out of her hand, dropped it on the floor, and brought his heel down on it with a sickening crunch. Corrie knew she looked convincingly dismayed; even though she still had Dudley Evans' phone in her pocket, she promised herself that she would replace J.D.'s phone for him. If they all survived this night.

"What do you all want?" she cried, making her voice sound more angry than scared. She wanted to let Rick know she was still all right and that she was still "in the game" even if J.D.'s phone had been retired. "Leave Myra and her family alone! They have nothing to do with any of this! You want to know about me and my family, well, here I am and you can let them all go and deal with me!" Okay, THAT might be a little more confrontational than necessary and she imagined hearing Rick groan on the other end of the phone line. She took a deep breath and clenched her fists to keep her hands from shaking. "Tell me what you're looking for!"

"We want the paperwork Billy hid for me," Robert Moreno growled poking her in the shoulder. "Some friend he turned out to be. He said he'd help me then he stabbed me in the back!"

"Was that before or after you and Bill Woods stabbed HIM in the back?" Corrie raged, spinning to face the man. Myra's gasp reminded Corrie that a weapon was in the room and in the hands of a angry, vindictive woman and she tried to rein in her temper. "What was it, Layla Woodson's original birth certificate, listing Toby Willis as her father?" She shook her head. "I'm willing to bet you gave my dad a sealed envelope and made him promise to keep it under wraps, then you convinced Layla—your own daughter—that her father was someone else. You tried to make Billy the scapegoat for your scams when they fell through and it was that birth certificate that gave him the leverage to make you back off. Bill Woods took the fall because you both had designs on a woman who was—or had been—very wealthy." She glared at Marjorie McMillan who glared back at her. "Did you own that parcel of land they wanted to buy to put a campground on? Did they offer to cut you a deal over a lot of drinks at a friend's bar?" The whole truth was coming together in Corrie's mind and she knew, by the looks of the faces on the McMillans and Toby Willis, she was getting it all right. "My dad wasn't even there that night, was he? You all got Bill Woods so drunk he didn't remember that night and he accepted the responsibility for Layla's parentage because you convinced him that MY dad was her biological father and he didn't want Billy's reputation and marriage to suffer from the scandal! Then what went wrong?" she asked. "My dad found out about your scams and threatened to reveal the truth if his name wasn't cleared? Did he tell Uncle Bill about Toby being Layla's father?"

"That's enough!" snarled Marjorie McMillan. "All that matters now is that Bill Woods turned out to have a conscience after all! He had borrowed the money for the land deal from Billy Black Horse, who didn't care when it would be paid off even when it put a huge strain on his own finances. He was willing to take a loss to help a friend until he found out that friend was scamming him. It was enough for Billy to write off the money as a loss. All he cared about was keeping his name clean. But then Bill Woods found out he didn't have much time to make things right in this life...."

"What are you saying?" Corrie said, her anger evaporating and her heart pounding with an emotion that she was having a hard time identifying. "Bill Woods was sick? Was he dying?"

"He died sooner than he was supposed to," Toby Willis said, his voice betraying a tremor of feeling for the first time. "And it was probably less painful than it should have been. But not before he tried to 'make things right'. After he heard your dad had passed, he was obsessed with trying to balance the scales. He insisted that the money should be yours, it should have been your dad's...."

"What money are you talking about?" Corrie said, her head spinning. Thomas McMillan finally spoke up.

"MY money," he said with a stony look on his face. "They played me for a fool for years, Margie playing the poor but brave single mother, convincing me that Layla's dad had abandoned them both and the whole time she was taking money from both Toby Willis and Bill Woods, their pay off for her keeping quiet about their scams, all the while she was milking me dry with her expensive tastes. Bill Woods approached me first when he got his diagnosis and told me everything... all because he wanted them all to come clean and make things up to Billy Black Horse, with MY money."

"YOUR money?" Marjorie McMillan screeched and both Corrie and Myra jumped while the two men flinched. "I was the one who made your fortune! I helped you make good investments when you frittered away all your savings and retirement benefits...."

"YOU sucked me dry! YOU frittered away my money! There would have been no money to invest if it weren't for me! Then you cleaned out my account to pay off Bill Woods...."

"Pay him off for what?" Corrie hadn't meant to blurt out anymore questions nor draw any more attention to herself. She had been fascinated by the in-fighting among her family's enemies and, despite the danger she was in, wanted to know exactly what was going on. Rick and J.D. were probably both going prematurely gray, wondering when the shooting was going to start and how they were going to get her out of the crossfire. She still had to learn where Andy Luna was before they stormed in, but right now, she was more interested in finding out the whole story behind the events of the last few days. "What did Bill Woods have on you?"

It was the wrong thing to say. Thomas McMillan's face turned a dark shade of red and his lip curled in fury. Myra gasped when he grabbed Corrie's arm and yanked her toward him, his other hand balling into a fist. Marjorie McMillan snorted.

"Well, that's all you had to do to let her know she hit the nail on the head!" She let out a dry laugh that sounded like a hiccup. "Of course, your dear Uncle Bill had something on my husband... your father was probably the only non-criminal he ever associated with!" she said. "What he had on Thomas is not important now. All that matters is that we get our money...."

"MY money!" snapped Thomas McMillan, releasing Corrie and turning to face his wife.

"Whatever," she said, waving her gun hand dismissively. "We get our money and we get out of here. And that," she added, aiming the gun back at Myra, "is where you come in handy, Corrie. You're here, ostensibly, to talk to Myra's grandmother about the 'truth' regarding your parentage. Now we all know where the truth lies, so what are you really here for?" Corrie stared at her as she began to nod her head. "Of course, you're here for the money your dear Uncle Bill was going to return to you, the money he was going to use to right the wrongs he visited upon your father, to pay back an old debt, to assuage his guilt over having used and abused an old friendship. His remorse drove him to do something stupid and it got him killed. And now it's going to get YOU killed, along with your friends," she added coldly. "What did Bill Woods do with the money?" Corrie swallowed hard.

"Uncle Bill left a letter to me... a letter claiming that my dad was Layla's real father. How do you explain that?" she stammered, wondering if stalling was going to do any good. Would it get her more information or just buy her a few more minutes of life? From the look of terror on Myra's face, she was running out of time and she still didn't know where Myra's grandmother or Deputy Luna were.

"Who knows and who cares?" Robert Moreno/Toby Willis snapped. Mrs. McMillan shook her head in disgust.

"You did it anyway, didn't you?" she said, addressing him. "You went ahead and wrote that idiotic letter and planted it on Woods' body. You probably left evidence all over it...."

"Layla was supposed to have given Corrie the letter, to prove her claim! Then Woods decided to flake out on us and the whole plan went to hell!"

"YOU wrote that letter?" Corrie said, turning to stare at Moreno/Willis. "So Uncle Bill really did know the truth and you were afraid he'd not only pay back his debt to my dad, he'd also tell me that I'm the only one with a legal claim to the Black Horse! That's why you killed him! You wanted Layla Woodson to claim her inheritance and then you'd dry up her finances just the way you've done to countless innocent people!"

"Does it make it better to know the whole truth so you can die in peace?" Mrs. McMillan said in an oddly calm tone. Corrie turned to her and saw the gun pointed directly at her. "With you gone, there will be no reason for the old woman to keep the secret of where the money is hidden, especially when it means her granddaughter will be the next to die if she doesn't tell us...."

"What did you do with Deputy Luna?" Corrie asked suddenly, keeping her eyes focused on the barrel of the gun. Thomas McMillan scowled.

"What's it matter to you?" He gestured at his wife and the gun in her hand. "The deputy saw you skulking around the house and accidentally shot you. Bad enough he shot the sheriff's girlfriend, but the girl and her grandmother witnessed it, so he had to kill them, too." He grinned for the first time at the look on Corrie's face. He went on, "Then he tried to hide the evidence by setting the house on fire, maybe hoping it would be blamed on a lightning strike, but then he had a fit of remorse and shot himself as well. But," he added, his smile evaporating, "this little scenario could have a much, much happier ending if you tell us what Bill Woods did with the money he was going to 'return' to you."

Corrie doubted any information she gave them, even if she had it, was going to change the outcome. She cleared her throat. "He didn't 'return' anything to me and if it were money, I wouldn't have taken it," she said slowly and clearly. "You're wasting your time here and hurting people who haven't done anything to you. Just let everyone go and leave. You're only making things worse for yourselves." Toby Willis laughed, a harsh, gritty sound.

"Oh, you're Billy's daughter, all right," he sneered. "He must have sure been proud of you. Maybe your 'Uncle Bill' would still be alive if he knew how you felt about the money." He gripped Corrie's arm and steered her toward the kitchen. "Let's see, the deputy would have seen you sneaking around the back door...."

"Why would I come to the back door?" Corrie asked, hoping the emphasis she put on "back door" wasn't too obvious. She tried to hang back, but the sound of the safety being released on Deputy Luna's gun behind her forced her to follow her captor.

"Why would the deputy shoot someone coming up the front walk?" he snapped back. He glanced in the direction of Marjorie McMillan. "All right, she says she doesn't know anything about the money. So let's get rid of her and see if that gets the girl or the old lady talking before...."

"NO!" cried Myra, half-rising from the wing chair. Marjorie McMillan swung the gun back toward her and Corrie gasped. "Don't hurt her or my grandmother! I'll tell you where the money is!"

"What? Myra, wait...," Corrie blurted, as the McMillans and Toby Willis spun in Myra's direction.

"I just KNEW it!" crowed Marjorie McMillan. "I knew he'd bring it here and entrust it to the old woman! Bill Woods knew that Elsa Kaydahzinne was the Black Horse family confidant and she'd be the one he'd approach." She waved the gun at Corrie and glared at Myra. "All right, honey, just tell us where to find it and we'll be on our way."

"Promise you won't hurt my grandmother?" Myra asked and Corrie felt her heart twist. Despite Myra's plea, she knew that none of them would survive the night once the McMillans and Toby Willis got their money.

What were Rick and J.D. waiting for?

"Just tell us where it is!" Thomas McMillan boomed out and Myra flinched. Then, for just a second, she made eye contact with Corrie and tilted her head toward the hallway. Corrie had no idea what she was trying to convey, if she was trying to give Corrie a message or sign, or if she was imagining things. She made a slight move toward the hallway and Myra shook her head vigorously.

"It's in there, the bathroom where you locked up the deputy!" Myra said, her voice louder than it had been previously. The three intruders glanced down the hallway and Toby Willis shook his head.

"What the hell? Well, we've got to pull the deputy out to set the scene anyway." He shoved Corrie at Thomas McMillan and strode toward the bathroom door. He paused and grinned back at Corrie. "If it'll make you feel any better, the deputy's still alive. We haven't killed him yet, just gave him a little lump on the head and used his own handcuffs on him." He turned the knob and began to tug on the door. "If he's lucky, he'll still be unconscious when we...."

The door flew open, striking Toby Willis square in the face and sending him staggering backwards as Deputy Luna, his hands still cuffed behind him and a little unsteady on his feet, charged through the door, keeping his head and shoulder down and connecting squarely with Toby's midsection. Corrie yanked free from Thomas McMillan's grasp and dove at Marjorie McMillan. Myra grabbed for the woman's gun arm just as the front and back doors burst open and Rick's shout, "Sheriff's department! Nobody move!" reverberated through the room. A flash and a loud explosion of gun fire, and then plaster showered down from the living room ceiling, along with the chandelier light fixture. Corrie ducked and covered her head as sparks, chandelier crystals, and shards of glass rained down and then the room was plunged into darkness once again, except for the faint, reddish glow of the votive candle burning on the small table by Mrs. Kaydahzinne's chair. She had no idea if Marjorie McMillan still had the gun in her hand and, while she was positive that neither Rick, nor J.D., nor Deputy Evans would fire their weapons in the dark, she had no illusions that Mrs. McMillan would be so cautious.

Shouts, grunts, and several cries accompanied the sounds of people scuffling, furniture being overturned, and several items breaking. Corrie winced when the table holding the votive candle rocked and then crashed to the floor, the candle's flame flickering weakly. She groped for the wall and started to search frantically for the kitchen doorway, hoping that the power hadn't gone out in the whole house.

Her fingers found the door jamb, slid across the wallpaper, and came in contact with the light switch. Before she could flip it on, a rough hand grabbed her wrist and pulled her into the kitchen. Her scream was cut off by another hand clamping over her lips and then her arms were pinned to her side and she was being dragged, struggling, through the kitchen to the back door. "You and your father have cost me enough money and trouble!" Toby Willis snarled into her ear. "Now it's payback and I don't care if those two idiots get their money or not!" He shouldered open the back door and hauled her out onto the back steps. The wind had kicked up and raindrops pelted them both. He paused a moment, as if to get his bearings, and Corrie took the opportunity. She shoved backwards as hard as she could.

As she hoped, he stepped off the edge of the top step and fell two feet to the ground, but he still managed to hold onto her and she landed on top of him, both of them getting the wind knocked out of them. She scrambled to her feet, gasping for breath. A sharp shove from behind sent her face down on the muddy ground. She got to her knees as lightning flashed and looked up in time to see Toby Willis sprinting toward the river that ran behind the Kaydahzinne house. "Rick! J.D.! Somebody!" she screamed, feeling as if the words were draining every last bit of breath and strength from her body. At first, she didn't think she'd been heard, then J.D.'s voice came from the top of the steps.

"Corrie?" She looked up and squinted as a powerful flashlight beam shone in her face.

"Toby Willis!" she gasped. "Toward the river! Hurry! I'm okay!" she added as J.D. leaped off the top step and tore after him. She struggled to her feet just as Rick and Dudley came down the steps with the McMillans in tow, securely handcuffed. Myra followed them, supporting Deputy Luna who finally had his handcuffs removed and was holding a handkerchief to his bleeding head. They were coughing and a cloud of smoke rolled out after them.

"Where's Wilder?" Rick asked as he reached the bottom of the steps.

"He went after Toby Willis. He ran for the river." Before she could say anything else, Rick jerked his head toward the furthest corner of the backyard.

"You and Myra take Andy back there, as far from the house as you can. The fire department is on the way. That candle ignited the rug and curtains and it's spreading fast."

Myra let out a cry and nearly let Deputy Luna fall. "My grandmother is still in the house! They locked her in the bedroom!" She turned to run back into the house but Dudley grabbed her arm.

"Myra, no! You go with Corrie and Andy! I'll get your grandmother!" He shot a look at Rick who started to say something.

Rick looked at Myra, then at Corrie. She wasn't sure what he thought when she gave a slight nod, but his jaw clenched and he turned back to Deputy Evans. "Go. Hurry!" Dudley nodded and gave Myra a gentle push in the direction of Corrie. Corrie put her arm around Myra's shoulders and urged her in the direction Rick had ordered them.

"Come on, Myra," she said. They followed Rick and his prisoners and a stumbling Andy Luna away from the house, with Myra looking over her shoulder the whole time.

Chapter 23

J.D. tried not to think about what was going on back at the Kaydahzinne house as he ran through the weed-choked field toward the river. He had helped Sutton and Deputy Evans subdue and cuff the McMillans when he'd noticed that Toby Willis and Corrie were gone. Myra had gone to help the courageous and badly injured Deputy Luna who had fallen in a heap near the wall after tackling Willis. He had looked up at J.D. and gestured weakly toward the kitchen. "He took her through there," he managed to say before slumping against Myra.

J.D.'s first impulse when he found Corrie outside the back door was to stay with her, but he knew that he couldn't let Toby Willis escape. His flashlight beam parted the night but didn't reveal the man he was after. He listened for noises ahead of him in the darkness, but the rising wind and rain made it hard to tell what was causing the thrashing sounds of the tall grass and bushes in the field. He hadn't seen a vehicle at the Kaydahzinne house that might have belonged to the McMillans or Willis; that had to mean they had parked it near the river. He wished he knew Bonney County well enough to know if there was a road that ran along the back of the property.

Presently he heard the sounds of rushing water. The river was just ahead. He kept low, the shotgun ready, as he searched the muddy ground for signs that Toby Willis had gone this way. His eyes swept the area, finally seeing a path of trampled weeds and grass that seemed to lead over the edge of the berm above the river bank. He crept closer and peered over the edge. He heard the soft patter of raindrops on metal and dimmed the beam on his flashlight. In the darkness, he could make out the shadow of a vehicle in the tall grass by the side of the dirt road. It wasn't Deputy Evans' cruiser and it was impossible for J.D. to see who was in the car. He slowly raised the shotgun then heard a twig snap to his left.

He spun, bringing the shotgun around and slammed the barrel against the bulk of Toby Willis who was charging at him, swinging a heavy tree branch at J.D.'s head. He missed but connected with J.D.'s shoulder, knocking the gun out of J.D.'s grasp, but the blow threw Willis off balance as well and he dropped the tree branch. J.D. scrambled to his feet, groping for the shotgun as Willis launched himself at him. The impact drove them both over the berm and sent them sprawling down the slope toward the river, landing a few feet in front of the car. J.D. twisted out of Willis' grasp, dropping the flashlight, and gained his feet before the other man did. They were both unarmed, but Toby Willis was panting heavily and clutching his chest.

"Give it up, Willis," J.D. said. "You're under arrest." The hand-to-hand combat skills he'd honed as a Marine hadn't been used since he had left the Houston Police Department, but he was fairly certain that he'd be able to take down Willis with little effort. He waited, tensed and ready to spring into action, then Willis reached out with one hand, groping toward J.D., his other hand still clutching at his chest.

"Willis?" J.D. said, taking a cautious step back. He eyed the man, wondering if the grayish pallor of his face was due to the weak beam of the flashlight or....

"Help... me...," Toby Willis gasped, staggering toward J.D., still clutching at his chest. J.D., not taking chances, caught the man's outstretched arm and twisted it behind his back as he slumped to the ground, his breathing ragged. J.D. put his fingers to the side of the man's neck and swore under his breath when he could only detect the slightest sign of a pulse. He reached for his cell phone and cursed again when he remembered that he'd given it to Corrie earlier. Not, he thought grimly, that any help he called would arrive in time to save Toby Willis.

Sirens pierced the night along with flashing lights from emergency vehicles. J.D. released the man and climbed up the bank as fast as the slippery mud allowed. He found the shotgun and snatched it up and then froze. He stared in shock as smoke billowed from the roof of the Kaydahzinne house and flames leaped from the windows.

Corrie! Forgetting about Willis, he took off at a dead run across the field back to the house. A hundred worst case scenarios scrolled through his mind until he reached the perimeter of the yard. To his relief, he saw Corrie with her arm around Myra's shoulders. The sheriff was keeping a tight hold on the subdued and restrained McMillans, while Deputy Luna was being tended to by an EMT worker. It was hard to tell how many emergency vehicles and firefighters were present, but J.D. noticed that two people were missing.

Deputy Dudley Evans and Elsa Kaydahzinne.

Sutton glanced over his shoulder and there was unmistakeable relief in his face. “Where's Willis?” he said, unable to keep his voice down due to the chaos. Corrie looked over at them, looking relieved to see J.D. but apprehensive about what he was about to answer.

“He's down by the river. He's not going anywhere. Heart attack,” J.D. said. Corrie looked stricken and her eyes glazed with tears. J.D. wasn't sure what to make of that. A couple of uniformed officers from the village had responded to Sutton's call for assistance and had arrived on the scene. The sheriff motioned them over. “Where's Evans and Mrs. Kaydahzinne?” J.D. asked.

“They had her locked in a back bedroom. Dudley went to get her. I had to stay with these two,” Sutton muttered as he turned the McMillans over to the officers. J.D. started toward the house and the sheriff restrained him. “I can't let you do that, Wilder. I'll go!”

“How does that make it better?” J.D. snapped, shaking Sutton's hand off his arm.

“It doesn't, unless they get out alive! This is my responsibility, Wilder.” He straightened up and his gaze slid over to Corrie. She was watching them both, fear and dread in her eyes. It didn't matter which of them won this argument; they'd all lose in the end. Then Myra cried out, “There they are!”

They turned and saw Dudley Evans stumble from the back door, catching himself before he fell down the stairs. He appeared to have a quilt-wrapped bundle in his arms and he made his way as quickly and carefully down the steps as he could. A volunteer firefighter and an EMT tried to intercept him and relieve him of his burden, but he shook his head vehemently and strode toward them, making a beeline for Myra.

“Grandmother!” Myra's voice was choked with sobs, as Deputy Evans reached them and knelt down, gently lowering the frail old lady till she was half-sitting, half-lying on the wet grass. “Oh, my God, is she all right?” she cried, reaching for her grandmother's hand.

“Get back, give her some room,” Sutton ordered as J.D. and Corrie both edged toward the trio. J.D. noticed he was talking to the EMTs who had rushed over with oxygen and medical equipment. They obediently stopped short and waited. J.D. spoke up.

“There's a man down by the river. Heart attack victim. I don't think there's anything to be done, but....” They nodded and hurried toward the river. A third uniformed officer followed them. That had to constitute half of the Bonney police force.

Deputy Evans was coughing violently and he gently removed his handkerchief from Mrs. Kaydahzinne's face. "The smoke wasn't too bad in the bedroom," he said hoarsely. "But I didn't want her to have to breathe it in while we were getting out."

"What took you so long?" Sutton said quietly. The deputy looked up at his boss with a wry smile.

"She asked me to move her bird cages to the carport... she was afraid her birds would die from the smoke in the house. And she refused to leave without something for Myra. She insisted I get it for her and it was in the living room, in the curio cabinet."

The sheriff looked like he was about to have a stroke. "You saved her birds and then went into the living room to get something for her? That room was in flames!"

"It was either me or her, sir," Deputy Evans said. "She insisted."

"Grandmother," Myra said, half-laughing and half-crying, "Grandmother, are you all right?"

The old woman murmured something that was a garbled mix of Apache, Spanish, and English. She blinked several times and tried to sit up. "No, no, Grandmother, lie still. The ambulance is here...."

"No ambulance," Mrs. Kaydahzinne said, deciding on English and waving Myra's insistence away. "I'm fine. I don't need an ambulance or...." She stopped, as she looked back at her home, engulfed in flames. Her mouth dropped open and she moaned. "My house... my house...."

"Shh, Grandmother, I know, I'm so sorry," Myra cried, the tears streaming down her face and mingling with her grandmother's as she embraced her. Deputy Evans' face was set like stone, but J.D. could see the anguish in his eyes as he stared at Myra, unable to tear his eyes away.

For several moments, there was silence as they watched the firefighters put out the flames, aided by a light rain that was falling. A Village of Bonney police car pulled away with the McMillans inside and then the ambulance made its way to the riverside to pick up Toby Willis' body. Finally, Mrs. Kaydahzinne struggled to stand up, assisted by both Myra and Deputy Evans, and they made their way to the sheriff's Tahoe.

"It's all right," she said, waving off helpful hands, though she continued to lean heavily on Dudley Evans' arm. "It will be fine. Myra is safe, thank God, that's all that matters."

"And you're safe, too, Grandmother," Myra said as they helped her into the front seat of the Tahoe. Sutton got in and started the engine and turned the heater on; the wind and rain made the night cold, despite the fact that it was the middle of summer. The old woman touched the young woman's cheek.

"Yes, but YOU are the one I care about. You've been so good, so generous, taking care of me. But who will take care of you, Granddaughter?" Myra stared at her, shaking her head slightly, as Mrs. Kaydahzinne fumbled with a small package clutched in her hands. "Here," she said, thrusting it at Myra. "This is yours, child. I pray you'll need it... soon."

Myra took the partially torn tissue-wrapped bundle. A pale-blue crystal rosary and a small white prayer book slipped out of the paper. She stared at it in confusion. Her grandmother smiled.

"They were mine when I married your grandfather. My godmother gave them to me. 'Something old, something blue....' I forget exactly what she said," she broke off, frowning. "But it doesn't matter. What matters is that I wanted you to have them for when you married. I couldn't let them burn," she finished simply and patted Deputy Evans' arm. "Thank you, young man."

"Yes, ma'am," he said. Mrs. Kaydahzinne looked up at him. In the glow of the Tahoe's dome light, they could see her eyes twinkling.

"Now, then, young man, by chance you're not married, are you? Do you have a girlfriend?"

"Grandmother!" Myra blushed furiously and it was all J.D. could do to hold back a grin. He saw that Corrie and the sheriff both had to look away as well. Deputy Evans cleared his throat.

"Well, ma'am, as a matter of fact, I do," he said seriously. Disappointment flickered across Mrs. Kaydahzinne's face. Dudley reached out and took Myra's hand and drew her closer. "And I'd be honored to have your blessing to make her my wife." The elderly woman's disappointment turned to confusion, then her eyes widened.

For a moment, time froze and J.D. could feel Corrie and Sutton holding their breath as well. Mrs. Kaydahzinne took a deep breath and tears shone in her eyes. "Myra," she said softly, "Myra, why didn't you tell me?"

Myra appeared to brace herself. "Grandmother...."

"All this time, I've been burning that candle for you to meet a nice young man. Now look at my house!" She waved in the direction of what was left of her home. "You could have told me it had already worked. We could have avoided all this trouble." She looked at Myra whose mouth was hanging open and began to laugh. "Silly child, I'm only joking with you. But I am upset that you never brought your young man around to properly meet me and we could have had a nice meal for him. Although now I know why you've been cooking such big meals for us and we never seem to have any leftovers." She clucked and shook her head. "Now, this might not be the best time, but I want to know all about you, young man. Starting with your name?"

Deputy Evans managed to pull himself together; he had looked equally flustered and amused at Mrs. Kaydahzinne's reaction. "Dudley Evans, ma'am. It's a pleasure to meet you."

Sutton cleared his throat loudly and signaled to J.D. and Corrie that they needed to make themselves scarce. "We'll go get your cruiser, Dudley."

No one voiced any objections to walking back to the river with a light rain still falling. They were silent till they reached the edge of the Kaydahzinne property. Not much was left of the front of the house. They stood watching the crews working in the eerie glow of the emergency lights. Corrie shivered and J.D. moved closer to her. So did the sheriff.

"It's unbelievable," she said softly. J.D. nodded, staring at smoldering ruins of the building. Corrie sighed. "I told Myra she should have just told her grandmother about Dudley right from the beginning. They could have avoided so much heartache if she'd...."

J.D. laughed; he couldn't help it. "Women!" he said, shaking his head. "These people just lost their home and all you can think about is Myra and Dudley's romance!"

Corrie backhanded J.D. in the chest and the sheriff chuckled. "They did NOT lose their home," she said firmly. She looked back in the direction of the Tahoe. "They lost their house, which is a sad thing, because it's full of memories and history, but their home is where they are."

"And from the looks of things, they're going to be making a whole lot of new memories and history now," Sutton commented.

"Urrrgh," J.D. said. "Sounds like you guys need to stick to the day jobs and stop moonlighting at Hallmark." He dodged another backhand from Corrie. "And not that it matters to you two hopeless romantics in the grand scheme of things," he added dryly, "but what are the Kaydahzinnes going to do now that their house," he emphasized, "is pretty much destroyed?"

“There's always family,” Corrie said. “Myra's parents still live in Tunstall. That's a bit of a drive for Myra to get to work, but it won't be a permanent arrangement. Mrs. Kaydahzinne is far too independent to live with family yet. My guess,” Corrie went on, a smile playing on her lips, “is that there'll be a new house built on this property before too long, with maybe a small apartment added to it.” J.D. groaned.

“Fairy tales still come true in Bonney County,” he said. The sheriff nodded.

“Now it's time for the elves to get back to work and wrap everything up before the clock strikes midnight.” He glanced at his watch. “And get this young lady home before the Tahoe and your Harley turn into pumpkins.”

Chapter 24

"How the heck did that votive candle start that fire?" J.D. asked.

They were sitting around the dining table in Corrie's apartment. All three of them were exhausted, but still too keyed up to go to their respective homes and get some sleep. Corrie hadn't wanted to look at all that needed to be done in the campground store before her business was back up and running, so she led them directly up the stairs and put two pots of coffee on. Rick shook his head.

"They had planned to torch the place all along. Myra's grandmother used scented kerosene in her oil lamp. We didn't notice anything but the scent of lavender... that's the scent she used. The sofa, carpet, and curtains were doused with it and they had planned on making it look like the candle was 'accidentally' knocked over and started the blaze." He sighed and took a long sip of coffee. "Of course, we'd have found evidence that it wasn't an accident, but by that time they had planned to be long gone and hopefully wouldn't be found."

"So much for Bill Woods' plan to balance the scales," J.D. said. "That package or box or whatever of money he had planned to return to Corrie was destroyed in the fire. I'm sure it made the McMillans sick to their stomachs to see their money go up in flames." Rick shifted in his chair.

"There was no money hidden in the Kaydahzinne house," he said. Corrie had been listening to them, half-asleep in her chair with her untouched coffee cup in front of her, and she sat bolt upright.

"What? But Myra said...." Rick was shaking his head.

"She said that to try to buy some time... she realized you had the cell phone in your pocket and that help was nearby. She was hoping it would distract them long enough for us to make our move." He gave her his half-smile. "The fact that Andy had recovered enough to make a move helped a lot, too. They weren't expecting him to come rushing out the door." His smile faded and he continued soberly, "But there was no money. She knew that would be the only thing that they cared enough about to drop their guard and it worked."

Before anyone else spoke, Rick's phone buzzed. He barely

repressed a sigh as he answered, "Sutton." He frowned. "Now?" He listened again. "Sure you're okay to come over? All right, we'll meet you downstairs." He flipped the phone shut.

"Who was that?" Corrie asked as he stood up.

"Mike Ramirez. Said he needs to give you something."

"I thought he was taking it easy after he got conked on the head," J.D. said, raising a brow. Rick shrugged.

"He says he's fine. He used to ride bulls when he was in college to earn extra money. I think he spent most of it on ER visits, but he never missed a class or a party," Rick said dryly. "Anyway, he said that FedEx dropped a package off for Corrie this morning while we were all gone. No surprise he forgot all about it."

"I wasn't expecting a package," Corrie said as they made their way down the stairs. She again averted her eyes from the mess in the store. Tomorrow, tomorrow, she told herself. Deputy Ramirez's cruiser pulled into the parking space in front of the door as she flipped on the porch lights. Mike got out of his car, moving a bit stiffly. He had a FedEx envelope in his hand.

"How're you doing, Mike?" Rick asked as the deputy made his way up the steps.

"Nothing a few aspirins, an ice pack, and good night's sleep won't fix," Mike said, his infectious grin not as cheery as usual. "In fact, I was just heading that way when I remembered this." He held up the envelope. "I had to sign for it, but I didn't just want to drop it on the desk in case it was something important, so I put it in my cruiser under my windbreaker. With all that went on, I forgot about it."

"You didn't have to go to all the trouble to bring it to me," Corrie said, taking it and wondering what Mike had been doing since he'd been found under a picnic table on the patio with a lump on his head a few hours ago. His grin widened as if he'd read her mind.

"Buster's fiancee, Noreen, was working the ER tonight when I went in to get checked out. She's got a friend who just started working there and, well, she needs to get some practice in with working with patients and her bedside manner and all...."

"Right," Rick said shortly. "We appreciate the trouble you took to bring this out. Think you'll be up to working tomorrow?"

"Oh, yeah," Mike said. "Cheryl gets off work at seven and I don't have to be in till noon. I'm taking her to the early Mass and then Rozey's Diner for breakfast." He grinned. "Well, guess I'd better get going. Sheriff, I'll see you tomorrow. Lieutenant, Miss Black, ya'll have a good night." He went back to his cruiser and left. J.D. sighed.

"Wonder if people are ever going to stop calling me 'Lieutenant' around here?" he said. Rick raised a brow.

"Not as long as you keep acting like a cop without officially joining the Bonney police force. I didn't have a chance yet to tell everyone I deputized you. It'll be in the paper Monday, so you might have to get used to everyone calling you 'Deputy Wilder'." J.D. groaned.

"We'll see," he said. Corrie wondered why he was stalling on his decision so long. He gestured to the envelope in her hand. "So who's it from anyway?"

She turned the envelope over, but no name other than hers was on it. The return address was... "The Black Horse Campground? This was sent to me from here?"

"Maybe not," Rick said, moving closer and looking over her shoulder. "Maybe the sender didn't want you to know who was sending it so he used this address." Corrie felt herself go cold. She thrust the envelope at Rick.

"Here, you open it," she said. "I have no idea what it could be and I have to admit that I'm nervous about what's in it."

"You sure?" Rick asked, taking the envelope. She nodded and wrapped her arms around herself. She hadn't bothered to change out of her clothes but she was pretty sure it wasn't their damp condition that made her feel chilled. J.D. moved closer to her and she welcomed his warm presence, along with Rick's. She felt safer. Rick tore open the envelope and fished out two sheets of paper.

One was a lengthy letter, written in firm penstrokes. Rick looked up at Corrie. "It's from Bill Woods," he said.

"Another letter?" she said, taking it gingerly. One glance told her that the writer was the same one who had written the first warning note to close down the campground. "This writing doesn't match the letter J.D. found in the cabin... so Uncle Bill was the one who tried to warn me. And Toby Willis planted that other letter in the cabin to try to take the focus off himself...."

"Layla Woodson was given that letter written by Toby Willis to give to Corrie. That was before Woods was killed," Rick added. "After she saw Willis kill him, she read the letter. She didn't know what to make of it and was afraid to go through with the plan to give it to Corrie. She panicked when she found Woods dead and hid the letter in the cabin before she disappeared. But things didn't add up for her and she found herself wondering what the truth was...."

"According to Uncle Bill," Corrie said, deliberately using the familiar moniker, as she read the letter quickly, "he'd been feeling guilty for several years, but he and Toby Willis and the McMillans were bound together in silence because they all had secrets to hide. It wasn't until he was diagnosed with pancreatic cancer that he realized that the only thing that would bring him peace was to make things right, clear Billy's name once and for all, and pay back what he'd taken from him."

"And that is...?" J.D. asked. Rick held up a folded sheet of paper he had taken from the envelope and handed it to Corrie.

"Let's find out," he said. Corrie took a deep breath and unfolded the paper. What she saw took her breath away and she grabbed for the counter to hold herself up on shaking knees.

"What is it?" Rick and J.D. said at the same time.

She looked at them. "It's a bank check. For ten thousand dollars." Tears stung her eyes and she brushed them away impatiently. "Uncle Bill said that the money was all his to give back to Billy... he didn't take anything from anyone."

"I guess he knew the kind of people he was associating with and that they'd claim the money was theirs," J.D. said. Corrie nodded.

"He said Billy had loaned them five thousand, all those years ago," she went on, skimming through the letter once again. "They were supposed to buy that campground and pay Billy back whenever they could after they got it up and running. But he said they ended up just wasting the money on stupid stuff, partying, drinking. Marjorie McMillan offered them a chance to make their money by helping her with the real estate scams, but the guilt of having lied to his oldest and best friend always haunted him." She shook her head. "That's why he'd come back from time to time but never leave a number or anything to contact them. He didn't want Billy to know they had blown the deal after all the help he gave them. Toby Willis never felt guilty about it. He was always jealous of Billy and what he'd had... he was the one who persuaded Uncle Bill to try to break up my parents. He had proof of all of Uncle Bill's illegal activities and he used that to make Uncle Bill do whatever he wanted. Uncle Bill was always terrified of going to prison, but then he says, 'The doctors told me I don't have much time left and I'm more scared of leaving this world without making things right. Toby and them can't hurt me anymore. But when I go, I want to be sure I'm where I can see your mama and daddy and tell them myself how sorry I am and I want to be able to tell them that I did what I could to make it up to you and help you.' That's all he says," she added, swiping at the tears streaming down her face. Rick nodded.

"He must have suspected that the McMillans and Willis were on to him and he wanted to make sure you received your due, so he had the check sent to you to arrive on Saturday. That's why he wanted the campground vacated; he wanted to make sure they wouldn't interfere with the delivery of it." He took a deep breath. "That note was a warning after all."

"I'm pretty sure I said that at the beginning of all this, but I'll refrain from rubbing it in," Corrie said with a faint smile.

"I somehow doubt that," J.D. said.

"I would have preferred that he would have just sent his apology and check without the involvement of his shady associates," Rick said. It wasn't just tiredness that darkened his expression. "He almost ended up getting you killed as well," he said to Corrie.

"Then they would have ended up with the campground without a fight. Once they convinced everyone that Layla Woodson was related to me, probate would have granted her ownership of all my possessions, including the campground, and it would have been the same as if the McMillans and Willis owned it. That poor girl only wanted family and a sense of belonging. Toby Willis even told us that Bill Woods' first wife had a son, not a daughter, and had her play at being a male to try to intimidate Mrs. Kaydahzinne. No wonder she felt so rejected. They used her," Corrie said sadly.

"She's being released in the morning, Corrie," Rick said. "And we're going to find her some help. She's going to need a lot of counseling and support. We got a few leads on family members back in Texas... as far from the Black Horse as possible," he added.

"What about the Carsons?"

"The sheriff here," J.D. said nodding at Rick, "suspected that they were being used as much as Layla Woodson was. Are they still being held in Bonney?" Rick shook his head.

"I gave Eldon the word to let them go. They were just a couple of scapegoats that the McMillans and Willis were using to muddy the waters and throw suspicion off themselves. I doubt they'll be accepting free vacations from anyone for a long time."

"I feel bad for them getting mixed up in this, but I still wish there was something I could do to help Layla Woodson," Corrie said. Rick's thundercloud expression returned.

"She needs more help than you can give and it's not your responsibility anyway. Your family's reputation for rescuing birds with broken wings is well known. Trust me, you have to look out for yourself and your own interests now," he said firmly and J.D. nodded.

"All the more reason for you to get a will written as soon as possible," he said. Rick inclined his head in agreement and Corrie sighed.

"Yes, sir," she said, giving him a mock salute. "Can it wait till I get some sleep and try to get my life and business back in order?"

"I guess it'll have to... it's Sunday already and I'm sure you can't get a lawyer till Monday morning," J.D. conceded. Rick cleared his throat and J.D. shot him a look. "You're kidding me, right?"

"I happen to know a very good lawyer who wouldn't mind working on Sunday for a good reason. That's all," Rick said, holding his hands up. Corrie grinned at J.D.

"No, not him," she told J.D. "He's talking about the Sutton family lawyer, who happens to be an old friend of the family and has brunch with Rick's mother every Sunday. Your secret's out, by the way," she added to Rick. He shrugged.

"It's only a secret to people who don't live in Bonney," he said. "But Wilder's right, Corrie. Time to get your affairs in order."

"Could you phrase it a little differently?" she asked with a shiver. J.D. laughed.

"And while you're at it, get yourself a cell phone. You've proven that you sometimes DO leave your desk and when you do, it's not a bad idea to have a way to get hold of you. Or for you to get hold of someone," he added. Corrie gasped.

"Oh, my gosh, J.D.! I need to get you a new phone! Yours got stomped on...." He laughed.

"No need, Corrie. It's insured and I was planning to upgrade anyway."

She sighed. "I shouldn't feel this way, but this money—if it's really mine...."

"It's yours," Rick said. She didn't question him.

"This money is going to come in handy with everything that's happened. I hated to think what a financial hit the campground was going to take with having to cancel people's reservations and all...."

"Plenty of time to think about all that tomorrow," Rick said abruptly. He looked at the clock. "If you're planning to make the early Mass tomorrow, you'd best get some rest. You'll be safe tonight," he added.

Safe. Corrie had almost forgotten what that felt like. "Thanks, Rick. You, too, J.D." She had the almost uncontrollable urge to hug them, but she wasn't sure if she should... and if she did, who would she hug first? Both men were looking at her in a way that both thrilled and frightened her. They cared about her. They proved they'd both lay down their lives for her. It was clear that they both had feelings for her that went far beyond friendship, even if Rick couldn't act on those feelings and J.D. hadn't done more than hint at them. And the last thing she'd ever want to do is hurt either one of them. And yet, if she did have to choose between them....

No, she wouldn't be the one to make the first move. Certainly not tonight. She took a deep breath. "Thanks again, guys. I guess I'll see you in the morning?"

"And the rest of the day," J.D. said. "I'll be here to help get things back up and running. I'm sure you'll have most of your friends and staff here as well." He smiled and Corrie felt her heart lift.

"Thanks, J.D. I really appreciate that."

"I'll be here, too," Rick said. "We'll get everything back to how it should be in no time. And then," he said, waving a finger at Corrie, "since you won't have any guests on hand, it'll be the perfect time for us to have team practice." Corrie snapped her fingers.

"Right. Softball practice which we were supposed to have had yesterday afternoon," she said and smiled. "It'll be good to have something normal to look forward to!"

"'Normal'? I think I've heard that word before," J.D. said as he yawned and stretched before they all burst out laughing.

Chapter 25

Corrie adjusted her ball cap and blew an enormous bubble. She waited until Rick looked her way in the outfield before she popped it and grinned at his look of exasperation. Nothing irritated him more than chewing gum on his ball field.

Guns 'n' Hoses, the Bonney County softball team that consisted mostly of members of the sheriff's department and volunteer firefighting department, had assembled for their first official practice. The fact that a few members were out due to injuries didn't seem to faze them all. Deputies Gabe Apachito, still recovering from his appendix operation, and Andy Luna, who was nursing a minor concussion from the previous night's events, were taking turns as umpire and water boy. Shelli had coaxed RaeLynn into taking Andy's place as second baseman. J.D. had been recruited to play Gabe's position as catcher.

Rick, as usual, was on the mound. He was impatient to get started; the first of their six games against their opponents, the Rolling Bones, was in four days and they were far behind on practices. The Rolling Bones, made up primarily of members of the Bonney County Medical Center and the Emergency Medical Services, included Noreen Adler as one of their players along with several officers of the Bonney police department who volunteered as EMTs. Corrie wondered where J.D.'s loyalties would lie once he submitted his application to the Bonney PD. Not surprisingly, Buster had jumped ship and was cheering on Noreen's team, but he and Noreen had both showed up this morning to help Corrie get the Black Horse back into operating order.

She'd been touched to see that the Pages and Myers were already hard at work when she and Rick and J.D. had arrived after Sunday morning Mass. In fact, most of her employees had opted to attend Saturday night Mass in case the campground was allowed to be opened on Sunday. They were all engaged in various chores, cleaning and straightening up the store and cataloging any damaged merchandise. Once Corrie had changed her clothes and she and Rick and J.D. had pitched in, they were done by noon and she made a run to the store to provide her friends with a cookout feast after practice: brats, chicken, burgers, and ribs. Jackie, Dana, Shelli, and RaeLynn had whipped up potato salad, macaroni salad, and baked beans. The men had hauled the grills out to the practice field next to the campground and filled coolers with ice and soft drinks. Red and Jerry continued to man the grills while practice went on and Jackie and Dana concentrated on keeping everyone hydrated and tending to minor injuries. Even Dee Dee was on hand for the practice, cheering them on as if they were playing in the World Series... or the Super Bowl. She dressed for the occasion in a cheerleader costume that appeared to be sized to a girl half her age. Corrie wondered if Rick was going to have trouble keeping his male players focused on practice.

"Okay, everybody!" Rick called in his team. "We'll start with some batting drills, then catching and fielding. Corrie, I know you need the most batting practice, but I need you in the outfield when everyone else hits, so we'll rotate you in last."

"Gee, thanks, Sheriff," she said dryly as she gave him a mock salute and then jogged to the outfield, her braid swinging. No one ever walked on Rick's playing field. The players were rusty and it showed in the first few swings they took, but before long, Corrie was having to work to catch their hits. She couldn't keep the smile off her face. Her life was back to normal. Myra and Dudley's engagement was official and Mrs. Kaydahzinne was fine. The threat to her life and livelihood had been averted and she had received an unexpected bonus to help her get back on her feet. And she had a surprise for Rick and the rest of the team when it was her turn to bat.

Things couldn't be better.

~

J.D. hung back and watched while the first few players took their turns at bat. The level of their performance wasn't as impressive as Corrie's. She caught almost everything that came her way and fired it back with a speed and accuracy that made him whistle in admiration. When his turn came, he hefted the bat and felt a twinge of apprehension. It had been a long time, years even, since he'd played softball or baseball. He tried not be self-conscious about how he would do; he just hoped he didn't embarrass himself too much.

"Go get 'em, Lieutenant Wilder!" Dee Dee cried, jumping up and down and shaking her pom-poms. She whooped and cheered a little more loudly than she had for the rest of the team, which gave J.D. the uncomfortable feeling of being center stage.

“You don't play, Miss Simpson?” he asked as he stepped up to home plate. She shook her head as vigorously as her pom-poms.

“Oh, no!” she said. “My talents lie elsewhere, Lieutenant. I'm told I have a great pair of pom-poms and I'm not afraid to shake 'em!” She shook the shiny, metallic gold and green pom-poms in front of her and winked. J.D. felt his face burn and he turned away. He caught sight of Gabe Apachito's face. The deputy looked glum at the amount of attention Dee Dee was giving J.D. and J.D. hoped that wouldn't influence the deputy/umpire against him.

J.D. swung the bat, getting the feel for it, then gave Sutton a nod. The sheriff's gaze locked with his and J.D. felt his heart start pumping harder.

The windup.

The pitch.

Crack!

At first, J.D. was so shocked that he connected with his first hit that he froze in place. Sutton stared at the ball arching high into the air then he turned and looked at J.D. “For the love of God, Wilder, RUN!” he yelled.

J.D. took off, not daring to see if Corrie had managed to catch the ball. Yells and cheers came from the rest of the team and he arrived at second base, nearly colliding with Sutton, who caught the ball a split second after J.D. reached the base.

“Safe!” called Gabe. J.D. grinned as Sutton raised his brows.

“Nice hit,” he murmured. J.D. nodded his thanks; he hadn't expected the sheriff to be that effusive in his praise.

“All right, Corrie,” Sutton called. “Let's see if you can hit as good as you catch! Wilder,” he said, “be ready to catch anything if it happens to get past me. You probably won't have to leave that spot,” he added dryly.

“Come on, Sutton, she can't be THAT bad,” J.D. said as he slipped on a glove that the sheriff handed him, but then he noticed the teammates on the sidelines evacuating the area. Corrie picked up the bat and planted her fist on her hip, glaring at them.

“You'll see,” Sutton said under his breath. He stepped to the mound and J.D. sensed that Sutton was warring with himself. He'd given RaeLynn a few easy pitches when it was evident that the poor young woman had never held a bat in her life and allowed her to get as far as first base. But with Corrie, it was different. As much as the sheriff wanted to give Corrie a few good, easy hits, they all knew that Corrie would resent the special treatment.

And she was holding a bat.

Corrie got into an impressive stance, gripping the bat perfectly, her eyes full of fire. Sutton stood motionless for a few seconds, glanced back at J.D and nodded, then fired off his first pitch. Corrie swung.

The crack of the bat connecting with the ball was even louder than when J.D. had hit it. Both J.D. and Sutton—indeed the entire team—had frozen in place as the ball went zooming into the outfield. Nothing seemed to move, except for a car that pulled up to the playing field behind the bleachers. Corrie was the first to shake off her immobility and she took off running the bases. J.D. barely had time to note the car's driver getting out of the vehicle as he took off after the ball.

First base, second base... J.D. scooped up the ball, turned and fired it back toward Sutton, who was covering home. Dimly, J.D. could hear the cheers from the rest of the team and the small group of spectators grow louder. It was going to be close....

He started running for the infield. “Go!” he yelled, not sure if he was talking to Corrie or the sheriff. Sutton was at home plate, waiting for the ball, waiting to tag Corrie.

She was ten feet from the plate when she launched herself at home. She connected with the base and Sutton's lower legs just as the ball smacked into his glove. He lost his balance and fell backwards, Corrie plowing over the top of him.

The impact jarred the ball from his glove and sent it bouncing onto the ground.

“SAFE!” J.D. yelled along with the rest of the team, drowning out Gabe Apachito's official call. Corrie scrambled to her feet at the same time Sutton did. She was jumping up and down with joy.

“I did it! I did it!” she screamed. J.D. wasn't sure how the sheriff felt about getting knocked over by one of his own players, but he was cheering as well and caught Corrie around the waist in mid-jump and lifted her high as the rest of the team swarmed around them excitedly. J.D. paused, not sure how he felt about the sheriff holding Corrie in his arms like that. Then he saw that he wasn't the only one who didn't seem overjoyed.

“Pardon me. Am I interrupting something important?”

The voice wasn't loud, but the woman who spoke commanded the attention of everyone present. The cheers died away and the group parted, allowing her to step forward toward Sutton and Corrie. Her bearing and looks matched the custom BMW in which she had arrived. She was tall, with golden hair and ice-blue eyes and the regal posture of a queen. Her designer outfit was perfectly fitted to her flawless figure. She allowed a slight sneer to mar her beautiful face as she studied Sutton and Corrie, hot and sweaty, uniforms rumpled and streaked with dirt. She stopped an arm's length away and let her gaze travel from Sutton to Corrie and back again. Despite her confident air, a spark of anger and some other, almost similar, emotion flitted in her eyes and tinged her voice. "Hello, Rick."

J.D. had stopped and watched. Corrie had slipped out of Sutton's arms and stood back just a little, but she didn't retreat and the shock in her face turned into defiance. She raised her chin a little and straightened her back. J.D. recognized the look of pride that flashed in her eyes. And then he knew who the woman was.

Sutton also straightened up. His face had turned to stone and his eyes were hard and cold. His voice, when he spoke, was devoid of emotion. "Hello, Meghan."

Meghan Stratham Sutton. The sheriff's ex-wife.

Other Books in the Black Horse Campground Mysteries

End of the Road Book 1

Corrie Black, owner of the Black Horse Campground, hopes for a successful summer season, but the discovery that Marvin Landry, a long-time guest, has been shot dead in his own RV and $50,000 in cash missing does not herald a good beginning, especially since the victim's handicapped wife and angry stepson show little interest in discovering who murdered him. Is the appearance of a mysterious biker with a shadowy past and a recently deceased wife merely a coincidence? Despite opposition from former flame, Sheriff Rick Sutton, Corrie is determined to find the murderer. But will she find out who is friend or foe before the murderer decides it's the end of the road for Corrie?

No Lifeguard on Duty Book 2

At the Black Horse Campground in Bonney County, New Mexico summer means warm sunny days, a cool refreshing pool... and murder? Corrie Black welcome the summer with a party to celebrate opening the swimming pool. The shock of discovering Krista Otero's body in the pool the morning after the party is bad enough. What's worse is that Krista's death wasn't an accident. And what's more confusing is that Krista's closest friends all have something to hide. Corrie is determined to find out who used her swimming pool as a murder weapon and who is using her home as a base for illegal activities. But someone wants to keep Corrie out of their business... even if it means killing again!

At the Crossroad Book 4

Trouble often comes in threes. It's no different at the Black Horse Campground. On his first day as detective with the Bonney Police Department, J.D. Wilder finds three cold case files on his desk – three women who disappeared over a fifteen year period. It seems no one has ever properly investigated them. Then a woman from his past arrives to ask for his help. Again. The timing couldn't be worse, since he's finally about to ask Corrie on a date. ButCorrie also has a visitor from her past show up. And Sheriff Rick Sutton has his hands full dodging his ex-wife, Meghan, who insists on digging up a painful memory. When three bodies are discovered that prove the missing women were murdered, J.D.'s investigation reveals that all of their visitors have some connection to the victims. But which one of them killed three women? And will there be a fourth victim

A Summer to Remember Book 5

Police detective J.D. Wilder's attempt to focus on his budding romance with Corrie Black, owner of the Black Horse Campground, is thwarted when the cold cases he thought he had solves are reopened, and the killer is poised to strike again. But who held a grudge against the three cold-case victims? And who is the next target? With the help of Bonney County Sheriff Rick Sutton, J.D. probes the memories of Bonney residents who knew the victims and begins to make connections.

Then another death occurs, and Corrie is attacked. The attacker and the cold-case murderer could be the same person, but Corrie's condition is critical and she's lost memories of recent events, including the identity of her attacker and even having met J.D. Will she survive long enough to remember what happened? Or will she end up as a memory?

Fiesta of Fear Book 6

Fun. Games. Food. Murder....Corrie Black, owner of the Black Horse Campground in Bonney County, New Mexico, has her hands full. She has offered to host the annual San Ignacio church fiesta at the campground, she's helping her best friend Shelli deal with a missing ex-husband and troubled teenager, and she's trying to keep the peace between the parish's two most vocal members.

When the high school principal is found dead in the church cemetery, Corrie needs answers: Who are the 'ghost girls'? What is causing Shelli's son to get into so much trouble? What is causing the tension between the church secretary and the church treasurer? Are these connected to the murder? And most importantly to Corrie, what is the secret her coworker and friend, RaeLynn Shaffer, is hiding?

With the help of Bonney County sheriff, Rick Sutton, and Bonney Detective J.D. Wilder, Corrie tries to unravel the threads. that connect all the mysteries to the fiesta and the Black Horse Campground. But the threads turn into a net that could snare Corrie and her friends in a deadly trap!

CPSIA information can be obtained
at www.ICGtesting.com
Printed in the USA
FSHW010749290721
83501FS